MARCH ROARS

MARCH ROARS

A Paradise Café Mystery by

MAUREEN JENNINGS

Author of the Detective Murdoch Mysteries

Cormorant Books

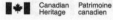 

We acknowledge financial support for our publishing activities: the
Government of Canada, through the Canada Book Fund and The Canada
Council for the Arts; the Government of Ontario, through the Ontario Arts
Council, Ontario Creates, and the Ontario Book Publishing Tax Credit.

LIBRARY AND ARCHIVES CANADA CATALOGUING IN PUBLICATION

Title: March roars : a Paradise Café mystery / by Maureen Jennings.
Names: Jennings, Maureen, author.
Identifiers: Canadiana (print) 2024036435X | Canadiana (ebook) 20240364384
| ISBN 9781770867246 (softcover) | ISBN 9781770867253 (EPUB)
Subjects: LCGFT: Novels. | LCGFT: Detective and mystery fiction.
Classification: LCC PS8569.E562 M37 2024 | DDC C813/.54—dc23

United States Library of Congress Control Number: 2024934030

Cover art: Nick Craine
Interior text design: Marijke Friesen
Manufactured by Friesens in Altona, Manitoba in July 2024.

Printed using paper from a responsible and sustainable resource,
including a mix of virgin fibres and recycled materials.

Printed and bound in Canada.

CORMORANT BOOKS INC.
260 ISHPADINAA (SPADINA) AVENUE, SUITE 502,
TKARONTO (TORONTO), ON M5T 2E4

SUITE 110, 7068 PORTAL WAY, FERNDALE, WA 98248, USA

www.cormorantbooks.com

For Iden, as always. What would I do without him?
And this time, in memory of dear friend, Larry Lalonde
who has left this life far too soon.

When March comes in like a lion,
it goes out like a lamb.

CHAPTER ONE

I WOKE UP with a start.

I was shivering, which wasn't surprising as I'd forgotten to close the window when I went to bed, and the temperature had dropped. But what had wakened me wasn't the chill air, it was the sound of Gramps coughing his heart out. He was already up, and I could hear him in the kitchen. His incessant coughing was becoming a source of anxiety for me. Stubborn old coot that he was, he refused to go to the doctor and said the cough would vanish when spring truly arrived. I thought it was more likely residual damage from the wound he had received three months earlier. He'd taken a bullet in the stomach when a case I'd been working on resulted in a scuffle at the Paradise Café. I shuddered at the memory.

I tugged the covers back over my legs and lay still for a minute. Daylight was making tentative forays into the room, and the March wind was tugging and howling at the window like a creature in distress.

At that moment, I heard knocking at the front door. We had an electric bell, but it had given up the ghost a couple of months ago, and neither Gramps nor I had yet got it fixed.

My alarm clock looked alarmed. It was only half past seven. A bit early for a friendly caller.

I got out of bed, grabbed my dressing gown, and headed downstairs.

Gramps was in the process of dealing with a young lad who was dressed in the uniform of a messenger from the post office.

"What's happening, Gramps?"

"This young fellow is delivering a letter for you."

"At this time of the morning?"

The boy tapped his cap. "Morning, ma'am. Sorry to wake you, but the sender said it was urgent."

"Who's it from?"

He looked at a slip of paper in his hand.

"Person by the name of Brodie. Mrs. O. Brodie."

"I don't know anybody by that name."

Again, the boy checked the paper. "I was given the recipient name of C. Frayne; T. Gilmore and Associates."

If this mysterious letter was including Mr. Gilmore, it had to be a business matter.

I held out my hand. "I'll take it."

He pulled back. "Sorry, ma'am, but there is a delivery charge."

"Didn't the sender pay that?"

"No, ma'am. My note here says payment is collect."

"Bit nervy," muttered Gramps.

I hesitated. I could refuse the letter, but I was curious. Who was this Mrs. Brodie who was trying to contact me so urgently?

"How much is it?"

"Two dollars, ma'am. Delivering outside of office hours is double."

"Highway robbery," growled Gramps. The boy didn't seem at all fazed. He was as undeveloped as a ten-year-old, but his face had already acquired the weariness of an octogenarian with too much life experience. He had on a navy-blue uniform with shiny buttons in a row down the front, a polished leather belt, and peaked cap with a braid around the brim. He resembled a diminutive admiral.

"Were you the one making all that noise?" I asked.

"What d'you mean, ma'am? I only knocked once."

"Never mind. I was making a joke."

"Oh. As you wish." He grinned obediently.

I grinned back. "Wait here. I'll just be a minute."

As I went to get the money from my handbag, Gramps stepped forward.

"Do you want a piece of toast?" he said to the boy. "I just made some."

The boy smiled. "Thank you, sir, that would be most appreciated. I didn't have no time for breakfast this morning."

"I'll get it," I called over my shoulder.

I returned as fast as I could with the two dollars, plus tip, and a piece of toast. I handed them to the boy, who put everything, toast included, into his pouch.

"Thanks. I'll be off, then."

"Don't you want to wait to see if there is a reply?"

"The lady said there was no need for an answer. It costs extra. She said just to make sure the message was received."

He whirled around and hurried off to his bike, which was propped up at the curb.

As he closed the door, the cold air brought on a fit of coughing in Gramps. I waited, emanating disapproval, until it subsided.

"You've still got your cough."

"We've got attached to each other."

"Gramps!"

He wiped at his eyes. "I know, I know, Lottie. I should go to the doctor. I'll be fine. Stop worrying." He peered at me. "I hope I didn't keep you awake. You look like you've been up all night."

"Thanks, Gramps. You don't look so hot yourself."

I put my arm around his bony shoulders and drew him away from the door.

"Come on. Let's have some breakfast, and I'll see what my mysterious letter is all about."

"The boy said the sender was a lady. I wonder why she sent it here and not to your office. How did she know the address?"

"I guess she checked the street directory."

Gramps muttered under his breath. For some reason known only to himself, he disapproved of Might's city directory, claiming it was a violation of privacy. I found it very useful, and no one had to be listed if they didn't want to be.

We went back to the kitchen, which was by now warm and cozy thanks to the woodstove Gramps had lit.

I patted him on the shoulder. "Sit down; I'll take care of the toast."

"No, no. I'll do it. You go and read your letter."

I had lived with my grandparents since I was two, when my mother, a young widow, had run off to find excitement and fulfillment with a circus troupe. Not that long ago, to our great shock, my Gran had died, leaving Gramps in my care, although I knew he saw it the other way around. Taking care of him was sometimes a challenge. I let him have his way and sat down at the table.

I had a look at the envelope. *C. Frayne*. The handwriting was neat and straight but unrevealing. I gave it a sniff. Nothing except a faint smell of tobacco. I assumed it had come from the messenger. He might look like a child, but I gathered he was a smoker like most of the boys in that line of work.

I pressed the envelope gently, but there didn't seem to be

anything untoward inside. Given our line of work, Mr. Gilmore had taught me to be cautious before opening unidentified letters or packages. You never knew if some disgruntled client had decided to punish us for our conclusions on their case. We had already experienced the dead rat in the letterbox scenario.

Gramps brought over a plate with two slices of toast slathered with butter.

"Coffee'll be ready in a minute." He went back to the stove.

I added some cherry jam — homemade, I might add — and took a bite.

"What's the letter say?" called Gramps from where he was fussing with the coffee pot.

"Don't know yet. I haven't finished my morning sustenance."

"Let's hope it doesn't contain a bomb. I can't afford to give you a fancy funeral."

"Gramps!"

I slit open the envelope. It contained one single page of lined paper, torn from a school notebook by the look of it. Same neat handwriting. Black ink.

Tuesday, March 9

To whom it may concern. My name is Mrs. Olivia Maeve Brodie. I wish to engage your services as a private investigator. It concerns a matter of grave injustice. Please call on me today at your soonest convenience. It is urgent. I am a resident at the House of Industry on Elm Street. Please do not reveal the reason for your visit under any circumstance. It is not safe to do so. Come at ten.

I am your faithful servant,

Olivia Brodie.

P.S. I will pay your fee.

Gramps came back to the table with my mug of coffee.

"So, is it good news or bad news?"

"I'll read it to you."

I did so, and when I finished, he gave a snort.

"Pay your fee? First of all, she didn't even pay for the delivery; second, she says she lives at the House of Industry. Her idea of 'grave injustice' may be somebody having more than their share of butter. And if she can afford your fees, she probably shouldn't be living in the city poorhouse on public relief."

His words were harsh, but I knew if it came down to it, he had a heart of mush.

"Are you going to see her?" he continued. "I thought you had an appointment today with a woman over on Gerrard Street. A *wealthy* widow. What was it again?"

"She said she's been robbed."

"Ha. She's probably dropped her diamond necklace down her new flushing toilet and wants to blame somebody else."

"Gramps, don't be such a snob."

"At least you can ask that one for a good fee."

"It's the same no matter who the client is. What's distressing Mrs. Brodie is quite as important as what is distressing Mrs. Calder."

"Sure it is. Tell that to the government."

I returned the letter to the envelope.

"I'm going to the office. Mr. Gilmore should be in soon. I'll run it by him."

Gramps shrugged at me. "You've made up your mind anyway. I know you. As soon as I said 'poorhouse,' you were ready to adopt the bloody woman and have her move in."

I batted him on the arm. "Stop it. I wouldn't dream of bringing anybody into this house with such a bad-tempered old codger. She'd run back as fast as she could."

That made him laugh, and that in turn made him cough.

"Are you coming to the Paradise for lunch?" he asked me when he could talk properly.

"I was planning to be there for the last sitting. Before I see Mrs. Calder."

"Any word on when Hilliard's son and daughter are arriving? Soon, isn't it?"

"Yep. Very soon. They're working out the time."

"How do you feel about that, Lottie? Stepchildren can be difficult to handle."

"Don't rush things, Gramps. They're not my legal stepchildren yet."

"They won't see it that way. You're their dad's new sweetheart. They'll be jealous."

I couldn't help but sigh. I was in love with a divorced man with children. I knew it wasn't going to be simple when I was finally introduced to the family. I was prepared to like the two children, and all I could hope was that they would like me.

"Well?" Gramps repeated. "How do you feel about having two youngsters underfoot?"

"Frankly, I'm a little nervous. We'll have to see. For my part, I'm more than happy to take them on."

"Let's hope they feel the same way. Their parents don't exactly get along. She may have poisoned their minds against you. Spurned women can do that."

"For heaven's sake, Gramps. What are you? A psychiatrist? Besides, she was the one who left the marriage."

"Doesn't matter. Spurned is spurned."

Suddenly, he reached over and squeezed my arm. To my surprise, I saw his eyes were watering.

"I don't want my girl to get hurt. I know my Lottie. You won't fight for what you want if you think somebody else deserves it more."

I handed him a serviette. "Here. Blow your nose and shut up. And if you're not better by next week, I'm taking you to the doctor, even if I have to drag you."

"I'll be fine. Calvin says he's got some medicine that he can make for me."

"*Make* for you?"

"He said it's an ancient Jamaican remedy. Something you rub on your chest."

I liked and respected Calvin Greene, the cook at the Paradise, but a homemade remedy of any kind described as "ancient" made me nervous.

"Let's see."

The wind flung itself at the kitchen window, howling and biting.

"Sounds like a bloody live creature, doesn't it?" Gramps winced. "Do you think we should let it in?"

"Better not. If I gather it in my arms to warm it and hold it against my heart, it will only mess up my hair. Besides, it's travelled across northern glaciers, and its breath will be icy."

Gramps gaped at me. "What?"

"Sorry, just waxing poetic."

"Warn me next time."

I left it at that, picked up the letter, and headed off to get dressed. At least the enigmatic Mrs. Brodie, resident of the poorhouse with a grave matter to discuss, had taken my mind off my worries.

CHAPTER TWO

MR. GILMORE WAS at his desk, perusing the newspaper, when I entered our office. He looked up and beamed at me.

"Good morning, Miss Frayne. Glad to see the wind didn't take you off to Oz."

Mr. Gilmore was fond of dropping literary references. Many of them went over my head. He also called me Miss Frayne, even though we'd known each other for almost two years, and I was now his associate. However, I addressed him as Mr. Gilmore to keep things even.

"It didn't take me, but it did seize my beret. I had to rescue it from the wheels of a streetcar on Yonge Street."

"Good heavens. I hope it's not damaged."

"The streetcar or my beret?"

Mr. Gilmore smiled in acknowledgement of my little joke.

"Get yourself settled. You look cold. I've made a fresh pot of coffee in anticipation of your punctual arrival. However, I'm afraid I have to leave in about an hour. I have a meeting with Mrs. Rundle and her solicitor to confirm her suspicion that her husband is committing adultery."

"Poor woman. I assume she will be devastated."

He sighed. "No doubt. She's a proud woman who has enjoyed her position in society."

"Will she sue for divorce, do you think?"

"I very much doubt it. She won't want the scandal."

The majority of divorce cases in which our clients were the wives fell to me, but this one had been Mr. Gilmore's. According to what he had witnessed, the well-to-do and ever-so-respectable Mr. George Rundle was not conducting business, as he claimed, but was having a rendezvous every Friday at the King Edward Hotel with an ever-so-young and pretty commercial typist.

I hung up my coat and somewhat muddy beret and went into the tiny alcove we pretended was a kitchen. As I poured myself a cup of coffee, Mr. Gilmore called out to me, "Remember that hue and cry about a house over on Edward Street getting robbed last week?"

"Weren't the thieves caught almost immediately?"

"They were. A pair of young Negroes. Brothers aged fifteen and thirteen. It says here the judge has sentenced them to ten days in jail, plus ten strokes of the strap each."

"Ouch."

Mr. Gilmore shook his head. "I know corporal punishment is supposed to act as a deterrent, but I doubt it will make much difference to those youngsters. I think their path in life is set. According to the newspaper, their father vanished years ago. The mother lives on the West Coast, and she states she doesn't want to have anything to do with them."

"Ouch again."

I could certainly understand the trauma inflicted by a vanishing parent. I walked back to my desk.

Mr. Gilmore gave the paper a shake to straighten it up. "It says here some people are asking for air raid precautions in case there's another war and a gas attack."

"A gas attack? Surely not."

"To my thinking, if there is a war with Germany, it will be far worse than the previous one. Our ability to kill and maim each other became more refined as that conflict went on."

He shook a little more sense into the news, then folded the page over neatly.

"I think I need another cup of tea before I face the pain and outrage of the wronged Mrs. Rundle."

"I want to run something by you before you leave."

I took Mrs. Brodie's letter out of my handbag and gave it to him. He read it quickly.

"It's certainly intriguing. Do you want to go?"

"Won't do any harm. As you say, it's intriguing. Why is it so urgent, and why so unsafe?"

Mr. Gilmore let out a sigh.

"Not to be disparaging, Miss Frayne, but the woman says she's a resident of the poorhouse. She is probably elderly, lonely, and most certainly she will be poor. And likely confused."

His words were echoing those of Gramps, and I had to admit they made me a bit more stubborn.

Mr. Gilmore affected a pince-nez when he was reading as if he were a nineteenth-century gentleman sitting in his club. I thought he just enjoyed fiddling with it. He gazed at me over the top of the glasses.

"Besides, weren't you supposed to call on a Mrs. Calder today? Didn't you tell me she was most insistent?"

"That's not until two o'clock. If I go now, I can do both."

"I'm sure you can, but I hardly need remind you, cases have a way of absorbing us, especially among our more affluent clients. Mrs. Calder is likely the type of woman who loses her jewellery on a regular basis and immediately assumes one of the servants is a thief. You could spend hours for nothing, and then she will complain about the bill."

"Mr. Gilmore. Cease and desist. You are showing a severe bias."

"Very well. I shall not clip your wings."

He handed me back the letter.

I went to get my coat.

Mr. Gilmore hardly seemed to notice — he was still focused on the newspaper. I knew the bad news coming from Germany worried him tremendously. He had family members living there. I wished there was some comfort I could offer him, but there was none. The Western world seemed paralyzed in the face of a rapidly growing threat of conflict coming from Germany.

"Will I see you for lunch at the Paradise?" I asked.

"Darn, I almost forgot. I promised Hilliard and Wilf I'd arbitrate."

"Arbitrate? About St. Patrick's Day, you mean?"

"That's it. They still haven't fixed the programme. Wilf wants to put on his play and use the opportunity to bring attention to the downtrodden, particularly veterans. Hilliard says he wants people to just have a good time."

"Good luck with that. They're both stubborn as rocks, and they both think they're right."

"Oh, just to remind you, as of tomorrow, I will be out of town until Sunday. I'm going up to Montréal on some business."

"And you can't tell me what it is."

"I'm sorry, Miss Frayne. I'm not at liberty to disclose the matter just yet. But I will let you know as soon as I can."

He was looking very sombre, and I had the feeling that the reason he was going was no ordinary issue. This was not the first time he had considered it necessary to keep secrets, but I'd learned to trust his assurances of disclosure when the timing was right.

"And good luck with Mrs. Brodie. Take care. Some rough types are over in that area of town. Wayfarers, most of them."

"I'll take that under advisement."

The wind gave an assenting howl at the window.

Mr. Gilmore frowned in that direction. "I'd better ask the janitor to take a look. There is a dreadful draft coming in. The frame probably needs caulking."

So much for poetry.

CHAPTER THREE

TORONTO HAD MANY sombre buildings, honest and respectable in appearance, as befit a city that aspired to those qualities. The House of Industry, or the poorhouse, as it was more familiarly known, would easily win a prize over all of them. It was a large, imposing building, standing alone on its own grounds. There were three storeys, the upper windows as narrow as arrow slits. A tall iron fence around the perimeter kept everything in order, and the brick was a dull yellow, the colour of despair.

I dismounted, leaned my bicycle against a tree that was looking doubtful about the coming of spring, and went up to the front door. In contrast to the sobriety of the building — perhaps again echoing the aspirations of the city — the door was surprisingly handsome, wide and tall with a brick arch and stained glass lintel window. There was an electric doorbell on one side and a brass sign that commanded me to Press, Wait and Enter. I obeyed, and after what felt like a suitable pause, I pushed open the door and went inside.

The foyer was square with plain white walls and low lighting. No concession to aesthetics here. There were two unrevealing doors on each side, and on the wall facing the entrance was a large desk. As I stepped inside, a woman was already coming out from behind it. She was tall and solidly built, perhaps of middle age, and was so soberly dressed in an ankle-length dark dress she might have been a nun. She came toward me, smiling pleasantly and professionally.

"Good morning. May I be of assistance?"

Perhaps it was her tone of voice, perhaps the smile, but for a moment, I thought I'd accidentally wandered into Timothy Eaton's department store. Coats? Lingerie?

I returned the smile. "I am here to see Mrs. Olivia Brodie." I didn't want to say more than that. The letter had asked me not to reveal the reason for my visit, and I thought that was a good idea until I got the lie of the land.

The woman nodded. "Oh, yes. Mrs. Brodie said somebody was coming to see her this morning. You are to determine which of her pieces you might be able to sell in your shop."

So it turned out that *lie* of the land had been an apt phrase.

"Er, quite so," I replied, backing up Mrs. Brodie's fabrication.

The woman clasped her hands together. "It's so wonderful when our residents can earn a little extra money. It gives them a great sense of pride."

"Does Mrs. Brodie sell many of her ... er, pieces?"

"She works slowly now because of her arthritis, but usually she manages to find customers for all of them. They really are quite splendid."

I still wasn't any the wiser as to what Mrs. Brodie's pieces actually were.

"I'm Miss Lindsay," the welcomer continued. "I'm one of the attendants."

"I'm Charlotte Frayne."

Miss Lindsay abruptly checked a silver watch that was pinned on her significant chest. "Oh, dear. Time is marching on." She smiled over at me. "Please come this way. Mrs. Brodie is in the sunroom. She went there directly after breakfast so she could make sure of her place. She hasn't stirred since."

A gust of wind must have found its way underneath the door, because suddenly a sheaf of papers on the desk flew into the air.

"Dear me, what a windy day it is today. One could get quite blown away."

I smiled assent, but I thought the wind would have a tough job blowing Miss Lindsay very far.

She gestured toward the end of the hall, where I could see the iron doors of an elevator cage. "We do have a brand-new elevator now. It makes life so much easier for our inmates."

She pulled down the lever to open the heavy iron door and dragged it wide.

"Shall we?"

The elevator was small and smelled strongly of carbolic cleaner. Miss Lindsay shoved down the lever and pressed a button, and we jerked upward.

She had referred to it as "new," but it seemed old-fashioned to me, and it clanked arthritically as we slowly ascended. Miss Lindsay stood facing the doors, at the ready to open up. Her plain dress definitely suggested a uniform, and I fought off an impulse to call out my floor: *Women's shoes, please.*

Instead, I said, "I have not actually met Mrs. Brodie as yet. How long has she been a resident?"

"Not long. Alas, her husband died last October. They had only just moved to Toronto from the north, and she had simply no resources. She was admitted just after Christmas. Frankly, she didn't want to come here, but she could no longer support herself. She has no family, or even friends, for that matter, who might help, and it was us or destitution."

Miss Lindsay spoke as if it were a choice between Muskoka or Mississauga.

The elevator shuddered to a stop, and she hauled open the door.

"We're down at the end of the hall."

I followed her along a linoleum-covered floor. Her rubber-soled shoes squeaked.

She continued, "The sunroom has been an absolute boon for our inmates. They make great use of it. Prior to this, there was really nowhere for them to gather. Now they can sit and chat together." She raised her eyebrows at me. "The men are even allowed to smoke their pipes in their section, which they do so appreciate."

There was a glass partition to our left, and I could see the aforesaid sunroom. The morning was, in fact, cloudy and rather overcast, but the deep windows on the opposite side let in cascades of light. I could understand why it was considered a boon. However, as we got closer, it became obvious there was a big fracas happening in the women's section. A crowd of men were gathered at the connecting partition watching whatever was happening on the other side. I could hear raised, angry voices.

"Oh, dear," said Miss Lindsay as she quickened her step and opened the door.

The room was in an upheaval, and the cause appeared to be emanating from the far corner, where there was a fireplace with a cheery fire on the go. Two of the inmates were engaged in an angry exchange. One of them was standing and appeared to be trying to pry the second woman's hand off the seat of the chair next to her. The smaller one was seated, and she was resisting.

"That's my place," shouted the standing woman.

"It's not. I'm saving it."

"You're not allowed."

Miss Lindsay hurried over to them. Not quite knowing what to do, I followed her.

"Mrs. Fitzgerald, Mrs. Brodie. What's going on?"

The woman who was standing turned her head. Her face was contorted with anger. "She's not supposed to save chairs. I always sit there, and she won't let me. I suffer bad from the cold, and I need to be by the fire."

The other woman was diminutive but clearly not feeble. She was holding off her opponent with what looked like a strong grip.

"I'm expecting a visitor."

"It's against the rules. Tell her, Nurse. It's not allowed."

Miss Lindsay's voice was calm and soothing. "Let's not argue about it, my dears." She put her hand on the standing woman's arm. "You know what, Mrs. Fitzgerald, I could use a little help with preparations for our mid-morning snack. Why don't you and I go down together and get started. Afterward, we can sort this out."

The woman thrust out her lower lip. "She shouldn't be saving seats. Not by the fire, she shouldn't."

"It's just this once, I'm sure."

Mrs. Fitzgerald saw me and sent a withering glare in my direction as if I were complicit in the crime.

"She's not allowed. You shouldn't sit there."

I had no idea what to reply, but Miss Lindsay, who seemed unperturbed, gave Mrs. Fitzgerald a little pat.

"You know what? I've heard Mrs. Foster was planning to bake some chocolate cookies."

Mrs. Fitzgerald looked a bit mollified. "I like them best. If I help, can I have two?

"Of course."

Gently, Miss Lindsay started to lead her away. Mrs. Brodie kept her hand on the chair.

There were some sofas scattered around the room, but

it seemed as if most of the women had stood to observe the squabble.

Miss Lindsay beamed at them.

"Everything's all right now, my dears. Just go on with what you were doing. Miss Colborne will bring you to the dining room when they're ready. Chocolate cookies today. Won't that be nice?"

"It's not time yet, is it, Nurse?" An elderly woman who could have been Mrs. Fitzgerald's twin spoke up. "We just had our breakfast."

"Not just yet, Mrs. Acton," replied Miss Lindsay, cheery as ever. "But we might go a little early today. Mrs. Fitzgerald is going to help."

She threaded her arm firmly through that of Mrs. Fitzgerald. "Come along, then."

The woman in question seemed to have completely given up her quest for equality and accepted with happy docility. Once at the door, she paused long enough to glance over her shoulder and glare in triumph at her erstwhile opponent.

Rather like a flock of disturbed sparrows, the rest of the women settled down, bending in to confer with one another. From the many glances in my direction, I thought I must be the subject of the conversations.

The sea of white beards on the other side of the partition also ebbed away.

The sunroom was by no means large and seemed at capacity with about thirty or so women. Most of them were sitting on the wooden chairs and sofas that were lined up against the far wall. At first glance, it appeared that almost every woman had a piece of sewing or knitting in her hands. Music was jigging away in the background, and I could see a gramophone on a side table. An overlay of chatter started up but not too loud.

Before I could introduce myself, Mrs. Brodie turned a distinctly unfriendly gaze on me. She was a tiny creature, colourful in the extreme, wearing a long-sleeved red-and-blue knitted cardigan that fit tightly and showed off how skinny she was. Her skirt also looked knitted and was emerald green.

To my dismay, she looked at me uncomprehendingly.

"Who are you?"

"I'm Charlotte Frayne, from T. Gilmore and Associates. I'm here in response to your letter, which I received this morning."

"I was expecting a man."

"I am an associate of Mr. Gilmore."

"What did you say your name was?"

"Charlotte Frayne."

She scrutinized me for several moments, then finally she smiled and patted the chair next to her.

"All right then. Please sit down."

I did so, and she reached for a leather Gladstone bag that was on the floor beside her.

"Let's pretend we're looking at these."

She took out a bunch of knitted squares and dumped some on my lap. They were brightly coloured and neatly made.

She gave a quick glance in the direction of the door where Miss Lindsay had left with Mrs. Fitzgerald.

"I can't stand that old woman," she said emphatically. "Because she's been here for years, she thinks she owns the place. Well, I say God made us equal, and equal we're going to stay, even in this dismal hole."

I suppose I must have expressed more reaction than I realized because suddenly she grinned at me. "I was just saying that. It's not a dismal hole. They treat us good, considering we're on charity."

"I'm glad to hear it."

She nodded at the door.

"Did you tell Miss Lindsay why you were here?"

"No, I didn't."

"Good. That's very good. I don't want nobody to know."

She picked up one of the squares and held it in the air as if we were scrutinizing it. She put me in mind of an exotic bird: her bright plumage, her slightly tilted head, her brown button eyes.

Our faces were barely inches apart. Her breath was minty. She was speaking so softly, I was having a hard time hearing her. I had no idea what to expect.

"I read in the newspaper this morning about those two unfortunate Negro boys who have been sentenced to be strapped."

It was the case Mr. Gilmore had referred to earlier.

"Yes, I heard about it. They were convicted of theft."

She glanced around again. Another attendant, also in sombre garb, had come into the room and clapped her hands.

"Tea and cookies, ladies. Come along."

The women obeyed at once, chirruping and fluttering. They began to pack up their needlework, and the room was soon emptying out. Only a couple of inmates remained, slumped in their chairs, presumably in a slumber from which not even fresh cookies could tempt them.

Mrs. Brodie watched them for a moment, then she leaned even closer. She was speaking into my ear.

"Those boys are innocent."

I nodded encouragingly. "Why do you think so, Mrs. Brodie?"

She paused. "Because I saw the real criminals myself."

She stared at me, waiting for my reaction.

"Can you say any more about that?"

"You see, I'm allowed to make my deliveries myself if the weather is fine. It's a nice change for me to get out — the cardies sell especially well. It's just that they take a long time." She held up her hands, and I could see they were lumpy and misshapen. "Arthritis. All that cold Sudbury weather. Gets bitter up there. Hurts if I knit too much."

As gently as I could, I resumed the conversation.

"You were saying that you thought the boys charged with theft are not guilty?"

"That's right. Monday last, it was. I went to see Mrs. Nielson. She's got a little shop where she sells woollen goods and such. She's a good customer, and she especially likes my Fair Isle cardies. I'd just finished one, you see. It was early. Hardly light, really. When I'm making deliveries, I always go early right before breakfast. It's more private that way. So, like I said, I went to call on Mrs. Nielson. Her house is right on the corner of Edward and Elizabeth Streets. I didn't see a light on as yet, so I thought I'd just wait for a few minutes to give her time to rise and shine." Mrs. Brodie pursed her lips. "To tell the truth, I felt a bit awkward waiting outside on the porch. There's a bench in front of the house, so I thought I'd go and sit there. Well, didn't I see two men come from the back of the house across the road. Number 122, it was." She paused, remembering. "There was something about them that seemed funny to me. I wondered what they'd been up to. But just then Mrs. Nielson saw me, and she called me inside. She didn't give me as much as usual because she said winter was almost done, and she wasn't sure she could sell many more woolly cardies." Mrs. Brodie frowned. "I thought that was a bit of malarkey. I mean, it's just the beginning of March. We're going to get lots more cold days, if I know my Canadian weather. She just didn't want to pay the proper rate."

She chewed on that for a minute, and finally I prodded her again.

"Where were they heading? The two men you saw?"

"They continued along Edward Street. Like I said, Mrs. Nielson came out just then, so I wasn't paying them any more attention."

"You said there was something about them that seemed funny to you?"

"That's right, but tell you the truth, I didn't give it any more thought until this morning when I read the newspaper. Two Negro boys being charged. It said they had been burglarizing a house on Edward Street. Early Monday morning, it said." She shook her head. "These two men I saw were most definitely not Negroes. The streetlamp was still on, and I could see them clearly. One was tall and skinny. He had reddish hair and a big moustache. One of the droopy kind." She made a gesture. "Made me think of a Viking. The other one was smaller and all muffled up, so I didn't see what colour hair he had, but I can tell you for sure they were men, not young boys." She paused again and glanced over at the door, where a couple of the other inmates were slowly exiting.

"Can you tell me why you wondered about them, Mrs. Brodie?"

"What? Oh yes. One of them had a bundle under his arm. It was wrapped up in some kind of white cloth. I always notice fabrics, and this looked like it might have been wool or cotton. I saw black stripes and some sort of tassels, but I wouldn't swear to that. It seemed sort of fancy. Not the sort of thing you'd expect a wayfarer to be carrying. I'm betting them blokes were the ones who nicked stuff from that house. Those boys shouldn't be strapped for something they haven't done."

"Was there anything else about the two men that made you think they were burglars? Can you be a bit more specific?"

She frowned at me. "Specific? No, I can't. They just looked like they'd been up to no good." She made a movement across her lap with her fingers. "They were scurrying. You know the way rats do when they've got the cheese and a cat is after them."

"And at no time did you see boys going along the street?"

"Nope. It was early. Nobody out and about except me and the birds. That's another reason why I wondered about those blokes. What were they doing at that hour of the morning?"

I held back my sigh. "Have you considered reporting this to the police?"

She thrust out her jaw and shook her head. "They'd just make out I'm some addled old biddy who's lost her marbles. Honestly, I didn't know what to do, but by good luck, I saw your advertisement in the paper. Right there at the bottom of the page. Said you were a private investigator. You are, aren't you? You're not just the secretary?"

"I assure you I am a legitimate private investigator."

"Never mind," she continued. "The important thing is that you're here. But like I said, it's urgent. You'll have to move fast."

I had to be frank with her. "Mrs. Brodie, I respect your desire to make sure the innocent don't suffer, but I don't know where I'd start to investigate."

"What I was about to say is that I recognized one of the men. The redheaded skinny one. I don't know his name, but I was watching out of the window here, and I saw him yesterday. He came in for the dinner meal with the casuals."

"You're sure it was the same man you thought had stolen something?"

She sighed. "See what I mean. You immediately think I'm wrong. Confused. Addled."

"I'm sorry. It's easy to get mixed up when it's semi-dark, as you said it was."

"I'm not mixed up. I recognized him right away. He's got a sort of squashed face like he was a boxer or something."

"What about the second man?"

"Him I didn't recognize. Mind you, he had a tattered old cap on and a dark brown overcoat. Looked too big for him, so it was probably second-hand; he's likely a casual too. He looked younger."

She certainly wasn't sounding like a confused old lady at the moment.

"Was he in the lineup yesterday?"

"Could have been. I wasn't paying him as much attention."

"Mrs. Brodie, as you said, this is a serious situation. I think the police must be involved."

She began gathering up her knitted squares and stuffing them back in the Gladstone.

"I don't want to talk to them."

"One of the detectives is a friend of mine, and he's a really good man."

She looked doubtful.

"I swear he's not the kind of man who's going to jump to hasty conclusions, and I know he wouldn't want innocent young men to be punished for something they didn't do. Let me speak to him."

"And if I don't agree? This has been a confidential conversation."

In fact, we had no legally binding contract. There was no such thing where private investigators were concerned. If we encountered some kind of crime, we couldn't keep quiet any

more than an ordinary citizen could. That said, Mr. Gilmore
and I insisted on maintaining confidentiality with our clients
whenever possible. Confidentiality and a solid base of honesty.

She was silent for several moments, and I knew my own
trustworthiness was being assessed.

Before we could settle the matter, however, Miss Lindsay
reappeared in the sunroom.

"All done, Mrs. Brodie?"

"Yes, miss." She turned back to me and whispered, "Can
you come back at four o'clock? The casuals start lining up then
for the dinner meal. It's likely those men will show up."

"And if they don't?"

She smiled in a rather cheeky way. "You get to see how
things are run here. Might come in handy in one of your cases.
Could be interesting."

I tried not to sigh. Spending a couple of hours at the House
of Industry wasn't my idea of excitement.

Mrs. Brodie called over to Miss Lindsay. "The lady can't
make up her mind. She has to come back at four."

The other woman looked surprised. "Very well. If that's
necessary."

I nodded briskly. "Thank you, Miss Lindsay. I'll just finish
up my business, and I'll meet you at the elevator."

I thought she might demur, but she didn't. She smiled her
saleswoman's smile at me and, with a slight squeak of her
shoes, turned and left.

Mrs. Brodie leaned closer again and, still in a whisper, said,
"I was even younger than those boys when my own family was
on the receiving end of a false accusation. Destroyed us. I don't
want to ever see it happen to somebody else. So, all right, you
can talk to that detective if you must."

"Mrs. Brodie, you said in your letter that it was unsafe. What did you mean by that?"

She leaned away slightly. "I think the men saw me. They might want to shut me up."

I offered to escort her to the dining room. As we left the sunroom, we were accompanied by the music of the gramophone. There was an unctuous tenor singing, *There is a small hotel, where there is a wishing well.* The record must have had a scratch because suddenly he was repeating himself. *Wishing well, wishing well.*

Once outside, I collected my bicycle and, buffeted by the wind, set off for police headquarters, where I hoped to meet Detective Jack Murdoch.

CHAPTER FOUR

IF THE DULL colour of the House of Industry conveyed despair, the brisk red brick of the police headquarters emanated confidence and vigour. A short flight of steps swept up toward the elegant arched doorway; two entrances — take your pick — led into the foyer and from there into the airy main hall.

The House of Industry had had a pervasive smell of carbolic; the police headquarters smelled of cigarettes. Many. This was pretty much a male preserve, after all.

I went over to the reception, where a young officer was assiduously clacking away on his typewriter. He was new, and I didn't recognize him.

He stopped immediately and greeted me politely.

"May I help you, madam?"

I experienced a small pang that I had moved so soon to young men referring to me as *madam* and not *miss*.

"I'd like to see Detective Murdoch."

"Is he expecting you?"

"No. This is a surprise visit."

He gave me a quick glance. "I'll see if he's available."

He rolled his chair to the console, put on his earphones, and plugged in. There was an immediate answer.

"There is somebody here to see you, sir. A missus ...?"

He looked over at me.

"Tell him Charlotte Frayne would like a word. *Miss* Frayne."

He repeated that.

"He will be right out."

I actually hadn't seen Jack Murdoch for a couple of months. Last year, our paths had crossed dramatically, his work and mine running on parallel tracks. We had promised each other we would keep in touch, have a family dinner and so on, but the time had flown by, and we hadn't actually done so.

The door leading to the offices opened, and Jack came through. He was smiling, and I smiled back. He was happily married, I was happily connected, but I admit I experienced the usual frisson of attraction he elicited. He was a good-looking man: tall, with a full head of dark hair, touched with grey at the sides. His navy suit was smart and well-fitting.

Today, he was sporting a narrow sling on his right arm.

"Good grief, Jack. What happened to you?"

"I wish I could say it was something heroic, but alas, it was sheer clumsiness. I tripped on a loose carpet." He lifted the sling in the air. "Result: a sprained wrist."

He extended his left hand, and, rather awkwardly, we shook.

"Charlotte. I was going to ring you just last week and see how things were going. Sorry about that."

"That's okay. We've both been busy, I'm sure. Crime doesn't take holidays."

He chuckled. "Ha. Wouldn't that be nice."

He certainly had to deal with far more serious cases than were in my purview, but I knew that, over the past year, I had gained his respect, and I appreciated it.

"How's Gramps faring?" he asked.

"He's got a touch of bronchitis at the moment."

"Sorry to hear that. He seemed to be recovering well from his injury when I saw him last."

"He was. This is a bit of a setback, but I hope it's short-lived."

"Is he up to going to the Paradise?"

"I think he'd crawl there if he had to."

"I was planning to drop in for lunch sometime soon. I'd like to see him."

"He's there every day."

"Even with bronchitis?"

"Even with."

I was being all chipper and so forth, but even talking about my grandfather's health made me anxious. I knew Jack would be sympathetic, but I didn't want to cry on his shoulder.

He beckoned. "Let's go into my office."

He ushered me through the door into the hall. Last year, I had been dealing with Detective Walter Arcady, and after a rocky start we had established a reasonably friendly relationship. Today, his door was closed, and no light showed.

Jack nodded in that direction. "Walter is taking a leave of absence. He's having some health problems."

"Oh, sorry to hear that."

"We're afraid it's cancer, but he'll know definitely by the end of next week. He's at home until then."

We went into his office. It was a small room, a little on the severe side, with functional furnishings softened only by a couple of shelves along one wall. Several books were interspersed with some family photographs and a cheery-looking pot of pink begonias.

"Please have a seat."

He went behind his desk, moving the chair with a slightly suppressed groan. The sprained wrist was causing him some discomfort.

"Great to see you, of course, Charlotte, but I assume you're here on business."

"Quite right."

I filled him in on the letter and the ensuing meeting with Olivia Brodie.

Rather bemused, he leaned back in his chair. "Let me get this straight. This lady was on Edward Street and saw two men who she thought were thieves."

"That's correct. And according to what she read in the newspaper, two Negro boys have been charged with breaking and entering on that street. You know the case I mean?"

"I do." He reached down and pulled open his desk drawer. "I didn't investigate it myself. It happened on the same day I landed on the floor. I've only just received the report."

He removed a folder from the drawer. Another groan escaped him.

"Are you sure that's only a sprain, Jack? It seems to be hurting you quite a lot."

He grimaced. "Don't worry, I'm just enjoying the moan."

I knew he'd suffered a severe wound when he was serving in the war, and, like most old soldiers, he was stoic. He looked in pain, but all I could do was make more sympathetic noises.

He opened the folder.

"Here we are. Acting Detective James McCready had the case." Jack gave me a little grin. "I warn you now, Charlotte, McCready is either going to make policing his career or he is going to write a bestselling novel and live on that."

"What do you mean?"

"You'll see." He started to read the report. "'Dated Tuesday, March 2. Police station three received a call at 8:40 a.m. on Monday, March 1. The caller identified himself as Howard

Zweit, a student who had come for his tutoring session with Dr. Morris Brandwein, who lives at 122 Edward Street. Master Zweit had found Dr. Brandwein lying prone on his kitchen floor. He was breathing but was an unnatural colour of grey, and he was unconscious.'"

I couldn't help but interrupt. "Were those the exact words of Master Zweit? 'An unnatural colour of grey'?"

Jack shrugged. "All I know is what McCready has written in the report."

"Go on. I'm waiting with bated breath."

"You'll have to tell me what that feels like. I never understood that expression."

"Jack!"

"Okay. I'll continue. 'The young man said he thought there may have been a break-in. The back door was slightly ajar, and the lock appeared to have been forced. Constable Littlejohn and I, Acting Detective McCready, were apprised of the nature of the call, and we went immediately to the house. The door was opened by the young man who had telephoned the station. All things considered, he was remarkably composed and obviously stout of heart.'"

I raised my eyebrow at this expression, but Jack kept going.

"'He led us at once to the kitchen, where we found Dr. Brandwein. He was on his back and just within the doorway from hall to kitchen. He was unconscious. Master Zweit said he had entered the house by way of the front door as he was accustomed to do. He had called out to announce his arrival, "Hello, Dr. Brandwein, I'm here," but he received no reply. He saw that the kitchen light was on and proceeded down the hall, thinking a cup of hot tea might be on offer. To his utter dismay, he discovered the prone body of his tutor. He waited only long enough to be able to see that the man was still breathing and then ran back to the front hall, where the telephone is situated. He rang the police station as reported above. When I questioned him, he said emphatically that he had seen no sign of an intruder. He was too shocked to check the backyard, but there was certainly nobody in the house at that moment. I myself made a point of listening intently to see if, in fact, an intruder might be hiding somewhere, but there was utter silence.'"

Jack glanced over at me with a grin. "See what I mean? Novelist."

He continued with the report. "'I made a fast, rather perfunctory examination, and there were no signs of trauma to Dr. Brandwein. He was still in his dressing gown, and I surmised he had come downstairs on hearing a disturbance. The back door was partly open. I instructed Constable Littlejohn to ring the station and order an ambulance, which he did. While we waited, I made Dr. Brandwein as comfortable as possible by placing a pillow underneath his head. He showed no awareness of our presence. I instructed the constable to draw a glass of water for the young man who had raised the alarm and escort him to the front parlour, where he was to wait. I stayed beside the doctor until the arrival of the ambulance, and he was lifted onto the stretcher and taken to the hospital. Constable Littlejohn and I went through the house to ascertain its condition. It is not a large house and might have been mistaken for a public library, it contained so many bookshelves and books. However, there was no obvious sign that anything had been summarily disturbed. Given the state of the back door, I assumed this was indeed a burglary. I returned to the station from where I rang the General Hospital where Dr. Brandwein had been taken. The doctor in charge, Dr. Sterling, confirmed that Dr. Brandwein had had a stroke. As of the writing of this report, he remains in serious condition. We were able to ascertain from Master Zweit that the doctor is a widower and lives alone. He is retired but formerly taught at Jarvis Collegiate. He took on a few students to prepare them for university. It was in this capacity that Master Zweit had come to the house.'"

Jack shifted in his chair. "All right so far?"

"Fine. When did they arrest the two boys?"

"Hold on. Here is McCready's comment. 'Although open to any possibility, I saw no reason at this stage to suspect Master Zweit. He was naturally shaken but seemed truthful. I gave him permission to return home until further notice. He scampered away in great relief. I decided to send two constables, Littlejohn and Nicholls, at once to go door to door and ascertain if any of the neighbours had any information on what had happened. Or if indeed anyone else had been robbed. The officers contacted five residents, but nobody had heard or seen any disturbance. They reported no burglary. In fact, they were shocked and alarmed by what had occurred. To a man (and a woman), they all declared this was a quiet street and law-abiding. One resident did add the comment, "Despite the proximity of the poorhouse." Referring to the House of Industry. A neighbour, a Mrs. Szabo, two doors down, also informed us that the previous day, Dr. Brandwein had announced his intention to visit his ailing sister who lives in Picton, Ontario. He also intimated he might move there. I include this in my report as it may be relevant to the case.'"

Again, Jack paused. "He could be right about that. If there were no other break-ins on the street, the doctor may have been specifically targeted. Someone may have known about his proposed visit and assumed the house would be empty."

"I was thinking that myself. Do go on."

Jack did so. "'However, at number 37, which is just east

of number 122 on the south side of Edward Street, Constable Littlejohn hit lucky. The resident of the house is a Mr. Soloman Glozier. He stated that he had seen two Negro boys running from Dr. Brandwein's house that morning. He had wondered what they were up to but did not consider a follow-up until the constable told him about the robbery. He immediately concluded these two were the culprits. He was able to give a clear description of the boys, whom he recognized. They are newspaper boys who are employed by a vendor on Spadina Avenue. Constable Littlejohn then went to question the vendor, whose name is Kenneth Biggles. He informed the constable that he did know the two boys and that they lived at the Working Boys Home, which is located on Gould Street. Constable Littlejohn telephoned this information into the station, and I set out right away to join them. The three of us went directly to the Home. The superintendent, Mr. James Donovan, informed us that the boys were, in fact, no longer resident at the Home. As of Saturday, he had evicted them. To be accurate, his exact words were that he "turfed them out." They had not paid the pitiful subsidy required for their board and "they were constantly picking quarrels and simply did not fit in." He said that he was holding a rucksack containing their possessions, which had been left behind on their rather hasty departure. I begged his permission to examine said rucksack, which he gave us forthwith. Inside, we found a few items of clothing and a relatively small, somewhat dusty, tin box. From the label, I ascertained it had once contained Christie biscuits. I opened it up, and inside were several items (see list below). On the basis of this evidence, we decided to pick up the boys in question. Mr. Biggles had said they would most likely be returning by four o'clock to pick up the evening editions of the newspaper. This turned out to be the case. Constable Nicholls remained with the vendor, and when the boys showed up, he arrested them and brought them to the station. The older boy is the one who speaks, and he protested their innocence. He explained the items in the tin box as items they had found at various times in the laneways as they traversed to work. He said emphatically they were not stolen. I said we had a witness placing them on the scene at the crucial time. The boy, whose name is Leroy, said they were on their way to work. That particular morning, as they were early, they had taken a detour. He agreed, albeit reluctantly, that they may have been seen by our witness, although 'that didn't prove anything' — his words. I then asked them if they had indeed burglarized Dr. Brandwein's house. They both became agitated; the older boy was even belligerent. He declared their innocence in no uncertain terms. Even, I am afraid to say, the boy laced this declaration with more than one expletive.'"

I couldn't help it. The expression made me burst out laughing.

"I'm surprised Acting Detective McCready didn't write down said expletives."

Jack laughed as well. "I warned you."

"Can I see the list of the items?"

He handed over a piece of paper. The handwriting was very neat. Maybe Detective McCready had been a clerk in his previous employment, drawn to police work by the allure of drama and excitement.

At first glance, all I could see was a list of a mishmash of articles: a couple of brass watches, one with leather band, one without; three hairpins; four single earrings (one mother-of-pearl stud, two silver hoops of different sizes, and one gold hoop, bent); three gloves (one woman's white kid, one cotton and lace trimmed, and one man's black leather, torn at two fingers). The only thing that seemed in any way valuable was a silver matchbox containing five unused matches. I pointed that out to Jack.

"Our good officer seized on that." He went back to the report. "'On examining the matchbox, I noticed a Star of David symbol engraved on the side. As Dr. Brandwein is Jewish, it seemed a reasonable conclusion that this was his property. Given the evidence in the rucksack and the statement of the witness, Mr. Glozier, I decided to detain the boys until they could be brought before a justice of the peace. This happened promptly, as Judge Carter was in locus. He thought the best course of action was to hold them overnight until he convened the juvenile court in the morning. It seemed the simplest thing to do was keep them on the premises, so we put them in one of the vacant general cells. That done, I decided to return to the house on Edward Street. Here, I encountered the housekeeper, Mrs. Venetia Ricci. She had heard what had happened from the constable who was temporarily stationed outside the door. She is a highly strung woman, and it was difficult to keep her calm enough to go through the house to ascertain what items were missing, but that is what I did. She said immediately that the solid silver menorah was missing. That is a special kind of candelabra that is used in Jewish religious rituals. It was kept on a shelf in the kitchen. I asked her about a silver matchbox, and she realized that was also missing. It was usually kept in Dr. Brandwein's smoking den, which adjoins the living room. Somewhat reluctantly, she agreed to poke her head into the den, which did indeed, as she had warned us, reek of tobacco. There was no sign of the matchbox. I had her go through the entire house very carefully, but she could find no evidence of other items being stolen. The doctor had an extensive library — in fact, it filled one entire room on the second floor — but Mrs. Ricci was unable to confirm that any of those books had gone.

I am of the opinion that the library was intact. It was neat and tightly packed. Books, however valuable to their owner, do not necessarily bring a good price on the illicit market. A solid silver candelabra would. As would a silver matchbox. As of the writing of this report, the boys, or more precisely the older boy, Leroy, continue to deny any guilt. Submitted respectfully, James McCready, Acting Detective, Toronto Constabulary.'"

Jack put the report down on his desk. "That's it. McCready brought the boys before Judge Carter the next day, and the judge found the evidence irrefutable. Then, as you now know, he sentenced the boys to ten days in jail and ten strokes of the strap. Actually, it was only eight for the younger boy, who the judge felt was more of a follower than a leader. Sentence to be carried out this coming Friday."

I jumped in. "Hold on a minute, Jack. Mrs. Brodie says that one of the two men she describes as suspicious was carrying something wrapped in a bundle. She said it was white with tassels and black stripes. It made me think of a Jewish *tallit,* a traditional prayer shawl. And you're telling me the victim of the robbery is Jewish?"

"That is correct. But the housekeeper doesn't appear to have reported a missing prayer shawl."

"That doesn't mean it wasn't stolen. She might not be that observant."

Jack gave me what I can only describe as a sharp look. "Point taken, Charlotte."

"Mrs. Brodie was adamant about seeing those two men," I continued. "The time and place fit. Early last Monday morning on Edward Street."

Jack was regarding me doubtfully. "What about our witness? He says he saw the boys running away from the house in question. Also early Monday morning."

"That could mean anything. Were they asked about that?"

"I don't know. They're maintaining their innocence, but that's a song a lot of criminals sing."

There was silence for a moment or two. I was still not happy.

"Jack, do you think the boys are innocent?"

"Frankly, no. It's true that the various items in the box might have been found goods; they seem cheap bits for the most part. But the silver matchbox is particularly damning. It certainly belonged to Dr. Brandwein. Why would it be in their possession?"

"I get your point, Jack, but Mrs. Brodie is certain it was two other men who did the burglary. As I said, right time, right place."

"But she didn't actually see them coming out of the house?"

"I don't believe so."

"On what did she base this supposition of guilt?"

"She thought they were 'scurrying' in a suspicious manner."

"Sorry, Charlotte, but that is a bit thin."

"Jack, if she is right, it would indeed be a grave miscarriage of justice, as she put it. Not to mention a painful one if the boys are to get the strap. What other evidence was there? Did you go over the house for fingerprints? Fibres?"

Jack exhaled sharply. "We didn't do that. It didn't seem worth the trouble. The candelabra is valuable, but not crushingly so. Neither is the matchbox."

"If they did steal the menorah, where is it?"

"They have admitted to nothing so far, but it wouldn't be that difficult to hide it somewhere other than their room with the intention of recovering it later."

"Is the newspaper vendor above suspicion? Could he have been doing a Fagin?"

"It's not out of the question, but I doubt it. He's been there for years. I've bought papers from him myself. There's never been a whisper of dark deeds concerning him." He shook his head. "The boys being incarcerated has left him very inconvenienced." Jack grimaced. "Many patrons haven't had the opportunity to read the latest bad news of the world."

It was my turn to do a little finger twiddling. I really liked Jack Murdoch. I considered him to be a compassionate man. He was also an officer of the law, and I knew it was sometimes difficult to dislodge such men from their final opinions. In spite of his making fun of McCready's wordiness, he seemed to have accepted his conclusions.

"You know as well as I do, Jack, lying is often the first level of defence. I'd say young Negro boys might have already learned to mistrust the law. They might not have expected they'd get a fair deal."

Jack leaned back in his chair and nodded.

"Didn't the boys get any sort of counsel, at least?"

"They were in juvenile court. They appeared before Judge Carter, and after questioning them, he determined they were guilty and gave sentence. He does have that authority. There was nothing to counter the conviction. There were no parents in evidence. The superintendent of the residence where they were staying gave a damning report. Case open and shut."

"Isn't that rather rushed?"

"I suppose it was, but as I say, the judge didn't consider it that serious a matter. I should tell you, Charlotte, when I myself spoke to the superintendent at the Home, he said the boys were highly impulsive and prone to hot temper. They had already had two nasty altercations at the Home. Both based on accusations of theft."

"McCready said they were sent packing. Where did they go?"

"The superintendent didn't know."

"How old are they?"

"The older one, Leroy Davies, is fifteen; the younger one, Jerome, is thirteen."

"Young to be on your own."

Jack wriggled his fingers. "You've made some good points, Charlotte. I don't want to be a lout here. I will talk to the boys again. As a matter of fact, they're downstairs in the cells."

"Still?"

"Judge Carter has ordered they be kept in custody until the sentence is carried out. He says he wants to teach the boys a lesson they won't forget. He thinks time in the cells should scare them straight."

"Who is going to administer the strap? Not you, I hope."

"At the judge's insistence, it will be one of the warders from the Don."

"When?"

"Punishment will be administered a few days from now. Friday at nine o'clock, to be precise." He sighed. "There's something else I should tell you. It hasn't got to the newspapers yet, but it could make things worse for the boys."

"Oh dear. What is it?"

"Dr. Brandwein may not recover. The stroke was severe. If he does die, it is very likely the judge, knowing his mindset, could hold the boys responsible. It is not inconceivable he will throw a charge of manslaughter at them."

"What would that mean?"

"Possibly a long term of incarceration."

"Proof of guilt seems imperative, wouldn't you say?"

"I would indeed."

As Mrs. Brodie had said, it was an urgent matter.

CHAPTER FIVE

JACK HAD SWORN me in on a previous occasion as a temporary official stenographer, and he did the same this time.

"We can talk to them in the office," he said. "Here, give me your coat, and I'll hang it up."

Nice.

I accompanied him down to the lower level of the police station, where the cells were.

There were six holding cells in the headquarters basement; they were intended for prisoners in transition to either a more serious incarceration like the Don Jail or the Kingston Penitentiary or release when bail was posted. I would never in a hundred years have described them as comfortable, but each cell had open bars rather than doors, which made them somewhat less claustrophobic than the usual jail. There was room for two men at a time, each having a narrow cot.

The stairs led to a narrow hall, at the end of which was the door to the cells proper. It was solid steel but barred halfway, giving the constable on duty a chance to observe his charges. An officer was at the desk, which was situated just outside the door. He jumped to his feet when we came in and gave Jack a military salute. He was definitely on the mature side of life, and everything about him suggested ex-soldier.

"Good morning, sir."

"Constable Weber, isn't it?"

"Yes, sir. Present, sir."

"We're here to interview the two boys who were brought in last week. The name is Davies. Leroy and Jerome."

"Yes, sir. They are in cell number three."

"How have they been?"

"Troublesome, in a word, sir. They don't seem to understand the word *quiet*. If they aren't trying to get my goat, they are provoking the other men in custody. I've had to threaten them with loss of privileges on two occasions. The last one was this morning."

"What privileges were they in danger of losing?" I asked. I genuinely wanted to know, but he darted a look at me as if I were one of those do-gooder women who had no idea what the darker side of society was really like.

"They would get only a cup of water and a slice of unbuttered bread for breakfast, and if they continued, the same for lunch and supper."

"Did they smarten up when you told them that was in the offing?"

"As a matter of fact, they did. Quiet as mice now."

Rather obviously, Jack cleared his throat. "Good. Let us in, will you, Constable? This is Miss Frayne, by the way. She's acting as my recorder for the moment."

I acknowledged him in an efficient sort of way.

"Madam," said Weber, and he made a curt bow of his head.

There was a long chain hooked to his belt with a key ring on the end. He selected a key and opened the barred door, standing back so we could go through ahead of him. There were high, narrow windows on each side, but the light was dim, and the air felt cold and stale. The only other occupant of the cells was a man in cell number two who was stretched out on his cot, reading. He lowered the book and called out,

"Good morning, Detective Murdoch. I hope you've come to tell me I can go."

"Not yet, Rick."

"Don't say you've come to take the curly-tops away? They've been keeping me company. Can get a bit dull in here."

He saw me standing behind Jack, and he swung himself off the cot and stood up. "I beg your pardon, miss. I didn't see you there. Good morning to you as well."

"And the same to you."

He gave me a rather formal bow. "Richard Wolfe at your service."

He was not the kind of man you might expect to find in a police cell. Medium height, slim and wiry, with smooth, close-cropped grey hair and a pencil moustache. Add to that wire-rimmed glasses and you could see him holding forth in a classroom, not here. He reminded me of Mr. Gilmore.

"I thought you were getting sprung yesterday, Rick," said Jack. "Did I get it wrong?"

"No, you are quite right. I was indeed supposed to depart yesterday, but the solicitor fell ill, and I have to wait."

"Sorry about that."

Rick's glasses seemed a little loose, and he shoved them up on his nose. "To tell the truth, things could be worse. The food is decent, if a mite boring; it's quiet; it's warm. I've been allowed a couple of books. Now all I need is some writing paper and a pen or pencil."

Jack chuckled. "I'll speak to the guard, and we'll get you some. Can't miss out on your epistles, can we?"

"Thank you kindly." He nodded in the direction of the cell across from him. "Don't tell me it's time for the lads to get whopped?"

"Not yet," answered Jack. "We're just going to have another chat with them."

"They're good boys, you know. They can be a bit rambunctious — at least the older boy can — but they're just lads. They haven't yet learned to accept that it's better to sail with the wind than against it. But they'll learn, I've no doubt. To my mind, they got a raw deal."

Rick's cell was opposite that of the two boys, and they had obviously heard us. I could see they had stood up and were both at the bars.

Given the bad report from the constable, I wasn't sure what to expect, but the boys were standing in silence, watching us. They were dark-skinned, small of stature, and in both cases the regular blue prison shirt and trousers that had been issued to them were loose and ill-fitting. Jack had said they were fifteen and thirteen years of age, but they both looked younger, not even in puberty yet. The thought of them being strapped by somebody who had lashed grown criminals was dreadful.

Jack turned to address them. "Morning, lads. Detective Murdoch here. I thought we could have a bit of a chat."

The smaller boy glanced over at his brother, who answered. I wouldn't say his voice was polite, but it was studiedly neutral, as was his expression.

"What would that be about, sir?"

"I want to go over your statements again."

The boy looked at him. "I'm not sure we can add much more, sir. Don't say you're going to tell us somebody else saw us robbing a house, 'cause it isn't true. We did nothing of the kind."

For such a young boy, he had the articulation of a hoary solicitor. Not that it was likely, but I hoped he'd have the chance to study law at some point in the future.

"Not robbers," whimpered the younger one. "Not fair wallop us."

At least that's what I think he said. He was hard to understand, as he had a cleft lip.

He looked as if he was going to burst into tears, and his brother reached over and pinched his ear. He was quiet immediately.

"Don't mind Jerome, sir," he said to Jack. "He's got the mithers. The food here don't agree with him. Gave him the runs."

There was a sanitary bucket in the corner of the cell, and even from where I was, I could smell it.

"Tell you what, I think we'd be more comfortable talking in my office," said Jack, and he turned and beckoned to Constable Weber.

"Before we do that, sir," interjected Leroy, "could we empty our bucket? Like I said, Jerome here has the runs, and he could do with using the latrine."

The constable said sharply, "You emptied your bucket this morning. Once a day is what you're permitted."

"I think if the boy has the runs, we probably should accommodate him," said Jack. His voice was pleasant, but I could tell Weber wasn't happy about being overruled.

"Very well, sir." He stepped past us so that he could unlock the cell.

To this point, everybody had been acting as if I were invisible, but Leroy now fixed his attention on me. If I'd seen him as a child before, I did so no longer. Briefly, I saw a depth of caution that was far beyond his years. Not hostile, but utterly without trust.

"May I be so bold as to ask who is this lady?" he said to Jack. "Will she also be at the meeting?"

"This is Miss Frayne, and she is currently assisting the police. I have invited her to be present when we talk. She will record what we say, and she will also ask questions if necessary."

Leroy nodded. "Look forward to it."

Jerome tugged at his brother's sleeve. He made a universal gesture indicating he couldn't hold his bowels.

"He's got to go and fast," said Leroy to Weber.

"Bring the bucket," snapped the constable, and he swung open the cell door.

The younger boy grabbed the bucket and came into the corridor; his brother was behind him. The exit to the outside courtyard where the latrines were located was at the far end. Jerome headed toward it, Weber close behind, Leroy behind him. Jack and I stayed by the cell.

The boy whimpered again as they stopped in front of the door. Weber hastily did the same manoeuvre with his key chain as he'd done at the entrance. As he did so, Rick called out, "Don't forget to empty your bucket properly, boys. Maybe the upholder of the law would dump it for you. It would give him a job to do."

His tone was full of contempt, and Weber looked over at him, momentarily distracted.

In a split second, the brothers moved.

"Go!" yelled Leroy.

Jerome swivelled and swung his bucket upward with all his might. It caught the constable just below his chin, causing his teeth to bite into his lip. A bright crimson stream of blood immediately spurted down his chin. Perhaps worse, he was splattered with urine and feces. He staggered back against the wall, and in a flash, Jerome darted through the exit. At the same time, Leroy leaped forward to follow him. As he passed the constable, he punched Weber so hard in his belly that, already stunned, the constable fell to the floor. Leroy was through the unlocked door in an instant and pulled it shut behind him. It locked automatically. Jack, with admirably fast reflexes, also started after the two boys. He was hampered by both the prone constable, who was lying on the key chain, and the sling on his arm. Rick added to the mayhem by yelling at top volume, "Go, lads! Go! Follow the flag!"

As for me, I didn't know what to do. The corridor was narrow, allowing only two people abreast. I was standing directly beside Rick's cell.

Jack managed to retrieve the key, but as he was struggling to unlock the door, Rick reached through the bars of his cell and grabbed me by the belt of my dress, pulling me over and effectively immobilizing me.

I didn't wait to give him a warning but did what I'd learned in my self-defence training over the past three months. I grabbed the little finger on his left hand and jerked it upward. He yelped in pain and let go of me. I didn't even need to give the right hand the same treatment because he let go on that side also. I jumped out of reach.

Jack turned. "What the hell?"

"Never mind, I'm all right."

The reeking constable staggered to his feet, but he looked in no shape to move far. Jack had by now unlocked the exit, and he rushed through. I was following, perhaps heedlessly, and I heard him shout out, "Leroy! Stop!"

I barely had time to register that I was in a small, walled courtyard. There was a wooden latrine hut to one side. On its steep roof, wobbling precariously, was the younger brother. Before we could do anything to stop him, he shoved himself from the roof, aiming for the high wall a few feet away.

He didn't make it.

He lost his footing and, with a cry, he slipped downward.

He landed on the concrete surface of the courtyard with a horrible thud.

And lay still.

Jack ran over to him. I went too. I was dimly aware that Weber had come into the courtyard.

Jack called over to him, "Fetch a doctor!"

Jack and I were both kneeling beside the injured boy. His right leg was twisted underneath him, but, more alarming, he was showing no signs of consciousness. His eyelids were quivering, his mouth was open, his breathing was harsh and rapid. A vivid gash had opened up just at his hairline.

Jack took the boy's hand.

"Jerome, stay with me. Help is coming."

I took the other hand, which was icy cold. I started to rub it gently. I had only met this lad a few minutes ago, but in that moment, I could feel that Jack Murdoch and I were locked into a primitive need to save this flickering life.

CHAPTER SIX

THE NEXT COUPLE of hours were a flurry of activity. The doctor arrived. Jerome, alive but still unconscious, was transported to the Hospital for Sick Children. Dr. Finney thought he would recover, but he "couldn't promise" — his words. As if he were able to dispense life promissory notes. Leroy, the older boy, was nowhere to be found. He had obviously climbed over the wall first, but where he'd gone from there, we didn't yet know. Jack assigned two of the duty constables to search the area.

"Jerome has a cleft palate, which is why he's hard to understand," Jack said. "It affects his hearing as well. I'd like to find his brother soon for his sake."

We moved back to his office to take a breather. Jack wasn't saying much, but I thought he was deeply troubled about what had happened. Finally, he said, "I blame myself, Charlotte. Those boys shouldn't have been in here. This is a jail for adults, not children."

"You didn't sentence them, the judge did."

"Doesn't matter. I might have been more insistent. They should have been over at the Children's Aid shelter, not here."

"My feeling is that if you're facing some pretty painful punishment, you're going to get desperate enough to attempt to escape no matter where you are."

He was still staring into space and hardly seemed to hear me.

"I swear," Jack said, "if the boy lives, I will make it up to him if it's the last thing I do." He gave me a wry smile. "My conscience is weighed down enough. I don't need any more guilt."

He didn't elaborate, and at that moment, a constable announced that, as requested, Richard Wolfe was here to be interviewed.

"Stay for a minute, will you, Charlotte? I'd like you to be in on this."

Rick was ushered in. Jack offered him a chair, which he refused, as if sitting down would make him complicit with the enemy. And enemy we were.

"We are considering charging you with obstructing police in discharge of their duty and aiding and abetting two convicted felons to escape."

"Hardly," Rick replied. "Doing a runner is not worth it in my book. I know; I've had a go more than once. You just make things worse for yourself."

I knew I should have kept quiet — it was Jack's interview — but my words blurted out before I could stop them.

"You were urging them on. I heard you."

Rick shrugged. "That was just in the heat of the moment."

His voice was calm and measured. I had to admit, except for the moments he was shouting to the escaping boys, he hadn't raised his voice.

I sensed he was the kind of man who liked to see somebody losing a bit of control, and I clenched my jaw.

"Do you know the whereabouts of Leroy Davies?" asked Jack.

"I haven't a clue."

"I believe the boys planned this carefully. They were simply waiting for the right moment."

Rick shrugged. "And you provided that for them by letting them out, didn't you, Detective? You and this lady here. I thought I was dealing with a wildcat."

My jaw undid itself all on its own at this. "*You* were the one who grabbed *me*. Why? That gave the boys a chance to get out in the yard."

Jack gave me a warning glance, and I clamped down again.

Rick frowned. "I was only trying to keep you out of harm's way. You're the one who attacked me. You could have broken my finger. As it is, it's sprained." He held up his hand, and the little finger did indeed look red and swollen. "The truth is, I'm considering bringing a charge against you. Unprovoked assault."

Jack interjected. "That's a case you're not going to win, Wolfe. I saw what you did. Miss Frayne was simply defending herself."

Rick peered over the top of his glasses. "We'll see what the law decides."

Jack tapped on his desk. "For the moment, our priority is to find this young lad. If you co-operate, I won't ask the judge to extend your sentence. Which I have every right to do."

Wolfe frowned at him. "Even if I was inclined to turn him in, which I'm not, I couldn't. I don't have a clue where he is. On a train to Montréal, I hope."

"Why would he go to Montréal?"

"Figure of speech. I hear they're nicer to coloured boys than Torontonians."

That was more or less it.

Wolfe refused to say any more except to further complain about his injury. Finally, Jack sent him back to his cell.

After he left, I asked Jack what the original charges had been against him. Why was he incarcerated?

"He said the wrong thing in the wrong place at the wrong time. He belongs to some kind of anarchist society. Doesn't believe in governments. Or authoritarian structures."

"I suppose that includes police officials."

"It certainly does. We are all simply agents of capitalism. Mindless minions. He trained as a lawyer, and as far as I can tell he ekes out a living defending the disenfranchised. Who rarely have money."

Jack's voice was angry. I'd already experienced the conflict between those who wanted fundamental social changes and those employed to maintain order. I sympathized with him, but to my mind it was a complex issue with no easy resolution.

"What is your sense, Charlotte? Do you think he's telling us the truth?"

"It's hard to tell. He's a smooth operator."

Jack rubbed at his wrist. "Yes, the lads seized the moment, but I'd say it was carefully planned ahead of time. They knew exactly what to do when they were let out of the cell."

"I agree, and Wolfe was right with them. That was piffle about keeping me safe. He wanted to make sure I couldn't do anything."

Jack stared at me. "Where did you learn that little self-defence trick?"

"I've been taking a course. In my line of work, you never know when it might be necessary."

He laughed. "I thought for a minute I was back in the army watching a demonstration on unarmed combat."

I was rather chuffed by that. Mr. Halston's lessons had obviously been sinking in.

Jack rocked back in his chair. "So, where is Leroy? He can't go back to the Home, but he's got to hide somewhere."

"And I'd guess it's not too far away. I agree with you that the whole thing had been thought out. He'd want to head for cover immediately. And that cover was ready for him."

Jack reached for his telephone. "I'm going to put out a broadsheet and have it posted everywhere in the vicinity. I'll mention that Jerome is seriously injured. That might draw the brother. Poor little sod." Jack's face was grim. "So much for you pursuing justice, Charlotte. I'm afraid those lads have made their situation infinitely worse."

"For God's sake, don't let the judge add more strokes of the strap."

"Over my dead body."

CHAPTER SEVEN

JACK HAD A lot to do, and officially I had no place. I was also going to be really late for my appointment with Mrs. Calder if I didn't make tracks. Jack said he'd do his best to meet me at four o'clock at the House of Industry, and we said our goodbyes.

I scuffed my shoes on the grassy verge outside of the building. I thought I might have stepped in the effluvium from the bucket. That would not give a good impression to a potential new client. I wiped off as best I could.

Mrs. Calder's address was on Gerrard Street, a wide, elegant boulevard that faced the Allan Horticultural Gardens, one of Toronto's jewels. An oasis of parkland, the gardens also contained a beautiful hothouse conservatory where flowers could thrive all through the dark days of winter. It had been a favourite place to visit with my grandparents when I was growing up. I thought it was another world in the middle of Toronto where flowers bloomed nonstop and it was always warm, even when there was snow outside piling up against the windows. I remember I'd asked my Gramps once why they didn't just open up the doors and let the warm air flow out into the park and melt all the snow. "It doesn't work quite like that, pet. I wish it did."

Now, as I cycled by, the park looked a little desolate. The winter snow drifts had melted, but the trees were not yet thrusting out their respective chests to celebrate their defiance of the bitter death-dealing cold that had been so recently visited on them.

A gust of wind grabbed me and actually lifted me and the bike a couple of inches. I was glad I didn't have too far to go.

Number 260 was at the corner of Gerrard Street and the well-coiffed Berkeley Street. It was in the middle of a row of houses, buff coloured with bay windows, nicely curtained; an iron fence enclosed each requisite small garden and short path. I couldn't call the house grand. It was too modest for that, but it looked satisfied with its lot in life.

I dismounted and propped my bike against a nearby street-lamp. My beret had kept my hair under control. I gave my shoes another quick scuff and rang the doorbell.

The woman who answered was clearly not a servant. She was dressed in a floor-length caftan of some iridescent gold and green material that flowed down to pointed, jewelled slippers. She was large-boned, and only a woman of her size could have got away with such an outfit. She was heavily made up, with wavy, jet-black, shoulder-length hair that I could only assume was a wig as she was probably well into her seventies. A miasma of exotic perfume wafted out.

"Mrs. Calder? I'm Charlotte Frayne." I tried to sound more confident than I actually felt. What was I getting myself into?

She frowned. "I was expecting you at least thirty minutes ago."

"My apologies. I was unavoidably detained."

"Very well. Come in. We're in the living room."

She stepped back, and as she did so, another woman came into the foyer. No Scheherazade here. Her plain navy dress with starched white collar and cuffs pronounced her "housekeeper."

"Mrs. Calder, I'm so sorry, I didn't hear the door. I was in the kitchen."

"Don't worry, Maria. I will take care of it."

The housekeeper gave me a most unfriendly stare. I wasn't sure what I'd done to deserve it, but it was obvious she considered me an undesirable visitor. This was the second time today I had been viewed with serious disapproval.

She addressed Mrs. Calder. "Will you be wanting tea, madam?"

"No, thank you. Miss Frayne is here on business."

"You should have told me, madam. We could have got things ready."

I wasn't sure what she meant by that but let it pass.

Mrs. Calder waved her hand. "I can take care of it." She beckoned to me. "Come this way."

The housekeeper was forced to step back, and Mrs. Calder led the way down the hall.

She actually moved quite fast, and I didn't have much chance to take in the surroundings, but I had the impression of paintings and furnishings that had lived a long life.

When we entered the drawing room, light and heat assailed me. An electric chandelier was emitting high-wattage light, and a big fire was crackling away in the hearth.

Mrs. Calder plonked herself down on a brocade armchair by the fireplace and indicated I could take the chair opposite. Nobody had asked me to remove my coat, but I did. It was that or boil.

I'll say this for Mrs. Calder, she was decisive. She didn't beat around the bush.

"Let's get to the point. As I said in my note, I am missing some very valuable jewellery, and I am afraid it has been stolen." She held up her hand as if I had interrupted her. "I know what you're about to say. No. I have not gone to the police. I thought I would start with you private people. It is a matter of some delicacy."

Before I could interject, she reached down to a sort of embroidery bag beside the chair and took out a long ebony cigarette holder. Another little rummage and she removed a packet of cigarettes, shook one out, and stuffed it into the holder. Then she looked vaguely around the room.

"Would you mind ...?"

I gathered she was in search of the lighter, which I could see on the mantlepiece.

"Allow me."

I got the thing — solid brass — and lit her cigarette for her. I felt as if we were in a movie: I was William Powell, and she was Myrna Loy.

She drew on the cigarette, deep into the lungs the way addicted smokers do.

"Thank you ... Miss ... er? Sorry. What was your name again?"

"Frayne. Charlotte Frayne. I'm an associate of Mr. Gilmore's. You got in touch with us because you said you had lost some jewellery and thought it might have been stolen."

"Oh, there's no question it was stolen. They could hardly have got up and walked away, could they?"

Another deep draw.

It was my turn to do some handbag fishing.

"I'll just take some notes, if you don't mind."

"If you have to. But as I said, this is a delicate matter. And most private."

What did she think I was going to do? Sell the story to the *Daily Star*?

"What exactly has gone missing, Mrs. Calder? Can you describe it for me?"

"Two items." Her voice was impatient, as if I were being deliberately obtuse. I was rapidly losing the desire to help this woman. "What is gone is a gold cufflink that belonged to my late, dear father. And a silver charm bracelet."

"Just one cufflink?"

She was still for a moment, her thoughts inward. "Yes. I'm afraid the other one disappeared some years ago."

"When did you last see these items?"

"I keep them both in a special box on my dressing table, and they were there last Sunday."

"And it wasn't until yesterday that you noticed they were missing?"

"That is correct."

"What time of day did you look?"

"In the morning. After breakfast."

"I presume you have done a search of the house?"

"Of course. We found nothing, and that was when I decided to telephone your agency. Both of these items have great sentimental value for me."

Her eyes actually met mine, and for a moment I thought I could see tears. On the other hand, it could have been the smoke, which was making circles around her head.

"Will you describe the cufflink and the bracelet, Mrs. Calder?"

"The link is gold. My father's initials are embossed. H.M."

I almost blurted out *His Majesty* but caught myself in the nick of time. "What do the initials stand for?"

"Herbert Moorhead." She looked over at me again as if expecting me to exclaim. I didn't. I had never heard of him before. "He was a city councillor. Very admired and respected. He died two weeks before my tenth birthday. His death was quite unexpected."

This time, for sure, the watery eyes were tears. Even after the lapse of all this time, the old grief was apparently still potent.

She pulled a handkerchief from her caftan and dabbed at her eyes.

"He was a good man and a most loving father. My mother was bereft. She herself did not live much longer. Hardly saw the year out. I was an orphan."

"I'm so sorry, Mrs. Calder. That must have been dreadful for you. Were there any other children in the family?"

"None. I was an only child."

There was an expression on her face that I couldn't quite decipher. I couldn't tell if she was happy about her single status or not. I decided to push it a little.

"I was the only one in my family too. I often wished I'd had brothers and sisters."

She stared at me. "Did you indeed? I must say, I was quite content. What contact I did have with other families, I noticed a great deal of enmity among the children. I thought they could be quite vicious with one another."

I pushed again. "I'll bet you made sure your own children didn't fall into that frame of mind."

I hadn't had the chance to check on her background other than that she was widowed. My mistake. She actually turned red and scowled at me.

"My husband and I were not blessed with issue."

Issue? I'd only seen that word applied to the aristocracy.

"If we had been so blessed," she continued, "I would have ensured they were amicable toward each other."

Lucky little mites they would have been. I myself thought

that love begat love, and so far, I didn't see a surfeit of it in Mrs. Calder's personality. I brought us back to the matter at hand.

"You said the other item is a silver charm bracelet?"

"That is correct. When I was four years old, my dear father gave me a silver bracelet for my birthday. There was one charm on it: a stork carrying a baby in a sling. The baby had the initial E for Emmeline, my Christian name. It was delightful. Papa said that on every birthday thereafter he would add another charm until I was all grown up and it was too heavy to wear." Again, she paused and took a journey into the past. "He kept his promise, and it became a very special moment when he gave me the latest charm." Her eyes met mine. "There were only six altogether. He died before my tenth birthday."

She'd already told me that, but it was obviously highly significant.

"I'm sorry, Mrs. Calder. That must have been very difficult for you."

"It was. I must say, I have always considered it an unnecessary death. He was in the prime of his life."

I wanted to ask her what had happened, but I sensed this was not the right time.

"Could you give me a description of the bracelet? What were the other charms, for instance? You said there were six."

She frowned at me as if I had been impertinent. "I said I was given one for each of my birthdays, but that was a long time ago, and things have a way of getting lost."

Another pause and a frown. I pushed on.

"How many remained, and what were they?"

"For my fifth birthday, I received a tiny gold skate. Lovely, it was. I was just starting to learn how to skate, so it was very appropriate. When I was seven, I received a knight in armour. It made me think of Papa."

"And when you were six?"

"I beg your pardon?"

"You said the knight arrived when you were seven, but according to what you've told me, you received a charm every year. Was one lost?"

She dragged deeply on her cigarette before she answered. "It was a little clock. It did somehow get lost, but I'm happy to say it was recovered."

"Are the others intact?"

"Yes. There is the ship that commemorated my eighth birthday. A beautiful sailing ship setting out in the world was how Papa described it. Just like I was."

The pause again.

"And the charm for your ninth birthday?"

"A church. Papa never missed one Sunday."

I looked up at her, forcing her to meet my gaze. "Let me make sure I have this right, Mrs. Calder. The charms remaining on the bracelet to date are a stork with your initial on it, a skate, a clock, a knight on his horse, a ship, and a church. Six altogether."

"I removed the little knight some time ago from the bracelet. It is in the jewellery box."

"So, five only then? A stork, a skate, a clock, a ship, and a church."

"Correct."

"And the box where you kept this jewellery is in your bedroom, is it?"

"Yes."

"Do you have any idea how a thief would have access to your room?"

"I certainly don't keep the door locked, if that's what you mean. There is only myself and my housekeeper, Maria, in the house. There is no need to act as if we're in a prison."

"Where is your room?"

She waved her hand. "I took over what used to be the breakfast room. Frankly, I was finding the stairs increasingly difficult."

"So, it is on this floor?"

"Precisely."

That added another dimension to the mystery. Rooms on the ground floor were obviously easier to break into than those on the upper floors. If that was what indeed had happened.

"Was anything else missing? Any other jewellery pieces?"

"No. I know exactly what I have, and the cufflink and bracelet are all that have gone."

That in itself was strange. Why not take the entire box? A single cufflink and a small silver bracelet with only five charms weren't exactly highly valuable, gold and silver notwithstanding.

I closed my notebook. "May I have a look at your room, Mrs. Calder?"

"Is that necessary?"

"You have hired me to investigate a theft. I cannot do that properly unless I can see the precise location where the items have gone missing."

My irritation must have crept into my voice despite myself, because she shifted in her chair, and her lower lip thrust out in a childish way.

"Very well. But it is my private space, and I would ask you to respect it."

Again, I wondered what she was afraid of. I suppose I could kick around a few cushions if I were so inclined. Or worse.

"In fact, I would prefer it if you were present while I do my inspection, Mrs. Calder."

"Very well." She balanced her cigarette on the lip of the fancy ashtray next to the chair.

Then, to my surprise, her face crumpled, and she looked genuinely upset. The overbearing, unreal, lady-of-the-manor demeanour vanished, and instead there was a lonely elderly woman who was in great distress.

"I'm sorry, Miss Frayne. I don't want to be obstructionist, and I really do need your help, but the truth is, I'm afraid the items could only have been taken by somebody who is known to me. By somebody I consider a friend. As you can imagine, that thought is most distressing."

"Was this person in the house over the past seven days?"

She took another deep draw on her cigarette. "Yes, she was. I am a member of a ladies' club. We meet on a regular basis, and the last meeting was here."

"May I ask the name of this club?"

"The Ladies' Pioneer Club. You've probably heard of us."

I hadn't, as a matter of a fact. There were a lot of clubs in the city that drew the allegiance of women from the more well-to-do level of society. The men had their fraternal societies and Masonic orders, the women their clubs. I should also say, they were mostly devoted to doing good work and helping the less well-situated. I murmured a noncommittal response.

"Is there one person in particular you are troubled about?"

She sighed. "Not exactly. There were five ladies present. I suppose it could have been any one of them."

"And they would all have been aware of the location of these items?"

"I made no secret of it."

"Why would one anybody in your club steal from you, Mrs. Calder?"

I thought it was a good bet that none of those women would be in financial straits forcing them to filch a silver charm bracelet and a single gold cufflink.

She shrugged. "Who knows the darkness that resides in the human heart, Miss Frayne? I can only suppose they wanted to render me a deep and painful wound."

I must have glanced over at her in surprise because she answered my unasked question.

"Why they would wish to do that, I do not know."

She stood up a little stiffly, and in a ripple of gold lamé she walked over to the fireplace and pulled on the embroidered bell pull that hung beside it.

The door opened, and in stepped the housekeeper.

She must have been close by. Very close.

"Yes, madam?"

"Maria, Miss Frayne wants to take a look in my bedroom."

"Of course. I've tidied up a bit." She smiled, more hospitable now. "Everything was upside down."

I took my cue from her. She was obviously in the know as to why I was there.

"I gather you have searched for the items that are missing?"

"We did indeed. We went through the entire house with a fine-tooth comb. And the grounds. We found nothing."

Mrs. Calder turned to me. "I would be completely lost without Maria. She is my lifesaver."

The housekeeper gave a little nod, accepting the compliment but suggesting it was something she was accustomed to. And perhaps deserving of.

"If you come this way, miss. I'll show you the bedroom."

Mrs. Calder retrieved her cigarette and waved it in the air. "I'll join you in a minute. I'll just finish my cigarette."

She scrunched up her face at me, rather like a child would. "Maria doesn't like me to smoke in my bedroom. She thinks it's an unhealthy habit."

"It is, madam," replied the other woman. "Very unhealthy."

I actually agreed with her, but this was not the moment to take sides. I was beginning to get a sense of the relationship between these two. Mrs. Calder might pay the salary, but Maria held the power. Not that unusual if I remembered my royal history.

I followed the housekeeper from the room. She closed the door to the drawing room behind us. There was something about the way she did it that made me think I was in for some revelations.

As it turned out, I was right, but before she could launch, there was a shout from the living room.

"Maria, will you come? I need you for a moment."

The housekeeper gritted her teeth. "Sorry, miss. I'll be right there."

She turned around and went back into the living room.

I felt a little awkward simply standing in the hall, and, as we were heading for the bedroom anyway, I could see no good reason not to start. I opened the bedroom door and went inside, leaving the door ajar to show my intentions were transparent.

Entering Mrs. Calder's "private space," as she had put it, was rather overwhelming. Like the mistress, it was extravagantly, colourfully furnished in a style that had been popular many years ago. Aztec, it was called: all hot, sunny colours. A canopied bed was draped with red striped curtains that matched those at the windows. White furniture, a purple chaise lounge. How you would even know something was missing in all the clutter, I don't know. The dresser was underneath the window, and I went over to have a look. Lots of Mexican-looking knick-knacks. Interestingly, only one photo. The print must have originally been sepia, but it had been colour-tinted. The photo showed a distinguished grey-haired man seated in a chair that had a distinct resemblance to a royal throne. A little girl with long ringlets was seated on his lap. She was wearing a pretty frilled dress edged with pink ribbon and a big pink bow in her dark brown hair. This had to be dear Papa and the child Emmeline. Beside the photograph was a square polished wooden box. I lifted the lid. It was indeed a jewellery box. Like the room, it was cluttered, and a tangle of pearl necklaces winked up at me. As carefully as I could, I removed the top tray. Underneath, the jewellery was a little neater and seemed to consist mostly of gold and silver brooches. Tucked to one side in the satin pocket was a postcard. I took a look. It was old, the style long ago replaced. On the "For Address Only" side was printed, "PLEASE FORWARD. Mrs. Brigid O'Rourke. Lakeview Avenue, Nr. Toronto." The handwriting was uneven but legible. I turned the card over. Same handwriting. "Dear Mam. I am well. As soon as I settle here, I shall send for you and little Sissie. Do not fret. Your loving son, Rory." I squinted at the postmark. It had been mailed from Winnipeg.

Just at that moment, the housekeeper came in, shutting the door firmly behind her.

"Oh dear, the mistress will be here in a moment. We have to talk quickly. I wanted to warn you about the nature of the situation here. I know she has hired you to find some jewellery items that she says have been stolen." She frowned at me. "Well, I can tell you, nothing has been stolen. Mrs. Calder, gets ... how shall I put it? She gets confused. She loses things and then gets into a state and is sure that she has been robbed." She paused and cocked her head, listening. "She's coming. I'll finish quick. She's hired investigators twice before, and nothing has come of it except she wasted her money. In every instance, the missing items showed up a short time later. She just forgot where she'd put them."

At that moment, I heard Mrs. Calder at the door. She called out, "Maria? Are you in there?"

The housekeeper just had time to whisper to me, "Don't take the job."

The door opened, almost knocking me over. Mrs. Calder came in, stopped, and looked at me in astonishment.

"Good heavens. Who on earth are you and what are you doing in my bedroom?"

CHAPTER EIGHT

BY THE TIME we sorted out the confusion, and I had been pressed to stay for a rather elaborate serving of tea and cakes, it was almost half past three. I had agreed to get to the House of Industry by four o'clock to determine if certain casuals were in fact thieves. I must say, the possibility of proving that they were or were not seemed a little easier than proving Mrs. Calder had been robbed by one of her dear friends, as she'd claimed.

In spite of the housekeeper's warning not to take the job, I had agreed to pursue further investigation. It wasn't the money, although the fee Mrs. Calder was offering was generous. I hoped that if I did fulfill my side of the agreement, she would have some peace of mind. Maria had said the missing items always turned up. If that was the case, I would return the money. Over tea, I questioned Mrs. Calder about her ladies' group. She said they had met in the drawing room. Her bedroom was adjacent. I asked her if she'd noticed anybody getting up and leaving the room at any time during the meeting. She actually laughed, albeit rather sardonically. "We met for over two hours, and during that time more than one of them left the room. Including me. It's called old lady bladder. I assumed they were heading for the bathroom."

The next meeting was tomorrow, at the club premises on Adelaide Street. A breakfast meeting at ten o'clock. She said she would introduce me as a potential new member, and I could use my skills to determine if one of them had taken the cufflink and bracelet. Frankly, unless one of the women decided to wear said items, I wasn't sure how I was going to know. What kind of club was the Ladies' Pioneers? *Our aim is to further the cause of the New Woman. We advocate for a society with no class structure, no liquor, and no wars. We raise money. We regularly hold lively and honest debates on all important matters affecting society, however controversial. Particularly controversial ones.* I liked the sound of that. Right up my alley. Not the *no liquor* part, but then again, that might fall into the category of controversial topics. Perhaps I should join legitimately.

However, I knew that the likelihood of their accepting me into the club was remote even if I could afford the initiation fee. I had no well-heeled, well-connected husband, after all.

As I was leaving, Mrs. Calder pressed upon me a rather battered copy of a cookbook the club had put together.

"It was a hot seller. We're thinking of reissuing it. Enjoy."

I can't say cooking was exactly a passion of mine, but I accepted the book. I'd pass it on to Calvin, the cook at the Paradise. He'd be the one to "enjoy."

I stuffed the book into my handbag, got my bicycle from the curb, and set off. This time the wind was behind me, and I sped along.

I'd been hoping to drop in at the café and at least say hello to Hilliard, but once again I was thwarted. I didn't have time.

I wondered if Leroy had been found yet and how his brother was doing.

With that thought, I lost my concentration for a second and turned too sharply, barely avoiding getting my wheel caught in the streetcar tracks. These were the bane of cyclists as they lay in wait, ready to rise up and seize the wheel of the unwary and throw the rider onto the hard pavement. I'd better pay attention to what I was doing, or I would end up doing nothing at all. Permanently.

CHAPTER NINE

I TURNED ONTO Elm Street and the familiar sight of the formidable House of Industry. A long line of men were waiting outside for the gates to open into the inner courtyard where the casuals were admitted. The relief was for men only. The women had to go elsewhere.

They put me in mind of the lineup of customers who waited for the Paradise Café to open. Thanks to Hilliard and his partners, the café served nourishing meals at reasonable prices. If deemed necessary, they allowed the customers to have credit, and nobody was turned away hungry. Perhaps because they were paying their way, the mood of that lineup was different from the one I was looking at now. Here, hardly anybody was talking to their neighbours; the clothes were poorer, the faces more weather-beaten.

I rode to the front door, propped my bike against the wall, and rang the bell.

Miss Lindsay welcomed me with a friendly smile of recognition.

"Good afternoon, Miss Frayne. Mrs. Brodie is waiting in the sunroom." She glanced over my shoulder. "She said you might be coming with a gentleman this time. He's a partner, she said?"

For a second or two, I didn't know what she meant, but then I realized I'd told Mrs. Brodie I was going to get in touch with Detective Murdoch. She was certainly intent on keeping the real reason for my presence a secret.

"He might be late."

"I'll watch out for him. Does he have far to come?"

"Er ..."

"I mean, where is your shop?"

"Queen Street."

Fortunately, she didn't pursue the matter. I followed her to the elevator, and we went through the same routine as last time and clanked up to the second floor.

"I do hope you will choose some of Mrs. Brodie's work. It would mean so much to her to know what she does is not in vain."

I felt a spasm of guilt. I'd gone along with Mrs. Brodie's little deception, but I hadn't followed it through in my mind. How would we proceed if she insisted that a couple of the casuals were thieves? I hoped Jack would arrive soon. It would be his call.

The sunroom was not as full as it had been earlier. There was no sign of the pugnacious Mrs. Fitzgerald, and only about half a dozen women were sitting in the sofas by the fire.

Miss Lindsay picked up on my thoughts.

"This is what we consider our turnaround time. At this time of day, we are getting ready to serve the evening meal. Most of our residents like to go to their rooms and freshen up." She gave a little shrug. "I know people think life here is highly regimented, but that is of necessity, really, and we try to make the meal a little special. The men are permitted to sit with the women, for instance. It so brightens up the day." She twinkled at me. "It's amazing the effect a little perfume or a well-polished pair of shoes might have on the spirits."

I can hardly describe the effect her words had on me. The utter dreariness of life in the poorhouse pervaded my very being. Day after day of routine and dependency enlivened by a dab of lavender water and shoe polish. Lord save me.

Mrs. Brodie was at the opposite end of the room this time, and she had obviously been watching the door. As we entered, she waved at me.

"I'll leave you to it, then," said Miss Lindsay. "Come and fetch me when you're done. And if you wish to stay for dinner, Miss Frayne, you would be most welcome."

That was kind, but I also had the feeling the residents were not the only ones who enjoyed a little variety in their lives. I wondered how they would react if Jack Murdoch also stayed for dinner. I had the feeling he'd be quietly and discreetly mobbed.

She left us, and Mrs. Brodie immediately got to her feet.

"Come over to the window, miss. The casuals are just lining up. I'll be able to see if those men have come today or not."

I took up the place next to her. It was true we could see clearly into the yard below. The surrounding brick walls were painted white, but the impression was not of good cheer and brightness but of sterility.

I guessed there were more than a hundred men in a snaking lineup that ended in front of the entrance to the dining room, where they were getting their welfare cards stamped by a dour porter. The afternoon was chilly, but most of them were fortified by winter overcoats, mufflers wrapped tightly, caps jammed on their heads — probably the only wardrobe they possessed. All of them looked shabby. Most were older, but there was a smattering of younger ones who were nevertheless moving slowly and obediently toward the porter. Even as I watched, I saw one bent old man being denied entrance. The porter was waving his card in the air and shaking his head. It was obvious the old chap no longer qualified to come in for a free meal. He didn't protest for long, just moved out of the line and shuffled away. Nobody came to his aid. The line closed up tight and continued to move slowly through the checkpoint.

Suddenly, Mrs. Brodie caught my arm.

"There. That's him. The one with the moustache."

I stared down into the courtyard. There were at least half a dozen men who would fit that description.

"There. Near the door. He's wearing a black oilskin."

There was indeed a man in a shiny oilskin coat and a blue cap moving slowly with the line. Not my idea of a Viking, which was how Mrs. Brodie had described him, except for the reddish hair that stuck out from under his cap and the matching moustache.

Mrs. Brodie shifted closer to the window and squinted her eyes.

"It's him, all right. And the other fellow. He's always the one behind. He's a follower. Same one. I can see him better now. I'd know him anywhere."

The men below seemed focused on getting into the dining room, but we were only one floor up, and if they had glanced our way, they would have seen us.

"We should nab them now while we can," she said. "They can't be let to get away with such a crime."

I hesitated. I could go down and talk to them, but what would I say? *Hey guys, were you out on Edward Street recently doing a spot of burglarizing?*

Mrs. Brodie was glaring at me with indignation. "Why don't you do something? It's them, I tell you. The burglars. Why don't you believe me?"

I was saved from answering such an impossible question by the men below us. One younger chap glanced up at the window. He pointed, and he must have said something out loud, because those near him also looked upward. I had the impression that whatever he'd said wasn't particularly flattering because there were a few grins flashing around. My gaze met his, and he touched his cap brim in acknowledgement. On the surface, the gesture might have seemed polite enough, but I didn't like it. There was something about it that was nasty. As if he was a man capitulating to the prevailing customs but only for convenience and under duress, and with underlying contempt and resentment. A couple of the other men also touched their caps, but they seemed much more genuinely polite. Then the attendant at the door beckoned for the next group to move forward, and the two men we were concerned about moved forward and disappeared from view.

Mrs. Brodie shrank back.

"They saw me."

I wasn't sure they had, but it was possible.

She caught me by the arm, her face full of fear. "You can't let them get away. You've got to do something."

This time it was Miss Lindsay who saved me. She came into the room and headed straight for us.

"Excuse me, Miss Frayne. We have just received a telephone call from a gentleman who said his name is Murdoch. He has asked us to relay a message."

She didn't look too happy about being thrust into that role. Before I could reply, Mrs. Brodie piped up.

"What did he say? Is he coming?"

Miss Lindsay was taken aback, and she looked at me for guidance.

I put on my best business voice. "Mrs. Brodie is right. I can assure you Mr. Murdoch would not make a frivolous call. What is the message?"

She blinked. "Simply that he will not be able to join you today after all. He said that he would like you to carry on with the task on hand. And he'd like to meet at the office afterward. He said he will be there until six o'clock."

Again, I didn't have a chance to get in a word in edgeways. Mrs. Brodie was fast off the mark.

"Miss Frayne was hoping you could take her to the dining room before she leaves."

"Really? I ... er ..." Miss Lindsay frowned. "I was under the impression that you were here to appraise Mrs. Brodie's work with a view to selling some of it."

This time I answered for myself. "Quite so, but to understand how the House functions is an important part of the picture, wouldn't you say?"

Miss Lindsay didn't look convinced. I pushed ahead.

"There has been such controversy in the newspaper reports lately about the conditions that exist here. I thought since I was here, I'd have a look for myself. Not that I believe any of the comments put forward by the unions. I myself have been most favourably impressed with what I've seen."

That was true.

"She mostly just wants to see the wayfarers' dining room," Mrs. Brodie added.

Miss Lindsay continued to look puzzled. "Are you interested in being a volunteer?"

"Possibly." I nodded and smiled. Great idea.

Miss Lindsay still looked doubtful, but she proved no match for Mrs. Brodie, who was demonstrating a lot more resilience than a few moments ago.

"I'd take her down myself," she chirped. "But you know how Mrs. Laughlen discourages us residents from mingling with the casuals. I heard her say it myself just the other day.

'Different kettle of fish,' is what she said. 'We have to protect the minnows from the sharks,' were her words."

Talk about creating a fog of innuendo and misdirection. It was masterful. Miss Lindsay was hooked.

"Very well. I'll take you down now, Miss Frayne."

"I'll wait here," said Mrs. Brodie. "I'm not going anywhere until I hear what you have to say."

She sat straight in the chair, a small, vulnerable bird with bright feathers. She didn't have to do any of this, but she wanted justice for two boys whom she'd never met. She'd told me, "My own family was once on the receiving end of a false accusation. I don't want to ever see it happen to somebody else." I didn't yet know what she was referring to, but what choice did I have except to protect her from the sharks?

CHAPTER TEN

I FOLLOWED MISS Lindsay to the elevator, and we shuddered down to the ground floor. She wasn't chatty this time, but I didn't mind. I was anxious about the message from Jack. I had an uneasy feeling it had to do with Leroy. But he'd said carry on, and carry on I would.

"This way," said Miss Lindsay as she dragged open the elevator door. "We'll go in by way of the kitchen. We'll be less conspicuous that way."

She started to head down a narrow passageway.

Her glance in my direction was surprisingly shrewd. "I'll have to drop by your shop for a visit."

I was momentarily taken aback. "My shop?"

"You're contemplating selling some of Mrs. Brodie's knitwear, are you not? You and Mr. Murdoch."

Fortunately for me, she walked fast, and by now we were through the passageway and at the entrance to the dining room. I was saved from concocting more fibs. I wished Mrs. Brodie hadn't been so insistent on keeping her secret. I liked Miss Lindsay, for one thing, and for another, I thought she might be a real asset in determining the truth of Mrs. Brodie's accusations.

The sound coming from the dining room was subdued. I knew there was a time, in the not-too-distant past, when all relief recipients had to eat in complete silence. Breaking that silence by talking was punished.

Silence was ever the great controller.

The door to the kitchen was on the left, and she ushered me inside.

Like most kitchens in the universe, this one was hot and steamy and smelled delicious. There were bright electric lights overhead and a large black range on one side. Two male workers, both rather elderly, were busy with the food preparation while a straight-backed, imposing man in a smart black uniform was overseeing them.

"How're the potatoes?"

"Potatoes ready," called out one man.

"Gravy needs a minute. Got to thicken," called out the other.

"A minute is all I'm going to give you," said the uniformed man. "We're ready outside." He noticed Miss Lindsay and me standing by the door, and he smiled. He slapped his hand to his forehead in a semi-military salute. He reminded me of Constable Weber. They must have been in the same regiment.

"Afternoon, ma'am."

Miss Lindsay smiled back. "Good afternoon, Mr. McKenna. Allow me to introduce Miss Frayne. She might be joining us as a volunteer. I'm showing her how things operate."

He saluted again, and I had to stop my own hand from jumping to my forehead. It was contagious.

"Mr. McKenna is our manager," continued Miss Lindsay. She twinkled away. "I truly don't know what we'd do without him."

Good gracious, they were actually flirting with each other.

"How was the beef?" Miss Lindsay asked him. "Loblaw gave us a nice discount, but I was afraid it might have been sitting around for a while."

Mr. McKenna bounced the question over to the gravy man.

"How was it, Trevor?"

"Seemed a bit on the tough side," he answered. "But I gave it a good pounding, and it's cooked for a while, so it should be all right."

"All set then? Shall we get started?" Mr. McKenna asked.

"How did the celery soup turn out?" asked Miss Lindsay. "I know Mrs. Laughlen was anxious about it."

Mr. McKenna answered in a hearty manner. "Best kind of soup. Economical and tasty. What more can we ask?"

There were two trolleys by the cutting table, and the cooks quickly transferred the food from the stove into the large steam dishes that were on each trolley. The stew looked a little, shall we say, homogenous. Pounding will do that to you. A third trolley was carrying the soup tureens.

I suddenly became aware of my own empty stomach growling at me. I hadn't had anything substantial to eat all day. Mrs. Calder's delicate cakes didn't count.

Miss Lindsay touched my elbow. "I have to get back upstairs. Will you be all right by yourself?"

Other than a slight misgiving that I might snatch food from one of the casuals, I thought I could manage.

"I'll be fine, Miss Lindsay. Thank you so much."

"Just take direction from Mr. McKenna. Perhaps you could set out the soup bowls. They're on the lower shelf of the trolleys. We need eight per tray."

"Right."

"It's always better to have a task, I find."

"Certainly."

"If you hear any comments, positive or otherwise, please tell me. We always want to know what our guests are thinking. Come back to the second floor when you're done."

She left, and Mr. McKenna faced the two greybeards, who had moved from the stoves to the trolleys. He raised his arm in the air.

"Ready then, Trevor? Jim? Let's get at 'em. Over we go."

And in we went.

CHAPTER ELEVEN

AS SOON AS we entered, the room dropped into silence. All the men focused on us. Or perhaps more accurately, they focused on the trolleys. The servers divided smartly like a platoon, one on each side of Mr. McKenna. He turned around and addressed the room. He still had his parade ground reach.

"All right then, I'm sure you're all ready to eat this delicious meal."

He paused for the response that came at him. Not loud, more muttered than anything. I heard, "Yes, Sergeant," which seemed appropriate. My two targets were seated at a table near the front. I didn't think either one had responded to Mr. McKenna, but I couldn't be sure.

"Excellent," he continued enthusiastically. "Most of you know the drill, but for those who are new here — and I see a few unfamiliar faces — this is what we do. One man is to be the corporal for the table. Volunteer or conscript doesn't matter, but he is delegated to come up here and pick up the rations. He will return to the table with said rations, and he will serve each of you. Of course, good manners and cheery words will prevail. Understood?"

Another murmur of assent from the group. They seemed to be enjoying him. He gave me a little nod, and I jumped to, setting out soup bowls on a tray.

"Righto, then. We'll start with the corporals from table one and table two. One to the trolley on my left; two to my right." He illustrated the command by pointing. He did not in fact have a swagger stick, but he might as well have. "Just remember, the faster you move, the better chance you have of eating hot food. And that means keeping the other lads happy. Corporals from the other tables can follow on as soon as tables one and two are served. In order, if you please. Anybody jumping the queue will be sent immediately to the rear." He clapped his hands and pointed. "Let's go, gentlemen. Mr. Hayden, Mr. Genik, you're up first. Hop to it."

As it turned out, Mrs. Brodie's suspected thief was the head of table two. Discreetly, I tried to get a better look at him as he approached the serving trolley. He was tall, perhaps fortyish. He was indeed skinny, but he had the broad shoulders and wide chest of a man who had done manual labour. I couldn't tell if the lack of flesh was recent or not. He was wearing a shabby demob suit, and I guessed he too had been a military man. Just as he reached the trolley, he was seized by a fit of coughing that bent him over. It seemed a long time before it subsided. Finally, he was able to move on, and he stood in front of me, waiting while Trevor began to spoon the soup into the bowls.

I took a chance and met his eyes. I smiled. Whoa. I didn't yet know if I was looking at a thief, but I did know I was meeting a man who I could see had very little to be happy about in the world before him.

He seemed to pick up something from me because he gave a half smile.

"My apologies for coughing like that. I'm not contagious, just bad lungs."

So that was what it was. Even though the Great War had been over for eighteen years, the effects still lingered in many of the men who had been there and suffered there. I wondered what had happened to this one.

"You're new here, aren't you, miss? I don't recall seeing you before."

Before I could answer, Mr. McKenna interjected.

"This is Miss Frayne. She's considering becoming a volunteer, so let's treat her nicely."

Genik nodded. "I saw you up in the sunroom with one of the inmates. A relative, is she? Comfortable, is she?"

"No relative, but yes, I believe the lady in question is comfortable."

Suddenly I felt nervous. The man was being polite and pleasant enough, but he had seen Mrs. Brodie and me together, and he now knew my name. I wondered why he'd made a point of referring to her. *It's not safe*, she had said.

Before I had time to assess the truth of my bit of panic, Mr. McKenna jumped in again.

"Hurry up, Genik. Your table's getting hungry. They'll be starting on the tablecloth in a minute."

The corporal from table one was about to return with his laden tray, and he heard this. The manager's tone had been jovial, but this man was obviously already angry. He halted and said in a loud voice, intended for the rest of the men, "Why not? Anything would taste better than this bloody bilge."

Mr. McKenna was not fazed. "Moaning again, Hayden? If you don't like it, don't come here. You should consider yourself lucky that a place like the House even exists."

It was like seeing a lit match drop on a tinderbox.

"Lucky!" roared the other man. "Sod that. The little food we do get is not fit for dogs. We line up for everything like we're jail-birds. Everything! If we stayed here, we'd have to line up to die."

He slammed the tray down again on the trolley. Some of the hot soup splashed out and caught Genik's arm, and he reacted.

"Hey! Watch what you're doing. That's good food you're wasting."

"Trust a Ukie to eat shit if he has to. Tastes good to him." Suddenly, Hayden addressed me. "Don't trust him, miss. He's light-fingered, is this one. Before you know it, you've lost your welfare card, your gloves. He'd take your socks if they weren't on your feet."

It was Genik's turn to erupt. In a second, he was inches from Hayden's face. He grabbed him by the collar, punctuating his remarks with a hard shove that almost knocked Hayden over.

"I've told you. It wasn't me took your miserable things. Take that back, you asshole."

Mr. McKenna had moved to one side of the room, but he rushed forward to intervene. "Tone it down, lads. There's a lady present, don't forget."

I appreciated his chivalry, but I rather thought not even the Queen Mother herself could have prevented the incident.

The two men were locked into a glaring competition. Some of the other casuals got up from their seats to watch. The air was saturated with anger and fear. However, Mr. McKenna, who clearly had dealt with such situations before, succeeded in separating the two, one strong arm pressed against the puffed chest of each man.

"Enough! Stop this immediately."

A handful of the men now left their tables and rushed forward to stand behind Hayden, literally and figuratively. A couple of others were behind Genik.

"It's about time you heard the truth," said one burly rough-neck to the manager. "We here did our bit to save your skin, and this is the thanks we get."

Mr. McKenna was not to be baited. "You think I didn't? You've no right to ride your high horse with me, Dales. If you don't like it, you can get out with him. More for your betters." He nodded at the redhead. "You too. We will not tolerate such behaviour in this establishment."

The younger man, whom I was linking to Genik as his companion, had also rushed forward, and he tried to put his arm around Genik's shoulders.

"Come on, Zav. Let's go. Doesn't matter."

Genik shook him off. "It matters to me what scum like this call me."

Perhaps emboldened by knowing he had some support, Hayden came up with another provocative sneer.

"Maybe I should have called you a bolshie. Would you like that better? How about a Ukie-commie-bolshie?"

I was still dithering by the trolleys, where the two elderly servers seemed paralyzed. I felt as if I was about to witness either the second battle of Agincourt or another Estevan. Knights or Strikers.

Thank goodness for ex sergeant majors.

Mr. McKenna still pressed his extended arms against each man. There was no way they could get at each other. He raised his voice, parade-ground trained.

"I'm giving you a choice, lads. Either I let go and you can go ahead and kill each other or you break it off right now. Seeing I have the heart of a pussycat, I'm not going to call the police, which I could do. I'm going to let you cool off, and when and only when you've calmed down you can have your dinner. Do I make myself clear?"

I'm not sure what would have happened next, but Genik was seized by another coughing fit and was forced to step back from the manager's barricading arm. Between coughs, he managed to speak.

"Don't worry, Sarge. We wouldn't want to eat under the same roof with shit like him. Marko and me will go."

His companion didn't look too happy at those words, but he was loyal, if nothing else. Still close enough to grab hold of Genik if necessary, he started to move away. Hayden shook himself like a dog shaking off water, and he too turned away. The indomitable manager took over. He pointed at the nearby tables.

"Okay. You, Smith. You, Barley; you take over the rations. Come on, soup's getting cold."

Order was restored, and I saw Genik and his friend heading out of the door. Whew. I could feel my heart beating faster. Incipient violence has a way of doing that to us. So far, it hadn't been what you'd refer to as a quiet day, but I can't say I was inured to it.

The dining room was still rumbling, but quietly so. Mr. McKenna's eye was inescapable. However, I had barely resumed my task of setting out the soup bowls when Miss Lindsay swished through the kitchen door. She came straight over to me.

"Miss Frayne, do you by chance know where Mrs. Brodie is?"

"No, I don't. Has something happened?"

Miss Lindsay's lips tightened. "I'm afraid she seems to have disappeared."

CHAPTER TWELVE

"WHAT? WHAT DO you mean, 'disappeared'?"

"After I left you in the kitchen, I went to fetch her for the meal, but she wasn't there, nor was she in her room. I asked at the porter's lodge, and he said she had gone out." Miss Lindsay clasped her hands together. "Apparently, she said she had to go on an important errand she'd forgotten about. She asked for a pass, and the porter wrote one for her. She got her outdoor things and left. He said she was carrying her Gladstone sample bag. I was wondering if she had made some sort of arrangement with you."

"No, I was going to come back upstairs to see her. Would she be waiting outside, by chance?"

"I don't think so." Miss Lindsay gave a wry smile. "It is not unknown for our older residents to wander off. We try to be aware. The porter thought she seemed quite *compos mentis*, as it were. In fact, he said he walked out with her, and she headed straight up Elizabeth Street. He was not alarmed."

"Does she have a curfew?"

"Yes. It's eight o'clock. But it will be dark by then, and we really don't like our residents to be out so late without a companion. I find it quite odd. Mrs. Brodie has never done this before. She never misses her dinner."

"She's an independent soul. I'm sure she'll be all right."

I was tempted to confide in Miss Lindsay, but I was still held back by my promise not to tell. I also wanted to believe my own words. I was surprised Mrs. Brodie had done a bunk. She knew I was coming back, and we hadn't finished our business.

While we were talking, the regular routine of serving had continued. Surprisingly, another ruckus seemed to be starting up. I could see Hayden at his table, but this trouble was happening a few tables away. More anger. The manager and a young, weather-beaten man were going at it.

"I was steamed yesterday," said the man, who might have been referring to the sun, by the look of his face. "Why the hell do I have to be done again?"

Mr. McKenna answered briskly.

"It's for your own protection. Who knows what you might have picked up while you were out."

"But I spent the day in the library."

"Doesn't matter. You know the rules. You don't follow them, you don't get to sleep in a nice clean bed."

With difficulty, the young man subsided. Some of the older men were looking nervous. They had long ago learned to stay out of other people's fights.

I turned back to Miss Lindsay, who had also taken in this little exchange. She shrugged. "Some men don't like the word *no*." She took a deep breath and straightened her spine. "I'd better get back."

"Would you mind getting in touch with me if Mrs. Brodie does show up? I'm concerned too."

"Very well. How shall I reach you?"

Good point. I couldn't yet divulge my actual line of work, and my home telephone was strictly, "If we're home, we'll answer." I decided to give out the number of the Paradise. There was always somebody there.

"I'll leave a number with your receptionist where I can be reached, shall I?"

"Please do. I'm sure we don't have a good reason to worry, but I appreciate your concern." She paused. "Do you think you might become a volunteer? We are always in need of cheery people like you."

"Maybe. I'll consider it. By the way, do you keep a record of the wayfarers? Names and such."

"Good heavens, why do you ask? You're not a journalist, are you?"

"Not at all. I was just curious. I heard one of the men referred to as Zav. It's such an unusual name, I wondered where he was from."

She gave me a distinctly skeptical look. "I understand it's a nickname. It's short for 'tomorrow' in Ukrainian. *Zavtra.* Viktor's always saying 'tomorrow,' as in tomorrow will be better, tomorrow the workers will take over."

"He's a communist, is he?"

"Apparently. We never ask, of course. I must say, he's usually polite and helpful. Did something happen?"

"You might say that, but perhaps you should speak to Mr. McKenna."

"Very well. I'll say good afternoon for now, Miss Frayne. Please consider joining us."

We left it at that. It was looking as if the controversial soup had been gulped down and the main meal was ready to follow. I didn't feel like staying any longer. I gave Mr. McKenna a wave and said goodbye to Trevor and Jim. They both gave me sweet smiles. "Come back soon," said Trevor. "Don't be put off by what happened today. They were just letting off steam."

I can't say I was in agreement with his assessment. Both men had seemed in deadly earnest to me.

JACK HAD SAID he'd be in the office until six. I decided to go straight there before it got dark. On the way out, I checked with the porter, but Mrs. Brodie had not returned. I had to remind myself of my own words to Miss Lindsay. *She's an independent woman.*

She was also elderly and frightened. It's not safe, she had warned me.

Where would she have gone?

CHAPTER THIRTEEN

ONCE AGAIN, I was helped along by strong blasts of March wind, and I sped along College Street toward the police headquarters. My route took me past the university. A small knot of twenty or so students were massed on the sidewalk. They were waving placards: STOP HITLER; NO BURNING BOOKS; DUMP MUSSOLINI. A police vehicle was parked nearby, and a couple of hefty officers were talking to the students. I slowed down. The students seemed orderly to me, but there was tension in the air. It was obvious the police were telling them to disperse. For a minute, I considered stopping and offering my support, but I'd had enough of conflict for one day. The students, who seemed to be mostly male, were starting to move back. They could still demonstrate without blocking the sidewalk.

I couldn't help but contrast them with the men I had just encountered. Not that long ago, so many of them had been young soldiers setting off to right the wrongs of the world, full of excitement and courage. Now what? Disillusioned, for the most part. Burning with the anger that comes from despair and frustration. The new world they'd thought they were fighting for had not materialized, and according to what I'd been reading it wasn't going to happen anytime soon. Far from it. The prolonged severe economic depression had taken its toll. All around, there were rumours of another war on the horizon. Pretty much the same enemy, pretty much the same need for strong young men to volunteer to get themselves killed or maimed. Would Hilliard feel compelled to sign up again even though he was close to forty? What about his partners in the café? They had all been so injured by the past war. And where were we women?

I allowed myself to contemplate for a moment what I would do if war were declared. I was single, no family commitments except for Gramps. I didn't think I'd be much good as a nurse. I also knew I couldn't spend hours standing in front of a conveyor belt checking artillery parts. What then? I guess I'd have to see.

I remounted my bike and set off again. I was glad to see the police headquarters: solid, dependable, not intimidated. My thoughts had been getting gloomy. Perhaps the pundits were wrong. Perhaps our leaders were smart enough to see the tragedy and the futility of entering into another world war.

Unless we were left no choice.

And perhaps I should think more seriously about what role I would take if that conflict did come about.

The constable at reception was friendly this time.

"Detective Murdoch is expecting you, madam. Please go through to his office."

I did as commanded. Jack's door was closed, but he answered my knock immediately.

"Charlotte. Come in. Sorry I couldn't come to the House, but I had to deal with things here."

I got settled in the chair in front of his desk. He too sat down. He looked tired.

"Did the men in question show up?"

"They did indeed. I got their names. Viktor Genik, called Zav, and a younger man whose name is Marko. I don't know his surname. I'm guessing Genik is an ex-soldier. He has that terrible kind of cough men get when they were gassed." I didn't miss Jack's sigh. He had that cough too, sometimes. "Ever heard of these men?"

Jack shook his head. "Can't say I have. I'll check the records. See if they've been previously acquainted with us."

He made a note in his book, wincing a little as he forced his hand to work. I filled him in on the altercation that had taken place in the dining room.

"In my view, Hayden started the fight. He called Genik 'light-fingered.' Could be accurate or just a way of insulting him. He also said he was a bolshie, commie, and Ukie. Genik took great exception. Just blew up. It was only because of the manager, Mr. McKenna, that there wasn't a full-scale riot."

Jack looked up. "Now, McKenna I do know. He's ex-military. I've met him at the War Vets Club a few times."

"I'd bet the bank he was a sergeant during the war."

"Sure was," said Jack with a grin. "I'll tell you his history one of these days. He's a good man. Underneath his tough as nails exterior, he's got a heart of gold."

It sounded rather metallic to me, but I thought the description was spot on, from what I'd seen.

"Here's a rather disturbing thing, Jack. Mrs. Brodie seems to have vanished."

I repeated what Miss Lindsay had told me.

Jack frowned. "And they don't know where she's gone?"

"No, I'm afraid not."

"Should we worry?"

"Possibly. She's not young, and she was frightened when she saw Genik. There's no doubt she recognized him."

"That does not, of course, mean he was up to a little breaking and entering."

"True. He certainly has a hot temper, but as you say, it doesn't necessarily mean he's a burglar."

I realized I might be indeed too alarmist, but I still felt nervous about Mrs. Brodie. I hoped she would be meeting up with Jack soon.

"If you hear from her, let me know. I would still like to talk to her about what she observed," he said.

"I will. Speaking of that, how's Jerome?"

Jack shook his head. "He's not much better. Not speaking. Movement restricted."

"And Leroy? Any development there?"

"We haven't found him yet. I went over to the Working Boys Home and talked to the superintendent again, but according to him, the boys have no relatives or friends in the neighbourhood who might have given him refuge. They kept to themselves while they were in the Home. They left in the morning and, most of the time, stayed out until the evening meal. They sold both the morning and evening papers. They were supposed to attend school in the afternoons, but when I telephoned the principal, he said they were constantly truant. He said he would speak to the other boys and let me know if they had anything useful to offer."

"What school were they going to?"

"Hester How over on Elizabeth Street."

That school had been founded specially to educate so-called troublesome youths and still had a bad reputation. I rather doubted Jack would extract much information from the Davies boys' comrades.

"I also went and spoke to the vendor. The brothers are only two of a fleet, as he calls it. He's got a dozen boys in total who work around the Yonge Street area. He says they come early in the morning, take their papers around to certain customers, then station themselves on Yonge Street, selling to passersby. They are usually sold out by noon. On good days. Then they go who knows where, return by four to pick up the evening editions, and go through the same routine until about six. No papers on Sunday, so they get that day off."

"Sounds like a tough life for such young kids."

"It is. I have to say, the vendor seemed decent enough, but he's trying to make a living himself. He doesn't have much time for hand-holding, as he puts it. Generally, he found our lads hard workers. They were punctual, which is a big virtue in his books. Nobody wants news that's already out of date. He said he had to speak to them at times about their manners, which he said were rough around the edges. If they thought they were being shortchanged by anybody, they weren't afraid to vent their anger." Jack paused. "I should be clear. The vendor was only speaking about the older one, Leroy. He said Jerome followed his brother's lead no matter what. He was surprised when I told him they were accused of theft. His comment was, 'I thought they were smarter than that.'" Jack frowned.

"I don't understand it. I mean, Leroy is going to be fairly conspicuous."

"So far there have been no reported sightings."

"Given what you've said about the lack of contacts, could he be hiding in a shed? An empty garage?"

"Not out of the question. I'm a bit short-staffed, unfortunately. Usual problems of close proximity. Too many men have come down with the flu. Tomorrow, if he hasn't shown up, I'll request some more officers from another division, and we'll do something more intensive. In the meantime, I've put out a broadsheet that's being handed around. See if that draws any information." He swivelled in his chair. "Thank goodness the weather's favourable. If he has to spend the night outdoors, he'll be cold, but he won't freeze to death."

The intercom on his desk buzzed suddenly. Jack flipped down the switch.

"Yes?"

I heard the tinny voice of the constable at reception.

"A Mr. Harry Toban would like you to drop in and see him. He said he has something you might want to take a look at."

Jack glanced at the clock on the wall. "Okay. Tell him I'll be right over."

He sat back in his chair. "Toban is a pawnbroker over on McCaul Street. If he says there's something I should see, he's probably in receipt of stolen goods. He makes sure he keeps his nose clean, and if he's suspicious, he lets us know." He grinned at me. "Do you want to come with me?"

"You bet."

Telling Jack I would meet him there, I collected my bicycle and rode off. My day was getting longer and longer, but I had the feeling this visit would be worth it.

It turned out to be even more useful than I could possibly have expected.

CHAPTER FOURTEEN

THE PAWNBROKER'S SHOP was in the middle of a row of residential houses. I wondered how the neighbours felt about this sore thumb. None of the houses looked particularly prosperous, but Toban's seemed even shabbier than the others. There was nothing illegal about its operations, but it was impossible for pawnshops to avoid seeming disreputable. Even today, with the Depression slowly fading, many people considered it humiliating to be in need. I had witnessed that at the House of Industry.

If churches and banks needed to look solid and prosperous, Toban's pawnshop seemed to be deliberately playing down respectability. *We are one of you,* was the message. The big sign over the front window declared, ANY ITEMS BOUGHT AND SOLD. The window itself was covered with handwritten notices that offered bargains and good deals, not to mention instant cash. Even without these, it would have been impossible to see inside. The window hadn't been washed since it was installed.

I had arrived ahead of Jack and felt a puff of childish pleasure. Bikes trump electric motors most of the time in this city. The black police car drew up a few minutes later, and Jack got out. He was still moving stiffly, and his injured arm seemed to be giving him trouble.

I got to the pawnbroker's door first and opened it for him.

We went in as a bell jangled overhead. Immediately, a man appeared from behind the long, glass-fronted counter.

Jack greeted him. "Hello, Harry. I got your message. What've you got for me?"

I suppose I'd expected an Irishman complete with an open, ruddy face and a big stomach. The proprietor, Mr. Toban, couldn't have been further from that stereotype. He was middling everything: age, build, hair, suit. No extreme anything. He looked like the kind of man you could confide in if you had troubles. He'd remember your name. A banker or an undertaker, not a pawnbroker.

He and Jack shook hands heartily, and Jack introduced me. Toban beamed a friendly smile at me, revealing rather white and unnaturally even teeth. I could only assume they were false.

"Pleasure, Miss Frayne."

The shop was empty, and as soon as we were inside, Toban flipped over the sign on the door to CLOSED. He pulled down the blind.

"Wait for a moment. It will be easier if I bring out the goods and show you here."

He trotted off behind the counter, and I had a chance to look around.

There were two large glass cases flanking the counter on each side, both cunningly lit and containing various items that winked at me seductively. Watches of an infinite variety were on the left, perhaps more easily parted with. The other case seemed to be devoted exclusively to men's goods, including several fancy ties. Jack was steadfastly resisting temptation and wasn't paying attention to the plethora of human tales, but I was drawn in. The glass-topped counter dominated the shop. All the price tags were prominent, and they seemed like bargains. Diamonds, sapphires, and pearls. You name it. Who had pawned that lovely gold and pearl ring? Were they forced to for need's sake, or were they only too happy to relinquish it? It certainly looked like an engagement ring. And that stunning emerald and diamond pendant? Who was the previous owner? Before I had a chance to speculate with Jack, Mr. Toban returned. He was carrying a cardboard box that he placed on a side table at the end of the counter. Here were his tools. A jeweller's eyepiece, a pair of white cotton gloves, a prim ledger, and an old-fashioned straight pen. Two bottles of ink waited next to it. One red, one black. The blotting paper was on a roller.

Mr. Toban removed a bundle from the box and placed it on the felt-topped table.

"These came in some days ago, and I wouldn't have thought anything of them until I read the broadsheet you distributed this afternoon. You said you were looking for a young negro boy, about fifteen years old. Possibly wearing navy pants and shirt?"

"That's right. Was he here?"

"Not one but two darkies came in. They wanted to sell these things." He flashed his splendid choppers at Jack. "As you know, I'm very careful. I don't want to get swindled, and I don't want anybody else to be swindled. They swore up and down they had found these items in various laneways. Over a couple of months throughout the winter, they said. They always check the newspaper's lost and found, but they hadn't seen anything relevant, so they thought they had the right to get a bit of cash after all this time. Finders keepers, they said."

He opened the bundle, which was wrapped in a purple striped neck scarf of shot silk. Smart looking. It held a variety of items: several lady's hat pins, one with a mother-of-pearl stopper; two plain white linen men's handkerchiefs, mud stained; a tie stud, chipped; a pair of black kid ladies' gloves; a locket, dented and tarnished, no chain.

Jack stared down at the rather pathetic haul. "It's plausible that people could have dropped these things. Did you believe the boys when they claimed to have found them?"

Toban shrugged. "They didn't seem like the sort of objects you would bother to steal. Not worth it."

"Did you give them cash or a loan?"

"Neither. I told them I'd have to assess the worth, and they could come back in a couple of days and find out." He poked at the goods. "It's junk. I mean, if I cleaned up the locket, I might be able to sell it for a dollar. Hatpins are a dime a dozen, literally. This one has a nice pearl stopper, so I'd maybe get fifty cents. The handkerchiefs are good for nothing. Not worth the cost of laundering. The gloves are fairly new. They might bring fifty cents."

"Have the boys come back?"

"Not so far. I put it out of my mind until I saw the police broadsheet. I'm positive the lad in question was one of the two that came in here. What's he done? Why are you after him?"

"Let's say he and his brother are up on charges, and he's run off."

"What sort of charges?"

"Breaking and entering. A couple of good items were stolen. The two boys were convicted. They were in jail until today, when they tried to do a bunk. The older lad got away, but the younger one didn't. Matter of fact, he's injured. We're worried about him."

Mr. Toban clicked his teeth together. "Must say I'm a bit surprised. I didn't pin them as thieves. This stuff here isn't worth stealing. If they do have other better goods, they didn't bring them in here."

"Was this all they showed you?"

"Yep. No, wait a minute, I lie. There was one other thing. A silver matchbox. Nice little piece. In fact, I offered them a couple of dollars. Generous really, but it looked quite new. Wasn't tarnished. The older boy turned me down. He probably thought he could get more somewhere else. Well, good luck to him. I make the best offers in town." He sighed in a rather ostentatious way. "My wife always complains. She says I'm forever putting us one step away from the poorhouse." He showed us the perfect teeth. "We do just fine, but I don't want to be comfortable by climbing on the backs of the poor, do I?"

I could see why Jack liked him.

"When were they here, exactly?"

"Last Monday, I think it was. Usually, I write everything down, but as I say this was no sale, and things got busy." Again, he flashed a smile, aimed at me. "As soon as the winter starts to leave us, I get a lot of customers. They want a little ready money to buy some nice things. Human nature, I suppose."

"So, you think it was on the first?" Jack asked him again.

"Could be. But don't put me on the stand."

"What time of day was it?"

"Early afternoon."

"Did you take down any particulars?" asked Jack. "An address, for instance?"

Mr. Toban frowned. "No, I didn't. As I said, it isn't necessary unless there is a sale."

"What else can you tell me about them, Harry?"

"I'd say they were brothers, for sure. The older one did all the talking. The shorter one didn't say a word. In fact, at one point I actually wondered if he wasn't deaf and dumb. Then he made some sort of grunting sound to his brother, so I could see he did have a voice, at least."

Jack nodded. "Has to be our boys."

Toban clicked his teeth. "Mind you, it seemed to me they'd been this route before. Not with me, like I said, but somewhere. They knew the ropes. They weren't put out, if you know what I mean." He turned to me. "A lot of people are ashamed that they've come down to this, as they see it. A woman needs to feed the kids, so she's forced to pawn a brooch; a man not wanting his wife to ever know he's sold his watch to buy booze." Mr. Toban looked quite mournful. "Listen. What I do is legal. I help them out. Why not? Half of the goods are redeemed come payday. What isn't, I sell for a fair price. Everybody gains."

I must say, I'd had my misgivings when I first met the man, but he seemed genuine. More to give him a little privacy than anything, I dropped my gaze to the display case. It contained mostly women's jewellery, all sumptuous. Gold rings, pendants, most of them studded with precious stones, and a couple of bracelets, one of which ...

Surely not!

"Excuse me, Mr. Toban. May I have a look at that bracelet? The silver one with the charms."

He switched immediately into sales professional mode.

"Certainly. Lovely little thing, isn't it? A child's bracelet, but any dainty woman such as yourself could wear it. There's plenty of room to add more charms as desired. I put it out only this morning. I'm sure it won't stay long."

He removed it from the display and laid it on the green felt. There were five charms: a stork delivering a baby in a sling; a skate; a clock, time eternally fixed to eleven minutes past eleven; an old-fashioned church; and a ship with full sails to the winds of life.

Mrs. Calder had described these selfsame charms.

"I'm afraid this bracelet is reported as stolen."

He gaped at me. "What? It wasn't on the police list. I always check. Why do you say it's been stolen, madam?"

Jack rescued me. "Miss Frayne is a private detective. We are actually working together on a case at the moment." He turned to me. "What's the situation, Charlotte?"

"I have a client who says some jewellery of hers was stolen recently. She described this exact bracelet. May I ask you, Mr. Toban, where you acquired this article?"

He smiled with his white teeth. "You may ask, but I cannot tell you. Anybody who brings in property to be surety for a loan is assured of complete privacy." Another smile. "I'm sure, Miss Frayne, you can understand how important this is for my business."

"And I'm sure, Mr. Toban," I replied, "you can understand how important it is for my business that I gain a reputation for efficiency."

At this point, Jack saved the day by bursting out laughing. "All right, you two. Let's not bruise our foreheads by bashing them. Harry, do me a favour. Take a look at your register, will you? Who brought this in?"

Reluctantly, the pawnbroker backed down. "You're asking me officially, I presume?"

"Of course." Jack tapped the ledger. "What are you avoiding, Harry?"

To my surprise, Toban turned quite pink. "To tell the truth, the person who brought this in was a lady. In some ways not my usual customer. She is a widow, recently bereaved. She had come out to do some shopping but left it a little late, and the banks had already closed. I have to say, she was most upset. She said she had wanted to buy a doll for her granddaughter's birthday, which was the next day. She had been told that to pawn an object was the same as taking out a small loan: you left your item as a guarantee." Mr. Toban nodded at me as if I'd asked a question. "That is true. I charge only a small interest, and I keep the item for a certain period of time as is mutually agreeable. If it is redeemed within that time, the owner loses nothing. If not, well ..." His expression shifted to what I was coming to think of as his undertaker's face. Full of gentle sympathy. "If the articles are not redeemed, I put them up for sale." He indicated the glass cases. "As you can see, excellent things at excellent prices."

"Was the bracelet the only thing she brought in?"

He pursed his lips. "As a matter of fact, there was another item. I didn't put it out." He reached in a drawer and took out a small white box. "She had this as well. She was most embarrassed as, of course, these are usually a pair, but she realized she only had one. She must have dropped the other somewhere in her home." As he was talking, he snapped open the box. Nestled in its satin bed was a single gold cufflink. "It's a nice piece, but as there is only one, it's not too saleable unless you want it for the gold, which is fourteen karat. And it's monographed, which makes it even less saleable."

He removed the cufflink so I could see it more closely. Sure enough, the initials were *H.M.*: Herbert Moorhead. Emmeline's father.

"She told me the link had belonged to her late husband." He sighed. "I probably should have waited, but it is now three days past the deadline. I assumed she wasn't going to return."

He was so doleful I felt like uttering soothing noises. Or better still, buying something.

"Most of my customers like dainty things like this," he continued, giving the bracelet a poke. "I have to admit, business has been a little slow lately, so I succumbed and put it out for sale. Now you're telling me it's stolen goods. What a pity."

I took my notebook out of my handbag and beamed at him. "I hope you don't mind if I take notes, Mr. Toban. Memory can be so unreliable, and notes are much more acceptable in a court of law, don't you think?"

Alarm flooded his face. "Jack. Please. I always check the goods that are brought in against the police list. If there's any doubt at all about the legal ownership, I won't take the article until I have confirmed them with you."

"I know that," Jack replied with a reassuring tone.

"I promise you, this was a most respectable lady. She must have a good reason for not redeeming her pledge. I should have waited."

I gave him my sweetest smile. "Excuse me, Mr. Toban, on what are you basing this judgement of respectability?"

He smoothed his hair anxiously. "Well, she was very well dressed for one thing, even though she was still in her widow's weeds. Her fur collar was black mink for sure, and it would have cost forty dollars easily. And she has a very good address."

"Do you have the lady's name? And address?"

"Just a minute." He opened the truth-telling ledger, turned to the last page, and ran his finger down the column.

"Here we are. Two items: one gold cufflink and one child's silver charm bracelet, belonging to Mrs. B. Libirori. Number 16 Glenview Avenue. Brought in on Monday, February 22, 1937. Cash credit of five dollars extended against retrieval of goods no later than Saturday, March 6, 1937. There's her signature."

I didn't point out to him that the initials on the link weren't consistent with the woman's story of it belonging to her deceased husband. On the other hand, she may have been married several times over, never mind apparently having the misfortune to be widowed more than once.

CHAPTER FIFTEEN

AT JACK'S REQUEST, Mr. Toban agreed to withdraw the items until further notice. His pleasant demeanour was being severely tested, and he made it clear he had to get back to business. With an emphatic swish of his sign to OPEN, he ushered us out.

"Let's sit in the car and talk for a bit," said Jack.

We did so.

"Do you mind if I smoke?"

"Is that a good idea for you?"

"You sound like my wife. And you are both quite right. I'm cutting back, I promise."

"All right."

He lit up a cigarette, rolling down the window for my sake. I waited until he'd got through the first few drags. And lots of coughing.

"I have to say, Jack, I'm finding all of this very odd. There is no doubt the bracelet and the cufflink fit the description of the items Mrs. Emmeline Calder claims were stolen. She has hired me to find them."

"I've known Harry Toban for a long time. I trust him. Beneath that soft exterior, there's a shrewd businessman. He's not likely to jeopardize his reputation." He flicked a bit of ash out the window.

"Who is this woman, then? How did she come into possession of these things?"

Another flick of the ash.

"Good question. As Toban said, a lot of people are ashamed of visiting a pawnshop. I'm sure that's not the only nom de plume he's ever been given. And probably not the first time he's been lied to. Any guesses?"

"Wilf would kill me for pointing at one of the working classes before anything else, but I must admit, my suspicions have fallen on the housekeeper, Maria. She's got access for sure, and she tried hard to dissuade me from taking on the investigation. But I have no idea why. Five dollars isn't exactly a fortune, is it?"

Jack took another draw on the cigarette, coughed, then, rather shamefaced, stubbed out the cigarette.

"I know, I know, I'm killing myself. Last one, I swear."

"Mrs. Calder said she suspects one of the members of her women's club stole the items, and I'm to meet them tomorrow morning."

"Okay. I'll leave that up to you. At least you'll be bringing members of Toronto's elite into the picture. Wilf can't fault you for that. Let me know if you need any help."

I knew Jack wasn't the kind of police officer who would automatically consider two small pieces of possibly purloined jewellery a trivial matter, but I could see it from his point of view. Crimes among society's well-to-do were not typically that serious.

Or that much aired.

"To change the subject for a minute ... there seems little doubt that the two boys Mr. Toban was referring to were the Davies brothers."

Jack nodded. "Unfortunately, that doesn't get us very far. I sure would like to locate Leroy. I'll put more constables on it when I get back."

Agreeing to connect up tomorrow, we parted company — he to hurry home for dinner with his long-suffering family, me to get over to the Paradise Café for the same reason.

As I collected my bike, a gust of wind swirled in the gutters, stirring old leaves. It was definitely getting colder. A young boy, an elderly woman. Not candidates for spending the night outdoors.

CHAPTER SIXTEEN

I ARRIVED AT the café just at the last sitting. I used the side door to slip into the kitchen, which was, as Hilliard liked to say, organized chaos. Calvin, the cook, had his head literally in the oven. Pearl, our lone waitress, was about to hoist the heavy tray of dinner plates and go into the restaurant to serve the customers. Hilliard and Gramps were nowhere to be seen. I presumed they were out there greeting everybody. By now, the café was so established and popular that most of the customers were repeat visitors. Good nourishing food, good prices, good company for the most part. What else do you want from a café? Oops, I almost forgot. These days, you could also have good entertainment. Wilf and Hilliard were already advertising the upcoming St. Patrick's Day festivities.

When she saw me, Pearl halted. "Look what the cat brought in."

This was not an infrequent greeting, so I no longer took it seriously. Pearl could be, shall we say, unpredictable. I didn't know when I would be in her good books or her bad books. The reasons were frankly unfathomable. Tonight, she made it clear. She was frowning at me. Bad books, obviously.

"Good evening, Pearl. How are you tonight?"

"What's it look like? My feet hurt, and I burned my thumb." She jerked her head in the direction of Calvin, who had emerged from the oven. "He might have the hide of a buffalo, but I don't. He didn't warn me the plate was hot."

Calvin shrugged. "Sorry, Pearl. I thought you'd figure that a plate I was taking out of the oven with a mitt might be a tad warm to the touch."

"I'm not a mind reader. You should've said."

She got a better grip on her tray and stuck out her foot to push on the swing door as she delivered her final sally in my direction. "Your granddad isn't well. You should take better care of him."

With that, she kicked open the door and disappeared into the dining room.

Whew.

Cal came over to join me at the table. "Good evening, Miss Charlotte. If you don't mind my saying, you're looking a little frazzled. How's the day been?"

"Frazzling. By the way, what's happening with Gramps? He insisted on coming here. How does he seem to you?"

Calvin pulled out a chair and sat down across from me. "He was coughing a lot. But he's not a complainer like others we know. He just soldiers on."

"He said you had some kind of old Jamaican remedy you were going to make for him."

Cal grinned. "That's right. My mom used it on us kids when we got coughs or colds. Gramps sounds like he has a touch of bronchitis, and this should put him to rights in no time."

"What is it?"

Before he could answer, the connecting door swung open and Hilliard came in.

"There's a big run on the bread and dripping, Cal."

He saw me, and his face lit up in a gratifying smile. He came straight over and planted a sweet kiss on my lips.

"Charlotte. Where have you been? I thought you were coming here at lunch."

"I was intending to ..."

The door opened again, and Pearl stomped in.

"This mob is acting like they haven't eaten in days. If you don't hurry up, I'll be on the menu next."

I felt like saying that dish might be a bit too sour for most of them, but I refrained.

Hilliard jumped to his feet. "Coming, my dear. Coming."

She returned to the dining room.

Cal had already got the bowl of dripping from the shelf and was spooning it into small dishes ready to go. Bread and dripping was a popular addition to the menu. Five cents extra.

Hilliard called to me over his shoulder as he put them on his tray. "You'll stick around after the sitting, I hope?"

"Sure will."

He blew me a kiss and zoomed out to the hungry customers before they turned on Pearl.

"Hungry?" Cal asked. "The chicken pilaf turned out pretty good. Do you want some?"

"You bet."

He went to serve some on a plate for me, and I grabbed my handbag and took out the cookbook that Mrs. Calder had given me. "Cal, I've got this for you. Special recipes by the Ladies' Pioneer Club. Have a look."

He brought my plate over to the table and picked up the book. "Thanks, Charlotte. I am in need of new recipes for sure, but I have to have something that is suitable for a large number, not too much preparation required but reliably tasty." He began to leaf through the cookbook. "Ah yes, roast venison. Even if I could get hold of the meat, I don't think that would be a big favourite with our crowd. They tend to identify with the deer." He smiled at me. "Thanks for thinking of me, but I know these women. They probably got the recipe from their cook and they wouldn't know a rissole from a ragout if their life depended on it."

I wouldn't know the difference myself, life-threatening or not, but I was too busy stuffing my mouth with rice to comment.

Interrupted briefly by the hard-working help — that is to say, Pearl — banging through the swing door, I cleared my plate. In the short interlude, I managed to give Calvin a brief synopsis of the two boys' situation.

"If you were Leroy, on the run from some nasty and unfair punishment, where might you hide out, Cal?"

"They were in the police headquarters jail, you say?"

"That's right. This all happened this morning."

He regarded me for a moment or two. "A good place might be the UNIA Hall. It's only a few blocks from the police head-quarters."

"Of course! I should have thought of that."

UNIA was the acronym for the Universal Negro Improvement Association. Initially begun in Jamaica by Marcus Garvey, it had blossomed in Harlem, New York, before dissolving, except for a few small divisions, one of which was in Toronto.

"It makes sense he might head there. But do you think they would shelter him? He'd have to give some explanation. They might not want to get mixed up with a fugitive from the law."

"That would not be unfamiliar to them, I'm sure. It's *within living memory*, as they say."

Cal's tone was ironic, and I was embarrassed. I knew he was referring to the past fugitives who had come up from the States fleeing slavery. I'd long ago stopped thinking of him as "coloured," but he was, and this was perforce his heritage.

"You sound as if you don't quite approve of this group, Cal. Why is that? I thought they were keen on bettering the lot of coloured people in society."

"Yes and no. The man who started it, Marcus Garvey, no doubt had good intentions. He wanted us Black folks to have pride in ourselves and show the world that we could run businesses, acquire money, rise in the ranks of society just as much as any white man."

He paused to see how I was taking all this in. I already knew his political and philosophical leanings. We'd had lots of great talks about them.

"And? You said 'good intentions.' What was the bad result?"

He chuckled. "The good was wanting to instill a sense of pride in those of us who have been told for decades we are an inferior race; the bad was the unquestioning acceptance of capitalism as the ultimate goal. Why should we consider being a fat and glutted plutocrat a sign of success?"

He was grinning at me when he said this, but I knew there was an element of seriousness in his comment. He and Wilf Morrow were nothing if not committed communists.

"Jack Murdoch considers the escape to have been well planned. They were just waiting for the right moment. Do you think Leroy could have been in touch with UNIA earlier?"

Calvin shrugged. "You should ask them. I happen to know the manager's name is Charley Dyer. He may tell you, or then again, he may not."

"Where's the Might's city directory?"

"In the drawer."

Before I could retrieve the directory, however, the door opened again. This time, it was my own Gramps coming through.

"Lottie! There you are. I was getting worried. Where've you been?"

"Nowhere special, Gramps. Just climbing up and down Toronto's social hierarchy."

Gramps was nothing if not quick. "I thought you looked a little dishevelled."

Cal gave a snort of laughter. "I've got to get back to work. Let me know how you get on, Charlotte." He picked up the cookbook and moved it out of harm's way. "I'll give it a good perusal, I promise."

Gramps started to talk to me, but he went into a fit of coughing.

I pulled out a chair and practically shoved him into it. "You think I'm dishevelled? You should take a look at yourself. How are you feeling?"

He flapped his hand at me to indicate he couldn't yet speak. I waited. Unasked, Cal came back to the table with a glass of water.

"Take a few slow sips."

Gramps did so, and slowly the coughing subsided.

"Cal, my granddad says your ancient remedy will make him live forever. Without a cough."

"I can only promise to make good on one of those things. Which do you want, Mr. Frayne? Immortality or good health?"

"Immortality sounds tiring; I'll settle for no cough."

"Done. Stay here."

Cal went over to the cupboard and returned with a jar that was still labelled as plum jam. He gave it to me to have a look. No jam now but a thick, greyish-brown substance. I gave it a sniff, and it almost took my nose off.

"What the heck is it, Cal?"

"Base ingredient is goose grease mixed with a little camphor oil. You've got to rub it on his chest every night for the next five days. Cover it over with a piece of warm flannel. Tuck him up in bed. Got that?"

"Got it."

"Also, before you leave, I'm going to give you some oregano leaves. Drop them in a pot of boiling water, then have him cover his head with a tea towel to make a tent and inhale the steam. Once in the morning and once at night. Got that?"

"Got it."

"Don't move, Mr. Frayne, I'm going to make you some tea."

"If you happen to have a tot of rum, I'd be happy."

"I just might," said Cal with a chuckle.

He bustled back to the stove, and I retrieved the street directory. I didn't like the look of my grandfather at all. His skin was grey, and he seemed shrunken. I knew better than to say anything to him, but I was very glad that Cal had stepped up.

"So did you get over to the poor folks' home away from home?" Gramps asked me.

"I did. Let me just look up this address, and I'll tell you all about it."

I leafed through to the street listings. There it was: 355 College Street, the Universal Negro Improvement Association.

I called over to Cal. "They don't have a telephone number, Cal. Any suggestions?"

"You'll probably have to go in person." He glanced up at the clock. "They might have closed up by now."

I looked over at Gramps. Between the fairly slim chance of locating a runaway and probably resilient boy and taking care of my ailing grandfather, there wasn't really a choice to be made.

"Come on, you. Drink up that tea, and then I'm getting you home."

"I'm not going to fight you, Lottie. Let's catch up on your exploits tomorrow morning."

His submissiveness was even more alarming.

Calvin had heard this exchange, and he went over to the telephone.

"I'm going to call for a taxi."

"Explain to Hilliard, will you, Cal?"

Just then, the man himself came into the kitchen.

"Explain what?"

"I'm getting Gramps off to bed."

"Good idea." He saw the jar of goose grease. "Cal fixing you up, I see."

Gramps had another fit of coughing. Hilliard and I exchanged worried glances.

"Go!" said Hill when the fit had calmed down. "And if I see you here tomorrow, Arnie, I'm going to call in the knackers."

That started a laugh going in my Gramps, which made him cough again.

Wordlessly, Hilliard went to the cupboard where we kept our outdoor things. He unhooked Gramps's overcoat and hat and brought them over.

As he helped him into the coat, however, Gramps's legs gave way under him, and he collapsed to the floor.

CHAPTER SEVENTEEN

FORTUNATELY, GRAMPS RECOVERED within a few minutes and sat up. He actually smiled as he took in all the anxious faces surrounding him.

"Sorry about that," he muttered.

"We're getting you to the hospital," said Hilliard.

"Nonsense! I'll be fine. I'm a bit tired is all. A good night's sleep and Cal's medicine will put me to rights in no time."

There was no dissuading him, and I gave in. Hilliard accompanied us home. Nice.

By the time ten o'clock rolled around, Gramps was safely in bed, oreganoed, warm and comfortable, flannel poultice doing its job.

Early on in the consummation of our relationship, Hilliard and I had decided there would be no overnights at my place. Gramps knew what was going on but was old-fashioned enough to be uncomfortable with his dear and only granddaughter sleeping with a man to whom she was not officially married. We'd all mutually decided not to draw attention to it.

Besides, I only had a single bed.

Tonight, we agreed, was not a good night for a sleepover, and Hilliard and I were making a rather lingering goodbye in the hall when the telephone began to trill. Darn thing ringing in the house at night always startled me, and I jumped to answer it. It was Jack.

"Sorry to call so late, Lottie, but I thought you'd want to know the latest development."

"Uh-oh. Not good, by the sound of it."

"No, I'm afraid not. I've been notified that Dr. Brandwein has suffered another stroke. The doctor doesn't think he will survive more than a few days."

"I'm so sorry, Jack. That is bad news indeed."

"I've informed Judge Carter, and he's up in arms. He says that he's holding the boys responsible. He's planning to extend Leroy's sentence to five months. Industrial school. He says he might even send him to adult prison."

"Oh no."

"Oh yes. Worse, he's increased the strapping punishment. Leroy will now receive fifteen strokes."

"Jack, that's barbaric."

"Tell me about it. The way the judge was carrying on, it's a wonder he didn't order the lash."

"They're boys. Surely, he can't do that."

"He can."

"What about Jerome? He's not included in this, is he?"

"Carter said the decision on him is temporarily on hold. He'll wait to see how the lad recovers."

"My god, Jack. Is there anything you can do?"

"I'm going to get the Children's Aid Society involved. I wish J.J. Kelso was still with us, but I have faith they have some other dedicated souls who would help. I'm going to contact them right away. See if they can advise us."

"Good move. This mustn't go through."

"Needless to say, the judge gave me a real dressing down. Blamed me for being careless for letting the boys run away."

"Hardly fair."

"Listen, my sergeant major, Pullam, would make Carter

seem like a kitten purring in my ear. You haven't heard a dressing down until you've heard Sergeant Pullam. He rivalled Shakespeare himself in the brilliance of inventive invective."

He was laughing even as he said it, but frankly it sounded horrendous. Man stuff.

"No sightings of Leroy, I gather."

"Sort of. There was a bicycle reported stolen on Murray Street. Probable time, right after our lad did a bunk, so I'm guessing he was the one took it. Gives him a lot more mobility, of course, so he could be hiding out anywhere in the city."

I filled him in on the information about the UNIA Hall and Cal's thought that the people there might know something about the missing boy.

"I'll send a constable up there to talk to them."

He promised to ring me at once if there was any more news, and we hung up.

I asked Hill to stay a little longer, and we repaired to the kitchen, where I repeated the conversation with Jack until I was momentarily distracted by the sound of coughing from upstairs.

Hilliard touched my hand. "He's sounding better."

I wasn't completely sure, but I tried to let myself be comforted. He leaned closer.

"Do you want me to stay?"

"Of course I *want* you to, but I don't think you should. I'm going to be too restless."

Hilliard looked as if he would try to talk me into it, and frankly, given everything that had happened today, he probably would have succeeded. Single bed notwithstanding. However, he backed off.

"I'll be going, then. I'll be close to the telephone if you need me."

I thanked him appropriately, and he left.

I sat at the kitchen table for rather a long time, drinking tea that had gone cold. Thinking about things. Listening to the wind.

CHAPTER EIGHTEEN

Wednesday, March 10, 1937

I HADN'T EXPECTED to sleep well, but surprisingly I did. Whatever was in Cal's ancient Jamaican remedy was helping Gramps, and I was awakened only twice by the sound of him coughing. Finally, my alarm clock's shrilling brought me to complete consciousness. Seven o'clock. I got up.

All was quiet from the sickroom, so I proceeded with breakfast. Gramps got up not long after, but with only a token struggle he agreed to go back to bed for the rest of the day. I was due at the meeting of the Ladies' Pioneer Club in a couple of hours, but my reflection in the mirror was not encouraging. I hid the dark circles under my eyes with some face powder, added rouge to my cheeks and lips so I looked healthier, and I was done. I vacillated a little in my choice of dress but settled on what I thought of as my working clothes. That is, a green striped blouse with crisp white collar and cuffs, a navy wool skirt, and a matching navy cardigan. Not ostentatious, just completely respectable.

That done, I went to make telephone calls.

First was to the café. Hilliard answered right away.

"Hey, I was just about to call you. How's it going? How's Arnie?"

"Seems better. Stubborn as usual, but he has agreed to stay in bed."

"Excellent. I'll have Cal put up some soup, and I'll bring it over this afternoon when we're done here."

"Thanks."

"How are you doing, Lottie? You looked a little rough last night."

"Let's say I'm alive, but don't push me on that one."

He laughed. "Okay. Good luck with the ladies. I'll see you later."

We hung up, and, with some trepidation, I dialled the police department.

Jack was already in his office. He greeted me in his usual friendly way, but he sounded tense.

"I don't have much new to report. The constable I sent to the UNIA Hall had no news. He spoke to a man named Dyer, who is charge of the place. He said he had not seen the boy in question and had no knowledge of his whereabouts. According to Constable Littlejohn, whom I see as a reliable officer, he wasn't sure we could rely on Dyer to follow up. Littlejohn impressed upon him the necessity of informing us if Leroy did show up, but he described him as defensive."

"As in hiding something?"

"Possibly."

"How's Jerome doing?"

"I called over to the hospital a little while ago. He's minimally improved, but the doctor was not giving a good prognosis. There seems to be damage to his spinal cord. He might be permanently disabled."

"Oh, Jack. That's terrible."

"Don't I know it." There was a pause, and I could hear him taking in a deep puff of smoke. "I feel guilty about what happened, Charlotte. I should have insisted the boys be moved to a children's facility."

I had no answer. I was sorry he was beating himself up, but he was right. The boys should not have been in the jail.

"Oh, by the way, has your poorhouse lady turned up yet? I'd still like to talk to her."

"I'm just about to find out. I'll get back to you."

"Please do. I'm putting this case on top priority."

My next call was to the House of Industry.

The telephone rang so long, I was on the point of hanging up when a breathless-sounding woman answered. It was Miss Lindsay herself.

"Miss Frayne! Excuse me for being out of breath. Our receptionist has not arrived yet, and I was going past the telephone, so I thought I should answer it. I was just on my way to supervise the breakfast."

"I was wondering if Mrs. Brodie has returned."

"Not as yet. Frankly, I'm in a bit of a quandary. This is by no means the first time she has left the premises independently, but it is the first time she has stayed away overnight. I thought I would give it until this afternoon, and if she has not returned, I might inform the police. I don't want to do that. Our residents who, shall we say, *wander* find it a rather frightening experience to be accosted by a uniformed officer. However, their well-being is paramount, wouldn't you say?"

"Certainly. And I would appreciate it if you would let me know what transpires. We have not yet finished our business."

I was about to conclude the conversation when Miss Lindsay said, "Dear me, I almost forgot. A gentleman actually telephoned here last evening. He wanted to get in touch with you."

"Me? Who was it?"

"I didn't take the call myself, but Miss Healy, who was at the desk, said he didn't leave a name. He said he thought you worked here, which, of course, you don't. As she rightfully told him."

"What did he want?"

"He didn't say."

"You're sure he asked for me personally?"

"Quite sure. 'I'd like to speak to Miss Frayne,' were his words. 'When will she be in?' Miss Healy told him she had no information on that matter." Miss Lindsay's normally pleasant voice became a little sharp. "As you can understand, Miss Frayne, our resources here are rather limited. We cannot tie up our employees' valuable time with conveying personal messages."

"I quite understand. It must have been a mistake. Perhaps the caller was looking for somebody else."

The only person who might think I worked at the House was one of the men I had encountered at the dinner meal yesterday. It had to be the man called Zav. He'd heard my name. He'd also made a point of mentioning seeing me with Mrs. Brodie. The woman who was prepared to accuse him of breaking and entering. And now she seemed to have vanished. I didn't like it. I didn't like it at all.

CHAPTER NINETEEN

CONSIDERING THE AMOUNT of accumulated wealth that entered its portals, the Ladies' Pioneer Club facility was a surprisingly modest three-storey building tucked in the middle of a row of other modest buildings. The oak door was solid and unpretentious. The only element that might have been considered remotely ostentatious was a stained glass window that gleamed above the lintel. It depicted a muscular-looking woman with a hoe.

I guessed the door would be unlocked so that there was no necessity for the members to linger on the sidewalk, and I was right. I turned the handle and went in.

Mrs. Calder was already waiting for me in the hall. She billowed toward me, her hand outstretched.

"Caroline, my dear. Welcome."

I didn't know if the misnomer was part of the subterfuge or a memory lapse, so I didn't correct her.

"Allow me to take your coat," she gushed. "No hat?"

"No. It's quite mild today."

Her blink of surprise made me realize her question had not been related to the weather but more to do with decorum. She herself was dressed much more soberly than when I'd last seen her, in a navy-blue, snug-fitting suit, rather masculine in style. The only startling piece of apparel was a plate-like yellow hat from which colourful purple feathers curved to her chin.

As I divested myself of my plain wool coat, she leaned in closer and whispered, "Everybody is in the meeting room having coffee. I've told them I have a guest, but I will introduce you properly when we go in."

I did a fast smoothing of my no doubt ruffled hair. "Any further thoughts on the matter at hand, Mrs. Calder? Are the same women present who were at your house?"

"Oh yes. They're all there." Again, she leaned closer. The tobacco from her recent cigarette, mingled with the dense fragrance of her perfume, assailed my nostrils. "Don't let appearances deceive you, my dear. One of these women is a viper."

She thrust open the door to the meeting room. I heard the tail end of somebody's speech. At least it sounded like a speech. Loud and well-enunciated, distinctly Anglo.

"We really must do something. We can't let her continue in this way —"

She stopped abruptly as we entered.

Mrs. Calder was ahead of me. She clapped her hands.

"Attention, everybody. Attention please. I would like you to meet my niece, Miss Christine Frayne. She's considering joining our club."

The lie slipped so easily from her lips I had the feeling my client was quite accustomed to the art of prevarication.

There were five women seated around a table. I glimpsed a bright room, businesslike in its furnishings but pleasant.

There were various muttered greetings from the assembled women. Mrs. Calder ushered me to a vacant chair and sat down beside me.

"Allow me to introduce everybody, my dear." She rushed along. "On my right is Mrs. Edelstone, our president and longest-living member."

I knew she was referring to how long the woman had been a member and not her age, but it was a gaffe, and the person addressed was obviously not impressed. She was a white-haired woman with what are often referred to as "strong features." That is, she had a rather long nose and matching jaw. Her hair underneath a small brimmed hat was seriously coiffed. I'd seen her picture on the society page of the *Toronto Star* more than once. She spoke, and this was the voice I'd heard when we entered the room. It was capable of deflating a hot-air balloon.

"Mrs. Calder, I haven't been president for the past six months. That honour goes to Mrs. Duncan. You must remember to say past president. And I'm not sure how I feel about being termed longest-living. It makes me feel rather dinosaurish."

Mrs. Calder did not seem the least intimidated.

"My apologies, Martha. You're always so emphatic, it's easy to forget you're not still our esteemed leader."

There was a ripple of laughter from the others around the table, rather quickly suppressed.

The woman next to the past president smiled at me.

"Welcome to the club. I'm Rosalynd Withers."

Her grey hair was marcelled back into a soft bun, her full bosom unconstrained, her tweed suit smartly classic. She was probably several years older than I and many dollars wealthier, but I felt a kinship with her immediately.

I smiled back. "Thank you."

Mrs. Calder continued the introductions. "On your left is Mrs. Lowdnes; next to her is Mrs. Duncan."

These two women were so similar in appearance they had to be sisters. Bobbed brown hair with firm finger waves and henna highlights, angular features, flowered dresses. Also wearing neat brimmed hats. We exchanged nods.

I was doing my best to see if there was any sign of serpent-like characteristics among the women, but so far nothing was apparent.

Mrs. Calder put her hands on the table.

"All right then, shall we get down to business?"

"Wait a minute, Emmeline, you haven't yet introduced me."

The remark, sharp and irritated, came from the woman directly across from us. Like Mrs. Edelstone, she was wearing a tight hat; her hair was dark rather than white but was also well-coiffed. Unlike the past president, there was nothing assertive or confident about her demeanour, even though she was clearly on the attack. She was scowling with a disconcerting hostility, but she had shrunk back into her chair as if she was also afraid.

This time, Mrs. Calder seemed flustered. "I beg your pardon, Bertha. My fault." She reached over and touched my hand. Her fingers were cold.

"Carol, my dear, allow me to introduce another long-standing member of the club. In fact, I might call her one of our founding mothers. Mrs. George Rundle."

I was totally taken aback.

Surely not *that* Mrs. Rundle? Mr. Gilmore's client? The cuckolded wife of respectable George; the Mrs. Rundle who was proud of her position in society?

To my knowledge, we hadn't met before, but it was obvious she wasn't at all happy about my presence.

I tried on a hearty smile. "Pleasure to meet you, Mrs. Rundle."

"I wish I could say the same, Miss Frayne."

Mrs. Calder gaped at her. "What on earth do you mean, Bertha?"

"I mean that we need to be discerning about strangers joining our meetings."

This time, Rosalynd Withers spoke up. "Miss Frayne will be getting a bad impression of us, Bertha. We have spoken recently about needing to expand the membership. I'm sure Emmeline would only introduce somebody she thought was suitable."

"Exactly so, Mrs. Withers," burst out Emmeline. "I have no idea what you are insinuating, Bertha."

Mrs. Rundle poked out her chin at the same time as she shrank further down in her chair. She made me think of a terrier who wants to bite but is afraid of retaliation.

"Let me say this. We must be very careful. I was speaking to Mrs. Sinclair only a few days ago. She said the Empire Club discovered that one of their new members was, in fact, a fraud. She was not at all what she claimed to be."

The others were staring at her in dismay. Mrs. Edelstone spoke up first.

"Are you saying that the person you refer to falsified her background in order to be accepted? Please make yourself clear."

Mrs. Edelstone had likely not had a paying job in her life, otherwise I would have pegged her as a former schoolmistress. You disobeyed her at your peril.

"That is exactly what I am saying," continued Mrs. Rundle. "The woman in question had been planted, as the expression goes, by the police themselves."

"Nonsense. Why on earth would they do that?" asked Mrs. Edelstone.

"They wanted to make sure the club was not preaching sedition like the anarchists and the communists."

"Nonsense," repeated Mrs. Edelstone. "The Empire Club is one of our most loyal organizations. Sedition is the last thing you are likely to hear."

"According to Mrs. Sinclair, the government has heard rumours that such talk has been permitted at more than one meeting."

"This is dreadful," said Mrs. Duncan, but whether she meant treasonous talk being permitted or the reaction of the government, I wasn't sure.

Mrs. Edelstone interjected. "Emmeline, can you clarify this matter?"

Mrs. Calder's suspicions were personal, not political, but in one sense, Mrs. Rundle was quite right. I was there to observe and report — in a word, to spy — and this had been instigated by Mrs. Calder. It was of course not up to me to admit or deny, but I had no desire to utter a bald-faced lie.

I turned to look at her. She jumped in.

"Really, Bertha, to listen to you, one might think you had something to hide."

Attack is the best defence.

Mrs. Rundle flushed. She reached for her handbag and got to her feet.

"I will return to the next meeting as long as I can be assured that our total privacy is guaranteed. Whether this young woman is genuinely your niece, Emmeline, and whether she is sincerely interested in our club, I rather doubt."

Mrs. Calder retreated a little but not much. "I could be insulted by these remarks, Bertha, but I have too much respect for our other members to take up the cudgel."

Hmm.

Mrs. Edelstone predictably pursued the matter.

"Mrs. Rundle, you are casting aspersions that cannot just

lie there on the table like a dead bird. Why are you saying these things?"

Again, Mrs. Rundle squeezed her handbag like a lifeline or a weapon.

"Very well. I am reluctant to say this, but if you insist … I happen to know that Miss Frayne, Miss *Charlotte* Frayne, is a private investigator. In other words, she is a detective."

All eyes swivelled toward me. I fixed my own gaze on the table.

"Is this true, Miss Frayne?" said Mrs. Edelstone, who had definitely stepped back into her former role of leader. Mrs. Duncan seemed totally at a loss for words. I glanced over at Mrs. Rundle, who was still on her feet. She seemed small and shrunken, and I actually felt a wave of pity for her. She was deeply distressed. Only yesterday, her world had fallen apart.

How, I don't know, but she had connected me with Mr. Gilmore and the whole sorry business of her philandering husband. I felt badly that I had obviously added to her hurt but perhaps not for the reasons she thought.

"Yes, it is true, I am a private investigator."

The other sister, Mrs. Lowdnes, spoke for the first time. "I don't really mind what work she does as long as it doesn't impinge on our mission, but I do think we need to be completely aboveboard in all of our dealings with each other. Is Miss Frayne your niece, Emmeline? Did you invite her here to see what we are about? Or is she here because of her profession?"

Mrs. Calder sidestepped in such an adroit way, I almost admired her.

"Did I say niece? Well, I meant it more in a spiritual way than genetic. As you said, Rosalynd, we have been talking about expanding our membership, so I thought I would bring

134 • MAUREEN JENNINGS

Karen to a meeting, and she could see what we are all about. It
didn't occur to me that she would be set upon in this unfortunate manner."

Mrs. Edelstone looked at me. "Miss Frayne, I'm sure we
would all appreciate it if you yourself would clarify your
position."

What was I going to say? It was apparent my client wasn't
going to come clean, and I didn't feel like getting into a lot of
lies. In some ways, prevarication was part of my job. I'd been
undercover more than once since I'd linked up with T. Gilmore
and Associates, but I can't say it was an aspect I particularly
enjoyed. Somehow, this felt different. I had been hired to do
more than observe and find out the truth. I was perhaps here
to perpetrate somebody's delusion. I flashed back to the housekeeper's warning. *She's hired investigators twice before. Don't
take the job. Nothing has been stolen.*

Mrs. Edelstone prompted me again. "Miss Frayne?"

"I'm afraid I'm constrained by reasons of confidentiality."

Mrs. Lowdnes spoke. "Are you saying that Emmeline
actually *hired* you?"

Mrs. Calder got me off the hook, but not in any honest
way. "Really, ladies, I find this all so objectional. I was not
aware that Miss Frayne was an investigator. She never said. We
met at some function or other, and I thought she might enjoy
joining our club. That's all there is to it. Why on earth would I
want to employ her services?"

"Miss Frayne," said the past president, "do you concur
with Mrs. Calder?"

I knew what I wanted to shout: *No. She hired me to spy on
all of you because she thinks you have stolen some jewellery.*

All I felt I *could* say was, "I'm afraid I cannot answer that
question."

Mrs. Calder was now the one doing the glaring. "It is obvious I misjudged this woman. I withdraw my nomination."

Mrs. Edelstone, who should have been called to the bar, addressed Mrs. Rundle. She was still hovering by her chair and looked utterly haggard.

"Bertha. You were the one who brought our attention to Miss Frayne's being a private investigator. I am wondering how you came to know that."

To everybody's horror, the little woman burst into wrenching, uncontrollable sobs.

"I know because I hired her associate."

"A private investigator?"

Mrs. Rundle could only nod.

"Why on earth did you do that, Bertha?"

"I needed to know the truth."

It was hard to make out what she was saying, her sobs were so engulfing. Mrs. Withers got up and came over to her.

"Hush, Bertha. Hush now. Come and sit down."

She led the unfortunate woman back to her chair. The others were frozen in their seats. Mrs. Calder seemed stunned.

There was a carafe of water on the table, and Mrs. Duncan got up, poured a glass, and handed it to the other woman. I dearly wanted to leave, but I thought that might create more of a disturbance than I already had. After what seemed like a long time, Mrs. Rundle calmed down, managed a few sips of water, and blew her nose. Finally, Mrs. Edelstone addressed her. Her voice was firm — I don't think she could speak any other way — but it was kind.

"When you say you needed to know the truth, what do you mean?"

"I have suspected for some time that George is unfaithful. I had to know for certain, and Mr. Gilmore confirmed my suspicions. George has been dallying with a young woman. For many months."

Saying that threatened to overturn her precarious equilibrium, but Rosalynd lifted the glass so she could take a sip.

"How could he? How could he?" whispered Mrs. Rundle. "We have been married for over thirty years."

"When George realizes the consequences of a public scandal, he will come to his senses," said Mrs. Edelstone in her legal voice. "Men always do." She turned to me. "Is that the reason for your presence here?"

"Absolutely not. I had no idea Mrs. Rundle was a member of the Pioneer Club."

It is easy to convince others you are sincere when you are.

"But you are not going to enlighten us as to the real reason?"

"I'm afraid I cannot do that."

"I must therefore ask you to leave."

Nobody was looking at me. Mrs. Calder was staring into space. The brief interaction that I had witnessed among these women made me think they weren't going to let her off the hook. I thought of the words I'd heard when we arrived. Mrs. Edelstone in her clarion, carrying voice.

We really must do something. We can't let her continue in this way ...

I got to my feet. "Good morning, ladies. I must apologize for any distress I have inadvertently caused."

I left them to it.

CHAPTER TWENTY

THE FIRST SITTING at the Paradise had just begun when I arrived. The customers were unusually animated, chatting more loudly than I'd heard in a while. Perhaps it was the hint of spring in the air — a choir of purple crocus in the flower box bringing hope and possibility for better times. Perhaps Cal had come up with a particularly delicious main. Perhaps Pearl was in a good mood.

That last possibility was scotched as soon as I walked in. She was about to put a peculiar-looking salad in front of one of the customers. I think it was beet and apple.

"Here you are, Mr. Mitchell."

Said customer was frowning.

"Tuck in. It's nice and fresh. Very good for what ails you."

Her working smile evaporated as soon as she saw me.

"Look who it isn't. Good morning, Miss Frayne. Or should I say, 'good afternoon'? We were wondering where you'd got to."

The usual stab of alarm pierced my stomach. "Has something happened? How's Gramps?"

"He's fine. He's in the kitchen helping Calvin."

"What! He's supposed to be home in bed."

Pearl harrumphed. "Good thing he is here. Mr. Morrow has disappeared, and Mr. Taylor has gone to the station to pick up his children."

"They weren't expected until next week."

"All I know is, he got a telephone call and off he flew. Who knows when he'll be back? Didn't matter I was the only one left to do the serving. We're busy out here, and I don't have four pair of hands, you know."

"My goodness, Pearl, I would never have guessed. You do so well with the ones you have."

Several of the customers close by smiled at this.

"I'll say," said one old codger with what might have passed for a leer in a younger buck. "She's the best there is. Not to mention good-looking."

"Oh, get out of here," rejoined Pearl, but she was mollified. Mood change. She nodded at me. "Don't worry about your granddad. He's tough as old shoe leather."

"I'll go check."

I headed for the kitchen, leaving Pearl to josh with the customers, who were mostly male. I was so intent on getting to the kitchen that I almost tripped over the feet of one of the men seated by the swing door. He yelped. I started to apologize, then I realized that the boots belonged to none other than the redhead I'd last seen in the dining room of the House of Industry. It was Zav Genik. The man Mrs. Brodie swore she'd seen on Edward Street. The same man who had flown into a murderous rage when somebody had taunted him. He who had presumably telephoned the House this morning inquiring about me. I guess he'd found me.

He stood up, and the young man next to him did the same. This was the companion who had hurried after Genik so anxiously in the dining room.

"Miss Frayne," said Genik with what was almost a bow. "I'm so glad to see you. I wish to offer you an apology for my behaviour yesterday. I had no wish to alarm you. You were, after all, only there because you desire to help those less fortunate."

Wow. What do you say to a speech like that?

"I understand you telephoned the House this morning and were looking for me."

He blinked but was still smooth as silk. His somewhat misshapen face was unrevealing. "That is correct. As I said, I wanted to make amends for my poor behaviour."

"How did you track me down?"

"Track you down? That is not exactly the case. I expected I would see you when Marko and I returned to the House. It is sheer chance that we have run into you here." He gestured. "I gather you are familiar with this café."

"The owners are friends of mine."

"I thought it must be something like that. You don't seem of the same ilk as the customers."

What the heck was that supposed to mean? This man was starting to give me the creeps. Sheer chance be blowed. I assumed he had been out to find me. But why? I didn't buy the apology garbage.

Even as I was chewing on my tongue, he turned to his companion.

"Allow me to introduce my friend, Marko Ryga."

The other man gave me a shy smile but didn't put out his hand. That initiation was up to me. I didn't either. He seemed more wholesome than Genik, but I was still most uneasy about their agenda.

"I'd better get going. Enjoy your lunch."

"Thank you. It certainly looks more appetizing than that we usually receive at the House."

I hadn't checked on today's menu, so I didn't yet know what Cal had made.

"Speaking of which, there was something I wanted to ask you, Miss Frayne."

Pearl chose the right moment to come bustling over. "What would you like, gentlemen?" She pointed at the blackboard by the register. "Everything's written down there. The main today is stewed mutton. Very tasty, I must say. Comes with beans and boiled potatoes. You get your choice of salad. Cabbage or cold beet and apple. I'll take your order for the sweet later. You can have the chocolate pudding, the oatmeal and raisin cookie, or the lemon tart."

Genik had turned to take a look at the board, and he seemed transfixed.

"How strange it feels to be given a choice."

I took the opportunity to continue through to the kitchen.

He called after me, "Will we see you later this afternoon, Miss Frayne?"

"Not today, I'm afraid."

I left the two of them in Pearl's capable hands, but I felt troubled. Why was he here? The café was not expensive, far from it. The partners made sure everything was quite afford-able for the customers, many of whom were, or had been, unemployed. But Genik and his friend had gone to the House of Industry for a meal. They needed a city-allotted ticket to do that. Had they run out? It was not impossible. Where had they obtained the money to pay for their lunch? What was it he wanted to ask me?

My dear Gramps was sitting at the kitchen table, peeling potatoes. Cal was at the stove dealing with the mutton stew. Wilf had returned and was writing something up in his notebook.

My grandfather greeted me with delight. "Here she is. Come and sit down, Lottie. Fill me in."

"What are you doing here? You're supposed to be in bed."

"Thanks to Dr. Greene here, I am feeling much better."

He did, in fact, look almost back to his old self.

"So how did it turn out this morning? Difficult, from the look of you."

"Give me a minute, Gramps. I just need to talk to Wilf."

"Do you want some stew?" Cal called to me over his shoulder. "It turned out quite well, considering."

"Considering what?"

"Considering the sheep probably died of old age," answered Gramps.

Cal stopped what he was doing and turned to Gramps in mock horror. "Are you insinuating the meat was tough?"

"Hey, don't worry about it, it's good for the jaw to have that much exercise."

Cal grabbed a fork and speared a piece of meat from the pot, blew on it, then took a nibble.

"It melts in the mouth. What are you talking about?"

Gramps shrugged. "I must have had one of the early bits, before you boiled it into oblivion."

Cal laughed. Me too. This repartee was long-standing with these two, and they both enjoyed it. Given how much work preparing for the servings entailed, I thought they were probably both right.

"I think I need something to take away a nasty taste. Maybe the chocolate pudding," I said to Cal.

Gramps looked at me in concern. "That kind of day already, is it?"

"'Fraid so."

Wilf had seemed totally engrossed in what he was writing, but he stopped.

"Your granddad said you had an appointment over at the Pioneer Club. Don't tell me they were roasting a striking miner over the fire. Regular club business, was it?"

Sometimes I got tired of Wilf's relentless politics.

"As a matter of fact, they were very nice women. They want to do some good in the world."

"Ha. Tell that to the peasants. They haven't noticed. So, what did you want to talk to me about?"

I didn't want to alarm Gramps, so I kept my voice even. "Wilf, did anybody ring here asking for me?"

He shook his head. "Not that I know of. Hill usually takes all the calls anyway. He doesn't trust me, for some reason. He says I'm always trying to recruit new members."

I returned his smile. That sort of banter was an ongoing thing between Hilliard and Wilf.

"Speaking of which, I'd like you to pop out to the dining room. There's a man sitting at the table by the swing door. Tall, thin fellow with reddish hair and a moustache. A sort of squashed face. He's wearing a black oilskin coat. He's with a younger man, clean-shaven, dark hair, brown coat."

"And what do I do if I see such a person?"

"Just tell me if it's anybody you know."

"A comrade is what you mean."

"Precisely."

"And if he is, what will you do with that information?"

"Wilf, for god's sake, what do you think? He might have been involved in a robbery that two innocent boys are in danger of being blamed for. It's a case I'm working on, and any information you can give me about that man might prevent a 'grave miscarriage of justice.'"

I couldn't help myself; Mrs. Brodie's words were burned into my brain.

Rather to my surprise, Wilf leaned forward and patted my hand.

"Come on, Lottie. I was only teasing." He jumped up. "I'll go look right now."

He was as good as his word.

Cal had heard all of this exchange. He picked up a dish of pudding and brought it to the table.

"By the way, the UNIA Hall is open this afternoon. I was thinking that I'd come with you, if you like. After the second sitting."

I was surprised. "Oh, you don't have to. I know where it is."

He looked at me for a moment. "Let's say they might be more likely to talk to you if I am there."

"Okay. If you say so. Thanks, Cal."

Gramps dropped his peeled potato into the bucket of water beside him.

"Are you going to let your nearest and dearest relative into the story, or am I going to croak on the spot and then find out?"

"Gramps, don't be silly. If you croak now, I'll be so mad at you I won't tell you a thing."

He nodded his head sagely. "Okay. I'll stick around. Fill me in."

Before I could do so, Wilf returned.

"Lottie, there is no one in the dining room that fits the description you gave me. I even went outside to see if he was having a smoke, but no. Nobody there. Pearl said she took the order from the man you were talking to, but he changed his mind. He and the other chap left. Pearl's ticked off, as she said he took up a table that could have gone to somebody else. We've had to turn away six people this morning."

"Maybe he heard about the mutton," quipped Gramps.

I chuckled more to make him happy than anything else. I wished I knew why Zav had left.

I addressed Wilf. "His name is Viktor Genik, goes by the nickname of Zav. His companion is Marko Ryga. Does that ring a bell?"

Wilf was startled. "Matter of fact, it does. He was at a meeting recently. He just came from out west. You say he might have been involved in robbing some rich cove's house?"

"Do you think that's likely?"

Wilf frowned. "Viktor was one of the miners persecuted in the Estevan strike. He was a returned soldier. Both of his parents died in the Ukrainian famine. He might have developed a short fuse for injustice. Comfort for the rich. Hardship for the poor."

His remark irritated me. "I don't know how well off the victim was, Wilf. Even if he was rich as Croesus, I don't think that's a good enough reason to steal his property. He's an elderly man, and he had a stroke, possibly when he surprised the robbers. He's had another one since. He might not live much longer."

Wilf was irritated in return. "Let's agree to disagree about what constitutes injustice. What do you want me to do about Genik?"

"I don't know if there's anything you can do. An investigation is underway concerning the robbery. Let's see what unfolds. I just don't want to see a young boy punished for something he didn't do."

"Fair enough. If Genik shows up here again, I'll have a chat with him, see what he has to say for himself," Wilf must have caught my expression because he threw up his hands. "Don't worry. I will be most delicate. Unlike the police, I won't accuse without evidence or throw him in jail on suspicion."

I felt like saying, "If he kills me or an old lady who might accuse him, on your head be it." But I knew I was overreacting.

Wilf grabbed his notebook. "I have to go into the dining room and take a survey."

"What kind of survey? Who prefers chocolate or lemon pudding?"

Wilf frowned, not amused.

"He's writing another play for St. Pat's Day," Gramps said to me. "I get to play a mine owner this time. I can fire people at will. Let them starve and so on."

Wilf broke into a grin. "You'll do a good job, Arnie. You'll find aspects of yourself you didn't know existed."

Gramps feigned alarm. "Hey, maybe that's too dangerous. Can I go back to being downtrodden?"

Cal called over to him, "No, you can't. That's my role."

I smiled falsely at Wilf. "Thank goodness you have no place for women in your plays. I'm waiting for the chance to be on an equal footing, but at the moment the only choice seems to be between the oppressor or the oppressed. Both male parts. Neither appeals to me."

Wilf was not appeased. "Write your own damn play. You can call it, *Look What We Women Have to Put Up With*. You never know, it might be a big success."

With that, he stomped out through the swing door, leaving us rocking in his wake like a small boat that the steamer has just passed. Or should I say the destroyer?

Gramps gave me a wink. "Stop needling him, Lottie. He's not going to change. Come and help me finish peeling these potatoes. Cal needs them."

I heard Wilf shout to the customers, "Listen up, everybody. I just want a show of hands. Who would like to be in a play for the St. Pat's Day celebration? It's about the striking miners at Estevan and what happened to them."

There was the sound of rather tepid responses.

Wilf again. "Who would like an Irish night? Performers and a singsong?"

This time the response was lusty. Definitely the preference.

"Seems like you won't be finding hidden aspects of your personality after all, Gramps."

He chuckled. "You don't think Wilf is going to take notice of what the crowd thinks, do you? He'll do what he wants as always."

"But that's not fair. Hill wants to do an Irish ceilidh."

"Listen. The miners could do a little song and dance while they're on strike. It'll work well."

"Speaking of which, what's the story with him and his children?"

"I don't really know. He got a phone call, I think from his ex-wife, that the children were on the train."

"They weren't supposed to come until next week."

"So I understand, but I guess plans changed. The train's due in to Union Station this morning, so he had to leave right away."

"Any message for me?"

Gramps grimaced. "He didn't have time, Lottie. It was very short notice."

There was nothing more to say, and I knew Gramps would worry if I showed signs of distress. Which I was most definitely feeling. As I'd said to him earlier, I'd been trying to be ready to meet Hill's children, but at the moment, I didn't feel at all prepared.

CHAPTER TWENTY-ONE

THE MUTTON MUST have softened up considerably by the end of the second sitting, because there were many appreciative comments. This put Pearl in good spirits, and she was only too happy to be left in charge of the café until Cal returned. Gramps volunteered to continue with the vegetable preparation, and she was also pleased about that. Gramps was one of Pearl's favourite people. Wilf had been even more outvoted when he did his second-sitting survey, but he wasn't daunted. He headed upstairs to do some more writing. "Fewer distractions," he muttered darkly. There was no word from Hill, and I wondered how the meeting with the children was going.

I kept an eye out for Genik and his companion, but they did not return.

Finally, the last customer, rather reluctantly, left. The café was tidied, dishes washed, and everything was laid out for the evening prep. I pitched in to help. Gramps continued to look healthy, and he insisted on starting a singsong while we worked. His repertoire was limited but lively. A couple of army marching songs and an old Irish ballad kept us going.

Calvin decided to simmer the mutton longer, added a lot more parsnips and carrots, and declared, "The evening menu will be mouth-watering." I planned to take his word for it rather than firsthand experience — I'd settle for a sandwich.

There was one more thing I had to do — I was well aware but had been avoiding it. I had to ring Jack Murdoch. Frankly, I was nervous about what I might hear.

The telephone was beside the cash register in the dining room, and I went in. The tables were all set, the plates and cutlery clean and sparkling, the fresh white tablecloths and folded napkins inviting. The walls were a sunny yellow. Even though it added to the cost of running the café, Hilliard and the partners had insisted from the beginning that they would make the dining room as cheery as they could. "For a lot of our customers," Hilliard had once said, "this is the only place they go where 'economy' isn't thrust in their faces." The choice worked. The Paradise was always full.

I paused for a moment in the silent room, taking in the brightness and order, the sense that it was waiting in welcome. It seemed to satisfy some need to believe that life was renewing.

I dialed the police station.

Jack was in his office and answered promptly.

"Good timing, Charlotte. I've just got back from the hospital. I wanted to see for myself how young Jerome was faring."

"And? What's the verdict?"

I could hear Jack take a drag on his cigarette before he answered.

"He's still not got much mobility, and they think he might have some bleeding in the brain. If that proves to be the case, they may have to do surgery. Otherwise ..."

He didn't finish his sentence. He didn't have to. Not much of a future for a young parentless boy with permanent brain damage.

"Still no sighting of Leroy?"

"No. And we can't find any next of kin willing to step in. Nobody."

"I'm about to go over to the UNIA Hall with Cal. He thinks they might be more forthcoming if he's with me."

"What about your missing lady? And the two men you're concerned about?"

"Nothing yet about Mrs. Brodie. I'll give the House another ring. But the two men showed up here at the café earlier today. I don't know why. Could have been innocent — this place is well known — but I believe they were specifically looking for me. And through me, Mrs. Brodie."

"Do they seem dangerous to you, Charlotte?" His voice was concerned.

"Not the younger one. He's totally controlled by the other man, Viktor Genik. Him, I can't quite read. He's certainly got a violent streak, but that might be reserved for other males."

"I'm going to reallocate some of my constables. We'll start with another house-to-house on Edward Street. See if there is anybody at all with information about the burglary. Sometimes a second go-around does yield something."

I knew it might also deliver false information. Not because the people questioned were being devious but because memory is so unreliable. Often, when there's a time lapse, recollection can be greatly elaborated. It had been more than a week now since Dr. Brandwein had been burglarized. In the absence of trace evidence, finding the real burglars was unlikely. I caught myself. I was already taking the position that the two brothers were innocent.

"Let me know how it goes at UNIA," said Jack. Another pull on the cigarette. "To tell the truth, Charlotte, it was distressing to see that little fellow in the hospital bed. This accident wouldn't have happened if we'd taken more care."

"Are you going to talk to Judge Carter?"

"I am. He's on furlough for the next few days, apparently playing golf somewhere, but as soon as he returns, I'll go and plead the case. I hope he will show some mercy."

"Fingers crossed."

But knowing the judicial system and its rigidity, I thought the chances were slim that the boys would be let off.

Even if they were totally innocent of any criminal action.

We hung up. The dining room looked less bright.

One more call to make.

CHAPTER TWENTY-TWO

THE TELEPHONE AT the House rang interminably until once again it was a breathless Miss Lindsay who answered.

"Miss Frayne, I'm glad you called. I don't suppose Mrs. Brodie has been in touch with you, has she?"

"No, she hasn't. She hasn't returned, I gather?"

"She has not. But I had a troubling call from our bank manager. She has apparently withdrawn all of her savings. When our residents come here, we encourage them to make monthly deposits from their pensions. It is their money to do with as they wish, but we've found it gives them a sense of pride to know they have a little money put by. Going off to the bank to check on their savings account is a regular excursion for them."

I had the feeling she could have waxed poetic about the benefits of putting aside money, but fascinating as that was, I didn't want to linger. Cal was waiting for me.

"How much money are we talking about, Miss Lindsay?"

"Almost fifty dollars. She has made a little extra from selling her knitted goods." She paused. "As you know."

Yikes, I had almost forgotten that was my cover story.

"You say you are troubled by this information from the bank?"

"What would she spend it on? She has no family at all. That's why she's in the House. Her regular needs are taken care of, and she hasn't shown any previous inclinations to extravagance in terms of clothes or jewellery. We don't encourage that. It isn't fair to those who have almost nothing."

Given what I knew, I was uneasy myself about Mrs. Brodie's vanishing act, but there wasn't much I could say. She was clear-minded and independent, and it was her money.

"Do you think I should notify the police?" continued Miss Lindsay.

"It hasn't been more than twenty-four hours, and I happen to know they are reluctant to search for missing persons unless they are sure the person is ... well, missing."

Like a young boy on the run from punishment.

"Very well, I will wait until tomorrow, but if she hasn't come back or notified us by then, I'm going to call the authorities."

"I think that is a good idea."

"How can I reach you, Miss Frayne, if I do locate her or if she returns here?"

"Er, I'm sort of on the move for the rest of the day. I will ring you again later this evening."

"Very well."

We rang off, and I went to fetch Cal.

He was putting the last touches to the main.

"Be right with you, Charlotte." He flung in a handful of chopped parsnips. "I'm sweetening it up a bit. It wasn't going down the gullets as fast as I'd hoped."

I had no intention of having it anywhere near my own gullet, but I nodded approvingly.

I went to get my coat from the closet, making a rather furtive appraisal of my grandfather's state of health as I went by. He was still cutting up carrots, briskly and efficiently, and I decided I could leave him for an hour or so. There had been no word from Hilliard.

Cal finished what he was doing and quickly removed his chef's hat and apron.

"I need some fresh air; all right with you if we walk to the Hall?"

"Sure."

I started to head for the dining room, but he stopped me.

"Let's take the side door."

"Okay."

He'd put on his own coat and a wool cap, which he jammed down tightly on his head, obscuring most of his face. There was something about what he was doing that seemed a bit odd, but I didn't really dwell on it, too preoccupied with my own thoughts.

As we stepped out into the laneway, a gust of March wind pounced on us. On its back was a sprinkling of chill rain just to ensure we weren't getting ahead of ourselves. Spring wasn't here quite yet.

"Are you sure you don't want to take the streetcar?" I asked Cal.

"Positive."

I pulled my jacket collar a little tighter, and we set off, Cal setting a brisk pace. We headed along McCaul Street, fairly busy at this time of day. I have to admit I rather prided myself on being a fast walker, and Cal and I were abreast, although he was keeping a few feet away. I realized I had only ever interacted with him in the confines of the Paradise kitchen. He had never seemed particularly aloof, but now he was.

Within a minute, I saw why.

There were two men coming toward us. They were workmen, ordinary cloth caps and tweed coats, not particularly scruffy or down at heel. Nothing about them signalled what happened next. Without pausing, they walked straight between us, knocking Cal out of the way so hard, he staggered and almost fell to the ground.

"You should watch where you're going," snapped one of them. The other glared at me.

Without even a backward glance, they continued on their way, leaving me spluttering in anger.

"Hey, you're the one who should watch out," I called.

Cal righted himself but immediately started to move again so fast I had to run to catch up.

"Cal, wait. Are you all right?"

He didn't slow down. "I'm fine. Let's keep moving."

"What bloody louts," I said, still seething. "What's wrong with them?"

Cal glanced over at me. "Let's say that some white men get disturbed if they see a negro man walking with a white woman."

"What! What on earth are you talking about?"

He actually gave me a little grin. "It happens more often than you might think. Even here in Toronto the Good."

"But that's ridiculous."

"Tell that to them."

Suddenly, I realized that what I had seen as rather odd behaviour was something that Cal probably did automatically. Side door ... no streetcar. Never walk side by side with a white woman, perhaps not even walk on his own in this area.

There were still a lot of people on the sidewalk. I regarded them much more closely. Most didn't pay any attention to us, I'm glad to say, but one or two glanced at us curiously; one couple even paused long enough to send a rather hostile scrutiny in our direction. I suppose what I had taken for granted, walking beside a dark-skinned man — albeit one I knew, liked, and respected — was not that common.

We continued on in silence.

Pedestrian traffic along College Street was thinner, and Cal kept up the fast pace.

After a while, I felt I could speak to him.

"I'm sorry, Cal. I didn't realize."

He shrugged. "Fortunately, it's not everybody has that attitude. But you can see why Marcus Garvey has had such a following. He advocates all us negroes going back to Africa where we can be our own bosses. He wants total segregation. No intermarriage, nothing. Tit for tat, you might say."

"Do you want to go back to Africa?"

"Not me. I was born and bred over on Augusta Street. I went to school here. I fought for this country, same as a lot of fellows." He grinned a little. "Besides, I don't like hot weather." He pointed across the road. "There's the UNIA Hall. Here's hoping they can help us."

The Hall was a flat-fronted three-storey building, in no way ostentatious.

Cal led the way across the road, barely missing a rather geriatric car that was wheezing toward us. Fortunately, the vehicle didn't seem capable of travelling at any speed, and Cal was able to dodge out of the way. After our previous encounter, I was suddenly filled with anxiety. Had it accidently moved toward him, or was it intentional?

I joined him on the sidewalk.

"Sorry, Miss Frayne. That was careless of me."

"It was. Are you trying to get yourself killed?"

"It wouldn't matter, would it? One less darkie to use up the oxygen."

"Cal! Don't say that. What's going on?"

"Nothing unusual. And nothing you can do anything about."

I wanted to press the issue, but the door to the Hall opened, and a group of young women flowed out. There were about half a dozen of them, dark-skinned and all dressed in long white dresses, white bonnets on their heads. Cal stepped back and lifted his cap politely.

"Good afternoon, ladies."

Two or three of the women responded with a little flutter as they went past, then one of them stopped.

"Hello, Calvin."

He seemed disconcerted. "Hello, Violet. I didn't know you were back in town."

"I've been here since Sunday. I was wondering if I would see you. I have a new assignment. We're moving on again next week."

"Oh boy. That is soon. I'll see if I can drop in next Monday afternoon."

"I'll be here. Bye for now."

She glanced over at me. Her expression was ambiguous. Not hostile, more curious than anything, but not friendly either. She hurried off to join her companions.

"Who are those women, Cal? They look as if they belong to some sort of group."

"They're Black Cross nurses. The Red Cross won't accept them, so they've started their own organization."

As I mentioned, my interactions with Calvin had been confined to the Paradise Café, and I was a little ashamed of myself. He had a room on the second floor of the café. He worked long hours. When he did get rare time off, he seemed to spend it in his room, catching up on his beauty sleep, as he put it. I knew nothing of his outside life.

"And Violet? Is she a particular friend?"

"Sort of."

There was something about the way he said this. Not a *the subject is closed* sort of tone, more *this is a sensitive issue*, tone.

"What did you mean, the Red Cross wouldn't accept them?"

"Exactly that. No coloured women allowed, no matter how efficient, dedicated, or competent they might appear. Only white women need apply."

I knew that even for white women, the reluctance of the medical profession to open its ranks had continued for a long time.

"When I burned my hands that time, Violet looked after me." He held out his hand, turning the wrist. "She did a good job. Minimal scarring."

I must admit I wanted to pursue the subject, but there was no more time. We were in the reception area of the Hall, and a man was heading in our direction. He was big and burly, with a rather battered face, and I guessed he had been a boxer in his younger days. He beamed at us, revealing several missing front teeth. Confirmed.

Calvin and the man shook hands heartily.

"Cal! How're you doing? We've missed seeing you. I thought you were going to enroll in my boxing class."

"I got caught up at work, I guess."

The other man slapped him on the shoulder. "You know what they say, all work and no play make for a dull day."

"I think you might be right about that, Charley."

"So, what brings you here today? I hope you don't have any ailments. The nurses have all just left."

"Yeah. I saw them."

The man gave Cal what I can only describe as a knowing look. "Violet Dorsett was with them, I believe?"

"Yes, she was." Cal hurried to change the subject. "Do you have a minute, Charley? I'd like you to meet my friend Miss Frayne. She would like to have a word with you. Miss Frayne, allow me to introduce Charley Dyer. He is in charge of the Hall."

We nodded politely at each other, but I caught the expression of wariness that flashed across Dyer's face. "What would you like to know, ma'am?"

Cal answered for me. "She's making inquiries about a lad who got himself in trouble. It's possible somebody in the community might be able to help."

"Coloured boy, is he?"

"He is."

"What sort of trouble are we talking about? We already had a copper here yesterday. Boy went missing, he said."

Cal shifted his feet, and I thought he had become uneasy.

"You know what, Charley? I'm going to let Miss Frayne explain. I've got to get back to work. All right?"

"Of course," said Dyer.

I had been expecting we would do this inquiry together, but I had no recourse but to agree.

Cal stepped forward and clasped Dyer's arm. "Don't worry. I can vouch for her." He turned back to me. "I'll see you at the café. Good luck."

Without more ado, he left us. A man in a hurry to get away, or a man in a hurry to get somewhere else?

Dyer watched the door close behind him and then nodded at me.

"We can talk in my office. Follow me, please."

He led the way down the narrow hall on the other side of the reception room.

There was something school-like about UNIA. It smelled faintly of carbolic disinfectant; it was clean, plain, and functional. This impression was reinforced as we walked past an open door on our right: I could see into a room where a dozen or so boys were seated in rows, facing one way. All were silent, no chatter or banter emanating. I glimpsed a tall, dark man, who might have been a teacher, standing at a podium, but there was no opportunity to linger or scrutinize them as Dyer was holding open the door to his office.

He took the chair behind his desk and indicated I should take the one in front. He was wearing a smart brown tweed suit and a striped tie, and other than his lived-in face, he reminded me of the vice-principal at my old high school. I felt as if I were back there and up on the carpet. Misdemeanour non-specific. My school days had actually been happy, and I rarely intentionally misbehaved. However, the rules were myriad, often arbitrary, but always strictly enforced. The VP and I had knocked heads on more than one occasion.

Dyer leaned forward. "How can I help you, Miss Frayne?"

"I'm trying to locate a young boy. He is ... er. " I stopped, not sure how much to explain. Dyer helped me out.

"Are you with the police?"

"I am a private investigator, and I am currently assisting the police with the case."

Dyer frowned. "Why do you think we might be able to help?"

"Calvin said there was a possibility he might be connected with UNIA."

Dyer scrutinized me. "How do you come to know Cal?"

"He's the chef at the Paradise Café. I'm there a lot."

"Are you? Cal and I go back a long way. We were in the same battalion in the war."

This was something else I hadn't talked much about with Cal. I knew he had served in the war, and it gave him a common bond with the partners of the café. But it was a man thing, as they often reminded me.

Dyer pulled a sheet of paper toward him and picked up a pen. "What's this boy's name? And what's he supposed to have done?"

He began to write as I answered.

"His name is Leroy Davies. He and his brother have been charged with burglary."

Dyer let out a soft whistle through his teeth. "Yes, I know him. They come here regularly. Jerome is the younger one, correct?"

"That's right. Unfortunately, Jerome met with an accident yesterday. It's serious. The police want to find Leroy as soon as possible. He may not know that his brother is hurt."

Dyer drummed his fingers on the desk. "I haven't seen them in several days. As I recall, they resided at the Working Boys Home on Gould Street. Have you checked with them?"

"Yes. Leroy has not been back there. Apparently, they were expelled recently."

Dyer grimaced. "That's not good, is it? So, what you're telling me, or rather not telling me, is that the boy is on the lam?"

I thought my dancing around the truth wasn't helping anybody at this point.

"Both boys were in custody. They tried to escape, and the younger one fell and has suffered a bad concussion. Leroy got away, but as I said, he might not be aware of what has happened to his brother."

Dyer put his pen down, raised his eyes to the ceiling, and tilted his chair. "You said a 'bad concussion.' How bad, exactly?"

"According to the hospital, Jerome may not recover completely. He may have damaged his spine, and there is fear he has a brain injury. The next few days will tell."

Dyer brought his chair down with a thud. "Good Lord. Have you notified their parents?"

"Neither the mother nor father can be located."

"So, to all intents and purposes, the boys are orphans ..."

Before he could continue, his voice was drowned out by a burst of sound from down the hall. Voices singing with perhaps more enthusiasm than musicality.

Dyer answered my inquiring look. "That's our youth choir rehearsing." He stood up abruptly. "You know what, some of those boys might have information about Leroy's whereabouts. Let's go and have a word with them." He grimaced. "I'd better do the talking — they'll be more comfortable with me. They haven't all had the best experience with police authorities."

"I'm not, strictly speaking, police."

"They won't necessarily make the distinction. You said you were assisting the police? In what capacity?"

"I was present when the boys made their escape. I had gone to see the detective in charge of the case. I happen to have taken a client who insists she can vouch for the boys' innocence."

"Can she now? How refreshing. But come along with me and we'll have a word with the members of the choir. I'll have to give them a bit of the story and explain why you are looking for him. You're not one of the community. They may not trust you right away."

I was digesting this as I followed him out of the office.

CHAPTER TWENTY-THREE

WE ENTERED THE room to the boisterous sound of "Rock of Ages."

Let me hide myself in Thee.

The choir director was waving his hand vigorously.

"Enunciate! Enunciate!" he shouted without perceivable impact.

There were half a dozen youngsters grouped together. A motley crew for sure, but they looked to be in the same age bracket as the Davies brothers. There was a girl seated at the piano.

Dyer addressed the music director. "Excuse me for interrupting, Mr. Burgess, but I wonder if I could speak to the lads for a moment. It's a rather serious matter or I wouldn't disturb you."

"Help yourself. We haven't really started as of yet."

The group had fallen silent. I could tell they were curious about me, but they were being discreet about it. Their eyes were fixed on Mr. Dyer.

"I am interested in locating a certain Leroy Davies. He has been a member of UNIA for a while, and I'm sure some of you know him. He comes here with his brother, Jerome." He paused. He certainly was receiving rapt attention, but I thought he was sorting out exactly what to say before he continued.

"Unfortunately, Jerome Davies has suffered a very serious accident, and, needless to say, we would like to make sure

Leroy has the opportunity to be with him." Another pause. One of the boys seized the opportunity.

"You say you are trying to *find* Leroy, sir. Can I ask why that is? They were always together when I saw them. Doesn't he know his brother has been injured?"

Dyer nodded at him. "Good question, Sammy. Leroy has run into trouble and has apparently thought it necessary to go into hiding. I don't believe he does know about Jerome."

"Is it police trouble?" asked another of the boys.

There was a ripple of alarm through the group, and I was reminded of a herd of cattle who have sniffed the air and found a predator's smell.

"Yes, it is."

This time, there were several fleeting sideways glances in my direction. The first boy, Sammy, took the lead and addressed me directly.

"Excuse me, miss, but are you from the police?"

Dyer answered for me.

"This is Miss Frayne. She is a private investigator, and she is assisting the police."

I wished he had allowed me to speak for myself, but it was too late. They were looking at me now, but I had suddenly become the fox circling the herd. Tension was thick in the air.

I plunged in. "Leroy and Jerome Davies were being held in custody because they have been charged with burglary. I have been contacted by a woman who swears she can testify that the boys are innocent. I went to the police station to talk to the detective in charge of the case. It turned out that the boys were being held in the cells. While I was there, they made an attempt to escape from the exercise yard. During this attempt, Jerome fell and suffered a concussion. Leroy had already managed to get over the wall and run off. That is why we doubt very much that he knows his brother was hurt."

Sammy whispered something to the boy standing beside him. I caught the word *strap*, and the boy grinned nervously. He knew about it.

"Anyway, if you do happen to know where Leroy is, or if you run into him, please ask him to get in touch with me. I just want to make sure he is safe and that he can see his brother."

"How will he find you?" another boy asked.

"My office is in the Arcade on Yonge Street: T. Gilmore and Associates, Private Investigators."

"Or you can simply inform me," interjected Dyer. "I will make sure to put him in touch with Miss Frayne. Any more questions?"

There was silence.

"All right then? I suggest you get back to your practice. You haven't got much time left. Mr. Burgess, over to you."

The conductor waved at the girl at the piano. "Rosa?" She gave them the chord.

"From the top," called Mr. Burgess. "And, one, two, three … *Rock of ages* …"

They burst into song. Louder this time. Affirming something they desperately needed to believe in.

I followed Mr. Dyer from the room.

Let me hide myself in Thee.

CHAPTER TWENTY-FOUR

"I WAS JUST about to have a spot of tea. Why don't you sit down for a minute and join me?"

"Er, thanks."

I was actually keen to get going, but I felt now that I had been admitted into this previously unknown world, I'd like to know more. I sat down while he poured me a cup of milky tea from a large thermos bottle on a side table. It was over-sugared; but I made myself endure it for the sake of hospitality. It was also tepid, which didn't add to its delectability.

He poured some for himself, sat behind his desk, and, with evident enjoyment, took a rather noisy slurp. I gave him a moment, sipped my tea, tried not to make a face, and put the cup back on the table.

"Anything else I can help you with?" Mr. Dyer asked.

"Hmm. I'm trying to get a sense of these two boys. How would you describe them? Apparently, the superintendent at the Home was finding them so disruptive he expelled them. He said they were always getting into arguments."

Dyer didn't answer immediately, just savoured more of his tea.

"I suppose which side you take depends which side you're on. When they've been here, they haven't caused arguments. The younger one has a speech impediment, so he doesn't talk too much. He sounds a bit funny, so at first, boys being boys, he was getting teased quite a lot. The older one, Leroy, wouldn't stand for it. Maybe he was a little too ready with his fists, but the teasing stopped real fast."

Another, longer sip.

"I had a word with all concerned, and I can assure you, there was no more of it. Either side."

"What did the boys do when they came here?"

"It varied. We've got a basketball court up on the third floor, and sometimes they have a game. The younger one was good even though he's short. Leroy was better at Ping-Pong. Fast on his feet."

I'd seen that for sure.

"If they didn't play, they'd just come on down here and sit with the choir. Jerome didn't sing, of course, but Leroy did." He chuckled. "More bellow than tenor, but that might even out if he practises." He sighed. "They didn't have a family life to speak of, so we were becoming that for them. It's the case with a lot of our members. We don't just have boys and girls. There are adults too, and we have several programs for them. You saw the Black Cross ladies. They have a meeting room here. We've got darts, billiards, an adult choir. Bible study classes, talks once a month. They are particularly popular. Last year, Marcus Garvey himself visited, and he gave a very good talk. Mind you, he wants us all to go back to Africa — the homeland, as he calls it. I don't fancy it myself. In spite of everything, I'm happy to live in Canada."

I would have liked to know what he meant by "in spite of everything," but I could guess. There was no legal policy of segregation here in Toronto as there still was in the United States, but for the most part, coloured and white occupied two separate worlds. I determined to talk more to Cal when I had the chance.

I started to gather my belongings together. "I'd better be off. Thanks so much for your help, Mr. Dyer. Please let me know if you hear anything. Anything at all."

"Will do."

I stood up.

"Hey, don't you want to finish your tea?"

"Thanks. That was plenty for me."

"I'll see you out, then."

I followed him out of the office. The choir room was quiet, and as we went past, the young girl who had been accompanying the choir at the piano came out. When she saw us, she stopped. An expression of fear ran across her face.

"Rosa? All done?"

"Yes, Mr. Dyer."

"See you next week?"

"Yes, sir."

She turned on her heel and returned to the choir room.

"She's a talented youngster, that one," said Dyer. "Taught herself to play the piano. She can listen to a song twice and play it right off the bat. Don't know how she does it. She could have a future as a pianist, but she's supporting two young sisters. Their dad was injured in an accident last year, and her mother is too sickly for steady work. They have to rely on what relief they get from the city and what Rosa brings in as a buttonhole maker up on Spadina. She comes here on her dinnertime. She's made some arrangement with the owner that she compresses four days of dinner into one. She works right through on the other days."

Again, I had no reply I could give easily. I'd heard her, and if she had picked this up on her own, there was talent indeed. I stashed the information in my idea pot to be brought out later. Unfortunately, I thought young Rosa was not the only violet born to blush unseen in the desert air. And I didn't mean the object of Cal's affections, who appeared to have found a way to blossom.

Dyer hovered at the threshold. He seemed wistful.

"I'll come over to the Paradise one of these days and have a visit with Cal. You say you're there a lot?"

Frankly, I was a little shy about being specific about my relationship with Hilliard. I prevaricated slightly.

"I have become friends with the partners. I help out sometimes if things get busy."

"Are you going there now?"

"Shortly. I've got some more work to do first. I want to have a chat with the man on Edward Street who says he saw the Davies boys on the street the morning of the burglary."

"Good work. It has been nice meeting you, Miss Frayne. Let's hope we can bring this situation to a righteous conclusion. Let's pray justice will prevail."

He turned and went back into the Hall. Rosa was coming out of the choir room at that moment, but again she shrank away, closing the door behind her.

CHAPTER TWENTY-FIVE

EDWARD STREET WAS a good brisk walk away, which was what I needed. I headed back along College Street. On the way to the UNIA Hall, I hadn't paid a lot of attention to the street itself. I'd been preoccupied with the encounter between Cal and me and the two men who had barged between us. How rude and angry they had appeared. I wanted to meet them again and give them a piece of my mind. A more sensible side of me knew that wouldn't be wise. Being a woman was a protection that wouldn't last long. *Gah.* I determined to increase my practice of martial arts. I'd been a little slack lately. I indulged in the fantasy of knocking Mr. Tweed-Cap to the ground with one swift throw over the hip. My thoughts had gone back to the scene, so I almost didn't notice that I was walking by the section given over to the two hospitals that dealt exclusively with consumptives. I saw that half a dozen inmates were being wheeled out onto the veranda in their invalid chairs. They were all children, all with thin, pale faces; each had a red blanket tucked underneath their chin. The day was getting colder and darker by now, but I assumed this was the usual time for them to get their fresh air. Not much sunlight left, but better than nothing. I was struck with a sudden memory.

I must have been about eight years old and coming home from school with my best friend, Penny Shawcross. We were giggling about something or other, not sure what, when Penny stopped dead in her tracks. "Look, Lottie. There's the TB nurse. Don't let her see us, it's bad luck." A youngish woman was walking across the road. She was soberly dressed in a grey suit, and she was carrying a black nurse's bag. Much later, recalling this incident, I'd realized she was probably on her way to visit one of the families who lived in the poor, fly-ridden district of the notorious Ward. The Ward was home to many European immigrants who were rumoured to have brought the White Plague with them.

Later, I'd told my grandmother what had transpired, and she was incensed. "Of course it's not bad luck. That is ignorant superstition, pure and simple. The nurse was on her way to help some poor soul. If you want to have good luck, she will bring it, not the opposite."

Not too long afterward, Penny vanished from my life. Gran said my friend had become ill and had to be sent away. Tuberculosis? Nobody would say, and I never saw her again.

I was on the opposite side of the road from the hospital, and as I walked by, I noticed one young girl struggle to pull herself up in her chair. She saw me and waved. A tentative and rather weak wave, but nonetheless, she was attempting to make contact with the outside world. I waved back vigorously. A couple of the other children saw this, and they too waved at me. We could have gone on like this indefinitely.

Fuelled by this encounter, I arrived at Edward Street in no time at all.

CHAPTER TWENTY-SIX

OLDER STREETS ARE sometimes described as having seen better days, but that didn't quite apply in this case. The street had never had good days, as far as I could tell. The small, decrepit houses were jammed together. Tiny, weed-covered front yards; tiny windows. Workers' cottages at one time. In other words, lived in by the poor, who didn't have the money, time, or even inclination to maintain their houses.

The man who claimed to have witnessed the robbers lived at number 37. It was identical to its neighbours in the lack of care that had been afforded to it.

There was no sign of a doorbell, so I thumped on the door as hard as I could. Twice. I was about to give up when the door was suddenly thrust open. A stocky, grizzled man was on the threshold. He was glaring at me.

"You don't need to break the door down. I heard you. I was in the back. What can I do for you?"

"Am I speaking to Mr. Glozier?"

"You are. Who are you? Do I know you?"

"My name is Charlotte Frayne. I am a private investigator, and no, I don't think we have met before."

I had my business card at the ready, and I handed it to him. He brought it up close to his eyes and frowned at it.

"Private investigator? What do you want to talk to me about? I'm not selling my house, if that's what you want."

I beamed at him shamelessly. "Not at all, sir. That's another line of work altogether. I was just wondering if I might ask you a few questions about the recent police case that you were a witness to."

"What? What are you talking about? That all got settled in the small claims court."

"I am referring to the charges laid against two young negro boys. They have been convicted of burglary, and a significant factor in their arrest was your testimony that you saw them emerge from the house in question."

He was still scowling at me in confusion. "Are you talking about the case I brought against Mary Szabo? Her blasted tree drops walnuts on my backyard all the time, and she refuses to cut it down. Ruins my lawn, spoils my recreation. Judge dismissed the case. Said it was natural. Work of God. Nothing he can do. Utter nonsense. God ain't going to cut that tree down. She has to."

I had to interrupt this flood.

"No, that's not why I'd like to talk to you, Mr. Glozier. I'd like to ask you about the incident that occurred a week ago. You saw two young boys leaving a house a few doors down. The house was burglarized, and the boys were later apprehended. Do you recall the incident?"

The light bulb went on.

"Now I know what you're talking about. Why didn't you say? It was a Tuesday morning. Two rapscallions broke into Morris Brandwein's house and stole his menorah."

"It was actually a Monday morning."

"Monday, Tuesday. What does it matter? They was still robbing the place. I saw them clear as day."

"As a matter of fact, Mr. Glozier, I understand it was barely daylight. So it wouldn't have been exactly clear as day."

He snorted in derision. "That's just an expression. It was light enough to see these two lads coming from Dr. Brandwein's house. Running, I should say, if you want me to be particular about my language. I saw them running away."

He waved vaguely to his left. I was still on his doorstep, and I looked in that direction.

"Were they coming this way?"

"Nope. Other way. Then they turned up the laneway, and that's all I saw." He turned his attention to me. "My tea's getting cold. Is there anything else you want to know? The police dealt with it. They were quick to make an arrest when it suited them. Brandwein can afford to lose a few bits and pieces. He'll buy more if I know him. What you can't never replace is peace of mind. Mine's gone and will be until that bloody woman cuts down her bloody tree. She's the one should be arrested."

Oops, the geyser was gushing again.

"I won't keep you much longer, Mr. Glozier. But I would much appreciate it if you could just answer a couple of questions."

"Okay. Hurry up."

"You said the boys were running. How fast would you say?"

"What do you mean? Running is running."

"Of course, but there's the running we might do to catch a train, for instance. That's usually a sprint. Short distance, flat out. Or the running we might do if we were late for work. We'd be moving fast, but we probably wouldn't be sprinting as such."

He waved his hand at me impatiently. "You're being too refined for me. Them boys were running, that's all I can say."

"Were they carrying anything? A bag? A sack of any kind?"

"Don't know. They were gone in a minute."

He stepped back into his doorway. "You've had your two questions. I'm going back to my tea. It's going to be stone cold."

He closed the door. Not exactly in my face, but as near as made no difference. I thanked my stars he wasn't my neighbour. I would be tempted to drop black walnuts on his head.

I returned to the sidewalk. Dr. Brandwein's house was not much further along. Even in poor morning light, it was plausible that Glozier would have been able to make out figures of boys running, but I doubted he'd have been able to make out features or skin colour. If the pair had indeed turned up the laneway, I thought the defence could make a case that Glozier might not have been able to determine they were negro boys as he was so insistent they were. Pity the Davies brothers had not been given a defence counsel.

I decided to have a look at the burglarized house.

Number 122 was in better shape than the house inhabited by Mr. Glozier. It looked better cared for; there were lace curtains in the front window. The blue trim was intact, no peeling. There was a narrow space separating it from the next house, which I assumed led to the backyard. Had the Davies brothers come from the rear? The back door was where the burglars had got into the house. A heavy silver candelabra had been stolen. Could the boys have been running if they were carrying that kind of loot? And why draw attention to yourself by running? None of it added up.

I decided to do the same check with Mrs. Brodie's statements. She had been at the southwest corner of Elizabeth and Edward Streets, calling at the house of Mrs. Nielson. She of the tight fists.

The house in question was small and tidy with brown trim and a handkerchief-sized front flower garden, currently bare. I'd been thinking of speaking to the stingy Mrs. Nielson herself, but there were no lights showing in the house, so I assumed she wasn't at home.

As Olivia had said, there was a city bench almost directly in front of the house. I walked over and sat down. Number 122, Dr. Brandwein's house, was across the street but easily visible. If, indeed, two men had come from the back and proceeded along Edward Street, Mrs. Brodie would have seen them. There was a lamppost at the corner, and they would have passed underneath it. She had declared emphatically that one of them was carrying something. They were "scurrying," as she'd phrased it. According to Mrs. Brodie, these men were the two she'd identified as casuals at the House of Industry: Viktor Genik and his young friend, Marko Ryga. She said they had seen her, and as I sat there, I thought that was entirely possible.

The afternoon was slipping into evening, and it was getting chilly. I thought my best plan was to go back to the café for some warmth, not to mention love.

I didn't initially see the bicyclist who came whipping around the corner and skidded to a halt so abruptly he almost fell off his bicycle. He was muffled, the lower part of his face completely hidden from me, but I recognized him immediately.

It was Leroy Davies.

"I understand you are looking for me. Well, here I am."

CHAPTER TWENTY-SEVEN

"LEROY. WHO DID you talk to?"

"Doesn't matter. A friend. But they said something about my brother being hurt." He pulled down the obscuring scarf, revealing a haggard face. "What happened to him?"

The street was deserted, but it felt odd to be delivering bad news while we were standing on the sidewalk.

I indicated the bench. "Come and sit down."

He hesitated, although I didn't know if he feared I could physically overpower him or if he suspected there was a constable hiding in the shadows. Finally, he propped the bike against the tree and sat down at the far end of the bench.

"What's happened?" he asked again.

"When you two made a break from the jail, Jerome fell off the roof of the latrine. He has a concussion. He's in the hospital."

He stared at me. "How bad is it?"

"I'm afraid it's bad."

Leroy jumped to his feet.

"Where is he? I've got to see him."

He looked as if he was on the verge of taking off on the bike. I caught him by the sleeve.

"Leroy, hold on a minute."

"Let go! I've got to see him."

He tried to shake me off, but I knew what that would mean, and I held on even tighter.

"You don't even know where he is. Sit down for a minute. I'm going to help you."

Edward Street was empty of pedestrians, but Leroy's voice was very loud. The last thing he needed was for a resident to take alarm and ring for the police.

Again, we stared at each other for a few tense moments, then he sat down at the end of the bench, not breaking his stare for a second.

"Okay. What have you got in mind?"

"First off, there is a warrant out for your arrest. You can't see Jerome if you're back in jail."

He glared at me but didn't move.

"Go on."

"He was taken to the Sick Children's Hospital. No, wait! Use your head. He's in a special unit. They won't let you in."

"I'm his brother. I'll make them."

"That won't work. I was thinking we should go together. I have some authority." I hoped that would prove to be true when we got there.

This time, he did grab the bike. "Let's go."

"Leroy, there's one more thing. I am obligated to inform the police that I have been in touch with you, but I promise I will not notify them until you've had the chance to see your brother."

He gave me more intense scrutiny. "Why are you doing this?"

"For one thing, I believe you are innocent of the charges laid against you."

He shrugged. "So what? That's not going to change anything. You should have seen that judge. He had his mind made up before he even saw us. Everybody did. Police, judge. Reporters. *Two coloured boys. Of course they're guilty. Whip 'em.*"

"Leroy, I assure you, Detective Murdoch won't let this continue. I believe I'm on to whoever actually committed the robbery, and you will be exonerated."

"What's that mean?"

"It means you will be found not guilty and be allowed to go back to your life."

Even as I said that, I had a qualm of doubt. Would the newspaper vendor take them back? Would the superintendent of the Working Boys Home allow them to return to the hostel? If neither of these options were available, what next? I got to my feet.

"Come on. You'll have to wheel your bike."

We set off. Leroy spoke only once.

"Is Jerome going to make it?"

I didn't think I could give him an honest answer without sending him off the deep end. That I didn't want. On the other hand, he deserved honesty.

"I'm afraid the doctor has grave concerns. He hit his head. But whatever the outcome, I promise you, we will help you through this."

I'd made two promises to this boy within the space of ten minutes, but frankly, I didn't hesitate. I meant both of them.

CHAPTER TWENTY-EIGHT

I HADN'T DONE so much walking in a while, and I soon remembered why I preferred my bike. My feet were getting sore in my "working shoes." Leroy was walking as fast as he could without breaking into a trot. He was silent for the most part, but I managed to get in a couple of questions.

"You made a statement to the police officer in which you said you were on Edward Street that morning on your way to work. Is that correct?"

He flashed me a wary glance.

"That's right."

"What time of day was it?

"I dunno. Early. Just getting light."

"Before eight o'clock, then?"

"I suppose so. Why are you asking? I said all this to the beaks."

"Because I have a witness who says she saw two men leaving the doctor's house about that time, and that is when the burglary must have taken place. It's possible they were the thieves. Did you see anybody on the street?"

He actually gave me a wan smile. "I wish I could say I did, and then we'd find out they was the burglars, but I didn't. We come through the laneways, and we didn't meet anybody."

I wondered how Mr. Glozier could have seen them if that was the case.

"You are aware there is a man who claims to have seen you and Jerome that morning heading along Edward Street. He lives at number 37."

"Yeah, the beak told me. Proof, he said. Silly asshole. Liked to hear himself talk, if you ask me."

"Did you yourself see this witness?"

"Is he a short, fat bloke with a whopping black beard that needs trimming?"

"That fits the description, all right. He lives at number 37. His name's Glozier."

"Yeah, I seen him, but not on Monday. I think it was another day."

"I thought you told the officer you were only on Edward Street because you were making a detour on your way to work."

"That's right, we were. Last time I looked there wasn't no law against it."

"So, I gather it's a route you've taken before?"

We were both still moving at a fast pace, but I could see Leroy's tension.

"Leroy, I'm on your side, I really am. But if I'm going to help you, I've got to get my facts straight."

He actually stopped in his tracks for a moment, and his eyes met mine.

"That'd be a change, wouldn't it? When did beaks ever care about facts?"

"I'm not with the police. I'm a private investigator."

He set off again; I kept up.

"It was in the laneway next to Centre Street that you found the matchbox, wasn't it?"

"That's right."

"Was that on Monday?"

"Might have been. I don't keep track of days."

"Did you take the matchbox to a pawnbroker on McCaul Street?"

"It's not illegal to pawn stuff. Finders keepers. We had a few other things. He didn't want none of them."

"So, that's a yes? You went to Toban's pawnshop with some items you'd found, including the matchbox?"

He was scowling at me. "We did, but we had the right. They didn't belong to nobody anymore."

"The detective said he found the matchbox in your belongings at the hostel. It was reported as stolen with another couple of items from Dr. Brandwein's house."

"What else was nicked?"

"A silver candelabra and a special shawl. Both religious items."

He halted and turned his bicycle so that it blocked my way.

"Look, missus. I appreciate the help you're giving me, and I think you are probably a decent person, but I'll telling you, once and for all, me and my brother had nothing to do with a robbery. We found every last one of those things." He shifted his bike. "I'm going on ahead. I'll wait for you at the hospital."

He mounted his bicycle and was off.

I had no choice except to follow as fast as I could.

CHAPTER TWENTY-NINE

FORTUNATELY FOR MY sore feet, the Hospital for Sick Children was only a ten-minute walk away. There was no sign of Leroy at the entrance, and my heart sank. I knew there would only be trouble if he'd tried to force his way in. I approached the entrance slowly, and as I did so, he stepped out from the corner of the building. He'd removed his toque and unwound his scarf, tying it neatly, cravat style, around his neck. It was surprising how much less sinister he appeared.

"Let's go inside," I said. "It might be upsetting to see Jerome this way, but please don't do anything. We can't jeopardize your position."

He nodded, and I hoped that whatever stress he was experiencing, he would contain it.

There was a reception area in the lobby, and I headed straight there, Leroy close behind me. A young woman was seated at the desk.

"Good afternoon, I'm here to visit Jerome Davies."

She smiled and pulled her visitors book toward her. She ran her finger down the list of patients, stopped, and looked up at me with some alarm.

"I'm afraid no visitors are allowed."

I guessed the ban on visitors was more related to the police quagmire he was stuck in than to health concerns. I could tell

Leroy had immediately become agitated. I shifted so that I was slightly in front of him.

"It is very important that we see him. Is there a doctor I can speak to?"

"I'll check."

She flipped a switch on her telephone console. "Is Dr. Sterling available? There is a lady here who wishes to visit Jerome Davies … Yes, that's right. I told her that. She has requested to speak to the doctor in charge."

I didn't hear the response, but she answered into the telephone.

"Very well. I'll tell her."

She turned to me, smile definitely tight now. "Somebody will be right out to speak with you. You can have a seat over there."

She indicated a bench beside the entrance. I took Leroy by the elbow and steered him in that direction.

We had hardly sat down when the connecting door to the ward opened and out walked a uniformed constable. The receptionist pointed at us, and he headed over. Leroy took one look and, before I could say or do anything, he jumped to his feet and shot away out the door. So much for my little boast about having authority. What a fiasco.

"Oi! You! Wait!" shouted the constable. He broke into a run. I too had jumped up and, also eager to go after Leroy, I accidently stepped in the constable's path, and we collided. He fell to the ground. The expression *like a sack of potatoes* seemed apt.

"Sorry, Constable."

With some difficulty, he scrambled to his feet and ran to the door. I followed right behind, and we went out onto the street. There was no sign of Leroy. The constable was angry, understandably. Except for our unfortunate collision, he might have been able to nab the lad.

He muttered a rather impolite curse under his breath. "He's got away."

I scanned the street. "Oh dear, so he has."

"I'll have to ask you to come back inside, miss. I'll need to make a report."

"Of course."

We went back into the lobby of the hospital. The young receptionist had come from behind her desk and was watching the scene unfold with a typical bystander mix of fear and excitement.

"What's happening?"

Before either of us could reply, the ward door swung open and a man in the white coat of a doctor came through.

He saw me and came over immediately. "I'm Dr. Sterling. I understand you wanted to see me?"

He conveyed that important things were waiting — heart surgery or some such vital activity. The receptionist chose sides immediately. "She was asking to visit Jerome Davies, Doctor, and I told her no visitors allowed, so then she asked to see the doctor in charge."

The constable added his aggrieved two cents' worth. "I believe this lady was in the company of the older brother, who is wanted for escaping custody while under arrest. She hindered me while I was about to apprehend the young man in question. He got away."

Now I had three people regarding me with varying degrees of annoyance. I addressed the doctor.

"My name is Charlotte Frayne. I have been assisting Detective Murdoch with this case. I had the opportunity to bring the older brother of the injured boy here to see him. I believe he was frightened when he saw the constable, and he ran off. I don't know where he has gone, but I would appreciate the use of a telephone so I can ring Detective Murdoch and inform him what has happened."

"There's one in my office — you can use that one." The doctor's voice was curt.

"I'd better get back to my post," said the constable.

It was my time to be chirpy, and I strove to keep the sarcasm out of my voice. "I'm surprised you've been assigned this job, Constable. I wouldn't have thought it was important enough to take up a police officer's valuable time."

He shrugged. "I'm just following orders. Apparently, one of the boys assaulted a police officer. The chief doesn't take kindly to that sort of thing. I've been told to keep an eye out for the brother in case he shows up. He is considered danger-ous. So that's what I have been doing. Then Miss Langford here said there was somebody wanting to see said boy, so I thought it was expedient to come and see who that said person was." He gave me what I could only call a malevolent scowl. "The rest you know. I would have apprehended the said crim-inal youth except that you stepped in front of me."

Dr. Sterling had been waiting rather impatiently, and now he held open the door to the ward and ushered me through.

"Miss Frayne, this way, please."

I followed him as we walked briskly down the corridor. I couldn't help but notice his rubber-soled shoes squeaked in the same way Miss Lindsay's did.

"How is Jerome, Doctor?"

"Not so good, I'm afraid." He shook his head. "The next few days will tell, but he gave himself quite a wallop on the head. He's in intensive care." He stopped in front of a glass partition. "There's the telephone. Help yourself."

The constable walked on past us and took up a position outside a closed door down the corridor. A lit sign above said, NO ENTRANCE. MEDICAL STAFF ONLY.

I went into the office and picked up the receiver. I was connected with Jack immediately, and I have to admit the sound of his voice gave me a feeling of intense relief.

He listened without comment while I related what had just occurred.

I finished with, "I feel wretched about the whole affair, Jack. I should never have brought him here. I didn't expect there would be a police guard."

"Apparently, Chief Draper is eager to make an example of these boys. Given that they ran away, he's designated Leroy as dangerous."

"Oh god, Jack. The doctor is concerned about Jerome. They're making noises that his condition is critical. I hate to think how Leroy would react if he dies."

"You say you encountered Leroy on Edward Street. Coincidence or intentional? Did anybody know that's where you might be?"

"I was coming from the UNIA Hall. I mentioned to the manager, Mr. Dyer, that I was heading to Edward Street."

I suddenly flashed back to the moment I was leaving. Dyer was seeing me to the door. Rosa, the brilliant piano player, was close by. She might have overheard what I said. Which meant she'd known where Leroy was and was able to inform him immediately. Unless Dyer himself had done so.

I passed this on to Jack.

"I think I should get up there and talk to these people."

"Jack, let me come with you. I think they might be reluctant to pass on information to the police, but at least we've already met through Cal."

There was a short hesitation on Jack's part, then he said, "Okay. I'll get a car and pick you up. Ten minutes."

We hung up, and I left the office and told Dr. Sterling that I'd finished. The next thing I did was spontaneous and perhaps rash on my part, but I didn't regret it. I asked the doctor if I could see Jerome Davies.

"Why? I don't want him disturbed. You can't question him or anything like that."

"I have no intention of doing that, Doctor. I only thought that he might like to know ..." I stopped. Know what? Vivid in my mind were the moments when Jack Murdoch and I had held that boy and tried to prevent him from falling into the abyss. Gramps might have said that I had some sort of saviour complex — that I couldn't stop Death in its tracks, much as I wanted to — but I didn't quite see it that way. All I knew was that the plight of this young boy had touched me deeply. If there was any way I could reach him and comfort him on the dark journey, I was going to try.

Rather to my surprise, Dr. Sterling relaxed. He smiled at me.

"Frankly, in these concussion cases, the more the patient can be drawn into positive exchanges, the better. I believe I can trust you to be a benign presence."

I could have kissed him.

"Thank you, Doctor."

He turned to the constable, who was standing stiffly by Jerome's door. "Thank you, Constable. I suggest you take a break for half an hour. I will handle this."

"Yes, sir. Very well, sir. I will be in the lobby if you need me."

He swivelled away but not before a parting glare at me. This man was not a rule breaker.

Dr. Sterling nodded at me to follow him, and we proceeded down the hall to the defending door.

CHAPTER THIRTY

I CAN'T SAY I've sat beside dozens of hospital bedsides, but I've sat by enough to experience the weight of the dying or seriously ill. The stark room, the narrow bed, the patient connected to various strange devices that hissed and beeped, the uncertainty of peering at that unknown country from whose bourn no traveller returns. All of this was familiar. The sight of Jerome Davies was not. He looked pitiably small underneath the white sheet; his head was immobilized in a leather constraint, presumably to stop him from thrashing around. Likewise, both hands were bound to the side of the bed bars.

Dr. Sterling had followed me into the room.

"He had a small bleed in his brain. There's a clot there. In an older patient, we'd call it a stroke. He also damaged his spine. He's in restraints so he doesn't move and aggravate the bleed. We are waiting to see if the clot will dissolve on its own before we attempt any surgery that may be too risky."

"If the clot does dissolve, will he be able to regain use of his muscles?"

The doctor pursed his lips. "We don't know. Maybe yes, maybe no. Depends on whether the spinal fracture heals properly."

"Is he conscious? Can I speak to him?"

Jerome answered for himself by opening his eyes. He saw

me, clearly knew who I was, and his eyelids fluttered. I thought he was afraid, and I hastened to reassure him.

"Jerome, it's Miss Frayne here. I just wanted to see how you were doing." He made noises, but I couldn't tell what he was saying. The impediment he'd already had was aggravated by the injury. I leaned forward.

"We want you to get better as soon as you can. Please don't worry. I promise you and Leroy won't be in any trouble."

Even restrained, he tried to move his head, and saliva started to dribble from the side of his mouth. Dr. Sterling, unasked, handed me a face cloth, and I wiped away the moisture.

I touched Jerome's forehead, which felt hot, but what I had meant to be a soothing gesture clearly wasn't. He struggled again. Dr. Sterling turned to the medicine tray and picked up a syringe.

"I'll give him a sedative."

He moved toward the prone boy, whose eyes widened in terror.

I spoke loudly. "It's all right, Jerome. The doctor won't hurt you. He just doesn't want you to hurt yourself." I stroked his forehead again. "I'm going to make sure your brother gets to see you as soon as possible. Don't worry. Leroy is fine. He wants you to be a good boy and get better."

Dr. Sterling had quietly and efficiently injected the sedative into Jerome's arm. It was fast-acting, and almost immediately the boy's eyes started to close. I bent over him.

"I have to go, Jerome, but I'll be back."

He was almost asleep, but he muttered something. I could barely hear him, but it sounded like he was trying to say, "… sent … Lee in sent."

That was it.

Dr. Sterling tapped my arm to indicate we should leave. I saw the heart monitor positioned above Jerome's head. The heartbeat line looked steady. What do you say to a monitor? How can you encourage a machine? Jerome was a tiny elevation of the sheet.

CHAPTER THIRTY-ONE

THE POLICE HUMBER had already drawn up outside the hospital. The driver's side window was rolled down, and I could see Jack Murdoch blowing cigarette smoke out the window. He saw me and waved. He seemed to have cast off his sling.

I hurried over and hopped in.

"What's the story?" he asked.

"I just was sitting beside a very young boy who may or may not live to see his next birthday. Who may or not be paralyzed for life. His only relative that seems to care about him has run away and is God knows where. That's the story, Jack, and it's a rotten one. I'd like to rewrite it."

He let out a deep sigh. "As would I, Charlotte. As would I." He pushed the starter button, and the Humber stumbled into life. "I was thinking from what you told me that we should go back to the UNIA Hall first. If that was where Leroy was informed about where you were going, there has to be some connection. He may have returned there."

He pulled into the road in front of a streetcar. The driver clanged his bell at him because he'd cut it too close. Jack waved apologetically and increased his speed to get out of the way. What I'd said about Jerome had rattled him too.

I waited for my heart to get out of my mouth so I could speak properly.

"The little lad seemed to be trying to tell me something, but it was very hard to understand. Sounded like, 'Sent. Lee sent.'"

Jack glanced over at me. "Any idea what that would mean?"

"I can't say I do. All I do know is what I've just said. I want to get the bottom of this whole mess so that when I say to this boy, 'It's going to be all right,' I don't feel as if I'm lying through my teeth."

"Okay. Let's lean on the folks at UNIA."

"Jack, I was also checking out the plausibility of what Mrs. Brodie said about seeing two men coming from the direction of the Brandwein house. It could easily be true. They would have been visible from the bench where she was sitting. Leroy said he and his brother were coming along the laneway, so she would not have seen them."

"What about our witness, Mr. Glozier?"

"I believe he's mistaken. He may, in fact, have seen the boys going to get their newspapers, but not on that particular morning. Leroy said that, and I'm beginning to think it's true."

"Has Mrs. Brodie shown up yet?"

"Not when I last called this afternoon ... Jack, I think you have to talk to the two men, Genik and his sidekick. I don't like the fact that Genik was trying to locate me and they tracked me down at the café."

Jack was pulling up in front of the UNIA Hall. This time, a small group of older men and women were entering. UNIA was obviously a popular centre for the local Black community.

I got out of the car and stood on the sidewalk for Jack to join me, just as young Rosa came out of the Hall. She saw me and, to my utter dismay, just as Leroy had done at a perceived threat, she took off. I wanted to chase after her, but hesitated as I had no desire to add to the fear. In that brief moment of hesitation, Rosa inadvertently helped me to decide what to do. She tripped and fell heavily to the ground.

I was beside her in a second. She was curled in a ball, her arms over her head as if warding off a blow.

"Rosa, Leroy's in trouble, and I want to help. I think you know where we can find him."

She peeked at me from underneath her arm. "I don't know." Her voice was a whisper.

"I think you do, Rosa. He followed me down to Edward Street after I left here, and he could only have known where I was going if somebody overheard me say that to Mr. Dyer. That was you, wasn't it?"

She shook her head. Jack had come over to see what was going on, but he didn't interfere, taking his cue from me.

I put my arm around Rosa. "Let's stand up. There's a girl. Oh my, you've given your knee quite a scrape. Why don't we go into the Hall and clean it up."

Slowly, she got to her feet. Blood was trickling down her shin.

She seemed dazed.

"Rosa, look at me. I am not going to hurt you. But I have just come from seeing Jerome Davies, and he is in serious condition. I know that his brother would want to be with him. The only way that will happen is if Leroy turns himself in. We have to find him. He ran away from the hospital."

This time, our eyes met. "Why did he run away?"

"There was a uniformed constable on duty in the ward, and Leroy got scared and ran from him. Do you know where he might have gone? Is he in the Hall?"

She didn't answer right away, still staring at a point just past my shoulder where Jack was standing.

"Is he a policeman?"

Jack answered. "I am. My name is Murdoch. I'm a detective. Miss Frayne and I are working together. I support everything she says. We want to find Leroy so we can take him to see his brother. We would appreciate your help."

Rosa blinked at him.

"He said he was going to get the strap."

"Unfortunately, that is true. But I have good reason to think he has been unjustly accused, and I am going to do everything in my power to make sure he is not punished."

Somewhere along the way in her young life, Rosa had had to rely on her instincts for survival. She could tell sincere from bullshit. She looked at me, then at Jack, and made the decision to trust us.

"He's in one of the empty houses on Centre Street. It's next to the shop that sells feathers."

"We'll go and take a look," said Jack. "And Rosa, if Leroy does get in touch with you, please persuade him to turn himself in. He can go straight to the police headquarters. I'll take care of him."

"Yes, sir."

She appeared so intimidated, I couldn't really tell how sincere she was, but there was no more I could do. I told her to go inside and get her knee washed, and without fuss she went. Jack and I regarded each other, mirroring our mutual concern.

"That must have been what Jerome was trying to say: Centre. Not *sent*. I'm going to assume that he wanted me to find Leroy."

"Let's get over there now, shall we?"

We headed back to the car.

CHAPTER THIRTY-TWO

JACK TURNED ONTO McCaul Street, and I could see Toban's pawnshop.

Jack saw it too. "That reminds me. Did you get any further with your other case of the missing jewellery?"

"Not really. I'm going to follow up as soon as I can, but frankly, I don't really have a clue what's at the bottom of it all."

With impeccable timing, the answer appeared in the shape of a woman who was walking along the street. A wide scarf was wrapped around her neck, and a brimmed wool hat was pulled down low on her head. Her tweed coat was unremarkable, but what *was* rather remarkable was that, even covered up as she was, she looked familiar. She moved fairly briskly but with a slight stiffness at the hips. Even as I was taking this in, she stopped in front of the pawnshop, glanced left and right, then pushed open the door to the shop.

"Jack, pull over for minute."

He did so and halted opposite.

"I'm sure that's Mrs. Calder's housekeeper, Maria Johnson."

"Do you want to go and see? I can wait."

"I think I will."

I got out of the car and hurried across the road to the pawnshop.

196 • MAUREEN JENNINGS

Too late. Even as I approached, Mr. Toban appeared on the other side of the door. Quickly, he pulled down the shade and simultaneously reversed the sign. The shop was now CLOSED. I couldn't tell whether he had seen me. I pressed the electric bell. Nothing happened. I tried again. Nothing. The inside lights were also off. Wherever Toban and the woman had gone, they were not interested in visitors.

I went back to the car. Jack got out and opened the passenger door for me.

"Well? Was it her?"

"I think it may have been. On the other hand, perhaps the woman was his dear elderly aunt come for a long-awaited visit. Mr. Toban has closed up the shop."

"Do you want me to call on him officially?"

"Not right now. The situation with the boys is far more urgent. I'd rather try to find Leroy."

"Okay."

We set off again, but I was troubled. I'd didn't like to be played for a fool or a gullible girl for hire. I had not enjoyed the position she'd placed me in at the Pioneer Club. I wanted to get this matter of Mrs. Calder's accusations settled.

CHAPTER THIRTY-THREE

CENTRE AVENUE WAS only a few minutes away. Jack drove slowly down the street with both of us keeping a lookout for a building that might qualify as a feather shop. It proved to be fairly close and among a rather interesting stretch of buildings. A plain building that had an equally plain sign over the double doors announced itself as a Russian Steam Bath. Presumably not exclusive to Russians, but where Jewish immigrants, among others, gathered to work on health and enjoy social interaction. I'd tried a steam bath once and hadn't fancied it. Too hot.

A couple of houses down from the bath was a small building that had a shop frontage. This seemed to be what we were looking for. The display in the window featured a couple of stuffed geese and a handful of pillowcases that were spilling out feathers. Fortunately, the geese did not seem perturbed by this. The sign over the window said the company supplied feathers and bedding.

Jack pulled over to the curb.

"This looks like it."

Next to the feather shop were two narrow houses. Each had a decrepit porch in front that looked as if it might collapse at any moment. All windows were boarded up, and a plank was nailed across each door. Vacant, obviously.

On initial sight, the houses looked impregnable.

198 • MAUREEN JENNINGS

"Let's check the back," said Jack.

There was the usual narrow dirt entry between the feather shop and the houses, and we made our way down to the rear. There was no yard attached to either house; each backed onto a laneway. A high, weather-stained fence sealed off a row of houses opposite that peeked timidly into the lane. Or frowned, depending on your perspective.

Jack examined the first house. All windows, like the front, were boarded up, and the door was nailed shut. The second house, which was attached, was the one we wanted.

It was clear that the board on the rear door was loose, and it was easy to pull it away. Jack tried the door handle, which turned without resistance. It was a squeeze to get through the board and the door, but we managed it.

If there had been a time when a happy, loving family had gathered here to enjoy a tasty meal surrounded by delicious smells, well-washed dishes, and a well-swept floor, that time had long gone. Not even ghosts would survive here. We were in what must have been the kitchen, now completely bare. This was obviously where the two boys had stayed when they were expelled from the Home. On the floor were two burlap bags stuffed with feathers. Sheets of newspapers were laid on top of the bags. The room was dark, only a sliver of light coming through the crack on the door. I could make out a candle stub on top of a brick. It was chilly in here and unutterably dreary. The air was dank and noisome.

I couldn't bear to think of any human beings living in these circumstances, let alone two young boys. I was about to share these thoughts with Jack when I was startled by the sight of a small black mouse who was scurrying along the baseboard to get home.

"Not exactly the Ritz, is it?" muttered Jack. "Poor sods. They must have been here for several days."

On the floor beside the makeshift bed was an open tin. A half a loaf of dried bread and a shrivelled apple gave mute testimony to the boys' last meal. One that had been shared by the mouse family, by the look of it. There was also a cracked empty bottle that had probably held water.

"Why did they end up in here?" I asked Jack, although I knew the answer.

"Where else? They're society's unwanted."

I thought that was even more true now that they had a criminal record, and this ugly space made me even more determined to find Leroy and, yes, rescue him.

There was nothing else to see.

"Let's get out of here," said Jack, and I was only too happy to oblige.

We squeezed our way out, and Jack replaced the board on the back door as securely as he could.

We returned to the car.

"I'm going back to the station and see if I can locate somebody at the Children's Aid to be on hand for us. Do you want me to drop you off at the café?"

"Yes, please. I need some warmth and light, not to mention food."

Jack sighed. "I know what you mean, Charlotte. I'll see if I can reassign some of the troops to do a more thorough sweep of the neighbourhood."

I debated going back to the UNIA Hall, but to tell the truth I was chilled and hungry. At least I was aware I was free to go to where I would be welcomed.

CHAPTER THIRTY-FOUR

THE FINAL SITTING was already in place, and through the window I could see Pearl was busy being sweet and chatty and Gramps was helping out. I wasn't sure if I liked that, but I knew he must have volunteered. The café was full, and I was glad to see we were now drawing in more families. It had been Wilf's idea to designate Wednesday as Family Day, with a small discount for each child. I could see at least six youngsters all concentrating on their plates.

I also experienced a little spasm of anxiety. I was due to meet Hilliard's children for the first time. As Gramps had reminded me, it might not be the easiest of situations.

I went in by the side door straight into the steamy, hot kitchen.

Cal was at the table, taking a break. Hilliard was across from him. Uh-oh. Something had not gone well. It was written all over his face. However, when he saw me, he beamed and jumped to his feet.

"What a sight for sore eyes. Come and sit down. Let me take your things. Have you eaten?"

I let him make a fuss and sat down at the table.

"I've got some leftover soup, Miss C. Would you like some?"

I must have looked a bit hesitant given our previous conversation, and Cal grinned at me.

"I modified one of the recipes from the book that you gave me. It went over very well."

"What was it?"

"Steamed fish eyes in a white sauce."

He'd said that to me deadpan and suckered me for a moment. Then both he and Hill burst out laughing.

"You should have seen your expression, Lottie," spluttered Hilliard. "Priceless."

I wasn't sure I was quite in the mood to be teased, but I tried to join in the fun.

"It's the white sauce I'm not partial to. Fish eyes? Yum."

Cal got to his feet. "You know what? I did make the potato soup that was recommended by Mrs. Pardoe."

"Who?"

"One of your Pioneer ladies. It was very popular today, so I'll make it again. She calls for starting with mashed potatoes, which is a bit different. Do you want to give it a try? There's some left."

"You bet."

He went over to the stove to fill up a bowl.

Harmony restored, I turned to Hill. "Where are the children, Hill?"

He frowned. "They didn't arrive. The train came and went. I didn't know what the hell was going on. Had they missed the train or what? And then the ticket man came out with a telegram for me. It was from Pauline. She said both children had come down with chicken pox and she had to keep them home. She'll let me know when we're in the clear."

I reached over. "I'm sorry about that. You must be disappointed."

He shrugged. "I am. I was looking forward to seeing them. But I dunno. They seem to get sick a lot. I hope this bout isn't too bad."

I made sympathetic noises. It was true what he said. His children did seem to come down with something whenever they were on the verge of coming to visit their father. I actually felt relieved. I had to admit, given the last two days, I didn't feel quite up to negotiating an undefined path across a potential minefield.

Cal put a bowl of creamy potato soup in front of me together with a plate of crusty bread.

"There's meat loaf if you want that, or if you want to go straight to the sweet I've got chocolate pudding with or without a dollop of whipped cream."

"No to the meat loaf and yes to pud. With dollops."

"Done." He went back to the stove.

It was Hilliard's turn to stand up. "I want to hear all about how things went for you, Lottie. But I can hear the mob is now stirring. I'd better make sure they leave." He planted a kiss on my head. "I'll let Arnie know you're here. He's been fretting."

"How was he today?"

"I'd say better, wouldn't you, Cal? Not as much coughing."

"I'd agree with that. The poultice helped."

This was another occasion for relief. I wiped the sides of the bowl with a slice of bread. Most of the time, Cal baked his own bread, and I think I could have lived for days on that alone. Crusty on the outside, soft on the inside. Come to think of it, that sounded like a character definition of dear Pearl.

Cal took the opportunity to come a little closer, and he asked quietly, "Any more word on the boys?"

"Nope. We found they had broken into a vacant house and were camped there, but Leroy has vanished again."

I filled him in on what had happened at the hospital. He leaned his head into his hands and groaned.

I felt wretched too. "I didn't expect there would be an officer keeping watch. Leroy bolted."

"I can't say I'm surprised."

"Any ideas, Cal?"

"He may have ended up at the British Methodist Episcopal Church. It's on Chestnut Street, which is in the area. Like UNIA, it's an important hub for coloured folks in the city. I know the minister. I'll see if he's heard anything."

"Thanks, Cal. I made promises to that lad that I didn't keep. I want to make sure, at the absolute least, he gets a fair trial."

"I'll go over when I finish here."

The door to the dining room swung open, and Gramps pushed his way through. He was carrying a loaded tray, and both Cal and I jumped up to relieve him.

"Gramps! What are you doing? You've just got out of your sickbed. Do you want to collapse again? You mustn't. It's too distracting."

Cal caught hold of the tray and took it off to the sink.

Gramps waved his hand at me dismissively, but I noticed he did go and sit down right away.

"I'm fine, Lottie."

He had a hard time making that sound convincing as he started to cough so hard his eyes began to water. Cal went over to the cupboard.

He returned with a bottle of brandy in his hand; he poured some into a glass and, in one swift movement, handed it to Gramps.

"Here. Take some of this."

Gramps didn't protest but took a big swallow. He spluttered and made a face at me.

"I can't understand why people like this stuff."

"Never mind. A lot of people can't get enough of it. Consider yourself lucky." I took his hand and lifted the glass. "Take another."

He had no choice and did so. Both Cal and I watched him anxiously. That went down easier.

"See! You liked it that time."

"Hmm."

"Don't get addicted."

The door swung open again, and Hilliard came in with Pearl close behind. They both had trays, which they dumped on the table.

"I swear, they get slower and slower leaving," said Hill. "You'd think we made good food here."

"I think they like the help," said Pearl.

I thought she was joking, but I wasn't sure. However, I grinned ostentatiously. "What would we do without you, Pearl?"

She scowled at me suspiciously. "Mr. Frayne does a good job too."

"He most certainly does," said Hilliard. "And let's make sure we don't wear him out. Cal? Can we excuse him from doing the dishes?"

"You bet."

"In that case, Arnie, I'm going to take you home in my newfangled motor car. Right now."

"Hold on, Mr. Taylor. That will just leave Calvin and me to clean up."

"No, I'll help out, Pearl. Many hands make light the work. I'd like to see my grandfather packed off."

"What about you, Lottie?"

"I've got my bike. I'll follow you as soon as we've finished."

"I'll wait for you at your house, then," said Hilliard.

Nobody was fooling anybody. Gramps was looking distinctly elderly, and the sooner he was back in bed the better. He didn't object. Cal got his coat from the rack and helped him into it. He didn't object to that either. I desperately wanted to go with him, but I knew it would help Cal and Pearl if I stayed.

I gave Gramps a kiss on the cheek and Hilliard a peck on the lips. "See you soon," I said.

They left.

"Mr. Frayne is looking quite peaked, don't you think?" said Pearl.

If there had been an expendable cup handy, I would have thrown it at her.

CHAPTER THIRTY-FIVE

IT WAS JUST after nine when we finished cleaning up. Cal had to do some preparation for the next day, but Pearl and I were free to go. She sailed off, and I got my coat and hat, said good-bye to Cal, and left.

It was dark out, but I had lights on my bike. I retrieved it from the hall and slipped away through the side door.

The street was deserted, but I don't know if it would have mattered whether there were people around or not. Maybe. Would I have called for help? Probably not. I wasn't sure of the threat level, for one thing, and after my experience with Leroy, I wasn't about to set the hare running if I didn't have to.

I had just mounted my bike when Zav Genik appeared out of the deep shadows by the café. He was by himself this time.

"Miss Frayne, can I have a word?"

He stood directly in front of me, blocking my path. I had no idea what he had in mind, but I didn't like being threatened. And his attitude and posture were indeed threatening.

"I don't appreciate your holding me up in this way, Mr. Genik. I'm in a hurry."

He didn't move.

"I won't keep you. But Marko and me were over at the House, about to go and get some grub, when this cop came over to us. A detective, so he says. Mac something or other. Says he wants to speak to us in private and asks us to go to the office. So naturally, I ask why, and he says there's been a robbery and some old lady says she saw us coming out of the house in question."

He paused and eyed me.

I gave him a shrug. "What has that to do with me?"

"The policeman, he says we've got to get ourselves down to police headquarters in the morning. To see if this old biddy will identify us. Not that she will, you understand, because we didn't do it."

"That has nothing to do with me. You should obey the police."

I risked a little movement forward, but he didn't budge. We were inches apart.

"You see, it's my understanding that you are acquainted with this same lady. I saw you with her. I asked the polly if we could do it there and then and get it over with, the ID thing, but he said she wasn't in residence at that moment."

I was about to interject again, but he continued.

"I was wondering if you knew where I might find this old dear."

"Why?"

He summoned up a grin that managed to be even more unpleasant than his scowl. "Just to have a chat, that's all. To reassure her it wasn't us."

His so-called explanation was so incredible, I almost burst out laughing.

Perhaps something of my reaction showed because he started to scowl again. I remembered how explosively he had reacted to the man in the House dining room. All I could think of was Mrs. Brodie and how tiny she was. How determined to ensure there was no grave miscarriage of justice. And here was this lout using every ploy he could to intimidate.

As I had learned in my self-defence class, surprise is one of the best weapons of attack. I didn't give Genik a chance to realize what I was doing. I shoved my bike wheel forward, hitting him hard in his solar plexus, and as he staggered away, I jumped on the pedals and shot off. I raced away as fast as I and machine could muster. Even if he had wanted to, Genik could not have caught me. He didn't even get up.

I WAS TORN about whether or not I should go straight to the police. I opted for getting home. Jack would have left the station long ago, and I didn't feel like involving a different detective or officer. Also, to be honest, I wanted to feel the security of Hilliard's arms. No matter how tough I might have seemed on the outside, the incident had been scary.

Hilliard and Gramps were waiting for me, loving and familiar. I stood for a moment at the kitchen door and took in the scene. They had already made tea and were partaking.

"Hey, my girl. What happened? Don't tell me your beret had another altercation with a streetcar?" Gramps said when he saw me.

That made me laugh, which helped.

"Do you want a cuppa?" Gramps asked. "Just made it."

I accepted, sat down at the table, and related what had transpired.

Hilliard stared at me. As did Gramps.

"What worries me the most is Mrs. Brodie. What if he does find her? Would he do her harm? At the very least, the way he was with me was intimidating. I can take care of myself; she can't."

"I think we should call the police," said Gramps.

Hill answered for me. "The problem is we don't know where Mrs. Brodie is, nor this Genik fellow. I don't know what the police could do. And he didn't actually lay a hand on you, did he, Charlotte?"

"Doesn't matter," said Gramps. "He was deliberately trying to scare her. He should be held accountable."

"It's okay, Gramps. I'm more angry now than scared."

I glanced at the clock on the wall. It wasn't yet half past nine. Genik had said the police officer, who had to be McCready by the sound of him, had been at the House around four o'clock. The chances were he was still on duty. I shared this with the other two.

"I'll ring the station and see if he's there," I added. Before I could act on that, the telephone rang. "Stay there. I'll get it."

We didn't receive a lot of calls at the best of times. The telephone was mostly there in case I had to deal with any business matters. A call coming in late at night created a rush of alarm. Did it signal an emergency?

I went into the hall where we kept the telephone.

"Charlotte Frayne speaking."

"Charlotte, it's Jack here."

Now I'd say that was good timing.

CHAPTER THIRTY-SIX

"JACK, I WAS just about to ring you."

"Oh, what about?"

"You first."

"Right. I thought you'd like to know I heard from a Miss Lindsay at the House of Industry. She said Mrs. Brodie has returned. Alive and well."

"What! That's great news. Where was she?"

"Apparently, she won't say. She says she wants to speak to the police. She's going to bed now, so it will have to wait until morning, but I have agreed to go over after they've had breakfast. I thought you'd like to come. Is that agreeable?"

"You bet. Oh, Jack, I'm so relieved."

I filled him in on my encounter with Zav Genik.

"Do you want to lay a charge, Lottie? For intimidation?"

"Maybe. More importantly, I want to sort out this burglary issue. Can you get a search warrant?"

"McCready gave Genik too much information." Jack's voice was angry. "Frightened him, by the sound of it. And we don't know what this man is capable of. I don't like it at all. Desperate men can do desperate things."

"Jack, can you ring Miss Lindsay and insist she keep a close watch on our Mrs. Brodie? And she must let you know at once if Genik shows up."

"I will do that right away. I assume they have a night porter. If I don't rouse anybody, I'm going to go there in person."

A man of action was Jack Murdoch.

"Do you want me to ring you back tonight?" he asked.

I was tempted, but I was also concerned for my Gramps. He didn't need to be rattled any more than he was. I thought I could trust that Olivia would be safe under the roof of the House of Industry.

"Let's connect in the morning, Jack."

"Will do. I'll come and get you at seven-thirty. Will you be all right tonight?"

"Fine. There's no reason to think Genik knows where I live."

That was true, but I also thought that just to feel safer, I'd invite Hilliard to spend the night. I could make up the couch in the living room.

It was also wider than my single bed.

CHAPTER THIRTY-SEVEN

Thursday, March 11, 1937

I HEARD THE clock chiming out midnight and knew my bout of insomnia was intractable. Hilliard snoring softly beside me wasn't helping, so I slipped out from under the coverlet and went upstairs. Gramps's room was quiet.

As I was wont to do when sleeplessness came to stay, I walked over to the window. It was a cloudless night, stars twinkling away in the dark sky; the moon was waning. An astrologer had told me once that this phase of the moon was a time of self-reflection and self-awareness. I'd forgotten whether I was *supposed* to do that or if that came about *because* of the moon. I couldn't say I was feeling particularly interiorly focused at the moment. Rather the opposite. I was thinking about Mrs. Brodie, who had gone somewhere with all of her savings and had now returned to the poorhouse. What on earth had she been doing? And then there were the boys. What was going to happen to Jerome if he came out of this disabled? There was only one facility that I knew of in the city. The Hospital for Incurables. Was he destined to spend the rest of his life in an institution? The victim of a grave injustice? And then there was the peculiar case of Mrs. Emmeline Calder and her missing bracelet. The memory of the Pioneer Club meeting was not a good one for various reasons. Had it really been her housekeeper I'd seen going into the pawnbroker? And if so, what was she doing there? I needed to go and pay my client a visit. Assuming she was still my client.

I drew the curtains. I was not sure I had come closer to sleep and briefly contemplated returning to the couch and Hilliard's warm back. However, I didn't want to disturb him either.

I got into bed. Happily, sleep did come to knit the ravelled sleeve of care, and before I knew it, my clock was ringing. It was half past six. Time to get up and deal with the day.

I WAS WAITING outside for Jack to pick me up. Daylight was being timid about taking over, and the street was dark and lonely with only a few houses showing a light. Even the wind was desultory, my beret not at risk.

I'd left Hilliard up and about and making breakfast for him and Gramps, who was still sleeping. Hill wasn't too happy that I'd left his bed when I had, but he understood insomnia all too well and didn't reproach me too much. I promised to let him know at once any developments.

Jack Murdoch was right on time. He didn't have to turn off the car engine, always a little dicey with these creaky old police cars. Furnishing up-to-date official vehicles was not a priority for the city councillors. Sometimes I thought they were still giving allegiance to our dear departed King George V, who thought a well-funded police department was an admission of defeat. Good Christian people didn't need policing.

Jack looked a little like I felt after only a few hours of sleep, and I guessed he'd had the same problem. He indicated the glove compartment.

"Fiona made an extra thermos of coffee if you want some. It's in there."

I did so want.

He was still driving somewhat awkwardly with his right hand, but his sling was still absent, so I assumed he was mending.

"Did you manage to get hold of a porter?" I asked him.

"I did, and he said he'd take care of informing Miss Lindsay we were coming. Let's hope he kept his word. He also said he'd check the register and see if they have an address for Genik and his pal. I have made up an emergency warrant, and if we need to, I can order some constables to do a search of their premises. We'll see. It depends on what our Mrs. Brodie does with the identification parade."

"Cal said he was going to check out some other sources in hopes of finding Leroy. Let's hope he has some luck."

By now the city was starting to wake up, and more cars were on the road. We manoeuvred around a clanking streetcar, which was carrying a paltry few passengers who, to my mind, looked fast asleep. I thought Detective McCready might be inspired to write a short story: "The Ghost Car."

We arrived at the House of Industry about the same time as daylight was affirmed. Lights were on. If a poorhouse could ever look cheery, this one did.

We were admitted at once by an anxious Miss Lindsay. I'd been preparing what to tell her about my previous subterfuge regarding Mrs. Brodie, but to my surprise she seemed to know already.

"Do come in. Mrs. Brodie is waiting for you in the reception room." She glanced over at me. "She's told me the real situation, Miss Frayne. I don't think there was any good reason for all the pretext, but she's adamant that it was upon her insistence."

She was clearly not happy about this, and I didn't blame her. Not for the first time, I was uncomfortable with the secrecy and deception of my position. When people found out what I was really up to, they often felt betrayed.

"I'm sorry, Miss Lindsay. As you say, Mrs. Brodie was insistent."

"And now she tells me she's going to the police station. You want her to identify some suspected robbers."

Jack answered that one. "That's right. It's important that we charge these men if they are indeed the actual criminals."

Miss Lindsay frowned. "I understand she believes the men in question have been casuals at the House. Do you have names?"

"I do. One is Viktor Genik, and the other is Marko Ryga. Do you know them?"

"No, I don't. There are sometimes two hundred or more men who come through our gates. Some stay only a few days. I don't know all of them. Besides, I deal mostly with our female population and permanent residents."

"Of course. That is quite understandable." He smiled reassuringly. Jack Murdoch was nothing if not gallant. Miss Lindsay obviously thought she was in dereliction of duty by not knowing the names of almost three hundred people.

"I was in contact with our porter," she continued. "He said he would check the register for me. This is considered confidential information, you understand. Many of our casuals do not have any kind of permanent residence, but a few do manage to cling to some derelict shack they call home. They come here when they cannot cope. They gain some sustenance, and then they leave again."

"This will be only for follow-up purposes if necessary."

She was melting a little in the face of his courtesy.

"Very well, I'll go and see if the porter has found anything. And perhaps I should fetch Mrs. Brodie. She is quite anxious about your coming for her."

"Of course."

She hurried away, and a minute later the connecting door was thrust open, and Mrs. Brodie marched into the foyer. She was wearing her outdoor clothes: a tight-fitting tweed coat that brushed her ankles, shiny beige boots, gloves, and a knitted cloche hat of startling colours. She had definitely dressed for the occasion.

"I thought I heard voices," she said. "Good morning, Miss Frayne. And you, sir, must be Detective Murdoch."

She thrust out her hand, and Jack took it in his.

"And you must be Mrs. Brodie." They shook hands. She didn't shake hands with me. I was in a different category, obviously.

"Are we ready to go?" she demanded. "I don't have all day, and I'd like to get this over with."

Miss Lindsay had said Mrs. Brodie was anxious, but she didn't seem that way to me. She seemed like a child who was barely suppressing her excitement about this new adventure that had opened up.

"We'll just be one minute, Mrs. Brodie," said Jack. "I need some information from Miss Lindsay."

Mrs. Brodie frowned at him. "Not about me, is it?"

"Not at all. I've asked for an address for those two men you saw."

"Good. I don't want to go to jail."

I didn't know why she would think jail was a possibility, but there was no time to question her. Miss Lindsay returned. She handed Jack a folded piece of paper.

"We actually do have some information. Mr. Brown asked for it when the men in question required an overnight stay. We were full that night, and he needed to know if they had any other resources."

Mrs. Brodie was already moving to the door. Miss Lindsay called to her, "Now, Mrs. Brodie. The policeman will bring you back here when you're done. We're serving your favourite cake today in honour of Mrs. Benny's birthday." She smiled. "She's eighty-four today, would you believe?"

Mrs. Brodie screwed up her face. "I believe it. She makes no sense most of the time. And she's light-fingered. She's always taking my wool."

Miss Lindsay laughed. "I think there's no ill intent. She just gets confused. But regardless, we were all so happy for your safe return. It was Cook who thought of baking the cake to celebrate both events."

Somewhat mollified, Mrs. Brodie made a little *harrumph* sound, and we made our exit.

As we were going down the steps, she caught Jack's arm.

"Are you going to switch on the siren?"

"We only use that if there is an emergency, Mrs. Brodie."

"Well, this is a sort of emergency, isn't it? We are in pursuit of some very wicked men."

Jack smiled at her. "You are quite right. As we approach the station, I shall switch on the siren."

We got into the car — me in the rear, Mrs. Brodie sitting straight as a queen in the front.

Jack started off. "By the way, Mrs. Brodie," said Jack, "where did you go when you left the House? I hope you weren't too distressed."

She shook her head vigorously. "'Course I was distressed, as you put it. You'd be if you were in my shoes. But that's behind me now. I just want to see justice done."

Jack gave her a little grin. "So, you're not going to tell me where you went."

She smiled back. "You must promise not to tell anybody. You too, Miss Frayne. I don't want it getting back to the House. It's my private business."

"I promise," said Jack.

"So do I."

She shifted a little in the seat. "I thought, 'Well, Livvy,' I thought, 'if these are to be your last days on this earth, you may as well enjoy them.'"

Jack smiled. "I'm sorry you even thought these might be your last days, Mrs. Brodie."

She looked at him impishly. "When you get to my age, you never know when your last day will be."

"Don't keep us in suspense," teased Jack. "Where did you go?"

Again, we got the impish look. "I went to a hotel. I've never stayed in a hotel in my whole life, and I've always wanted to."

"Good for you," answered Jack. "I only hope it met your expectations."

"Not exactly. You see, I used to live in Toronto when I was just a child. My mother was in service, you see, and she got a good placement in a grand house out in the east end. There was a hotel a couple of streets away. It faced onto the lake, and on the few occasions I got away from my chores, I'd go there. I couldn't go in, of course, I just stood across the street and watched who was coming and going. They all looked like real princes and princesses to me. With horses and carriages, in those days. And servants. Lots of them. So, I would say to myself, 'One day, I am going to stay here, and those bellboys will bow and scrape to me just as they are doing now to these people.' And I will say, 'I desire a room that faces the water, if you please. No other will do.'"

She halted, lost in memories. Jack prompted her gently.

"Is that what you did?"

"More or less," she said with a sigh. "When it came right down to it, I didn't want to go to that hotel. It's too far, for one thing. How would I get there? Besides, there were only bad memories there anyway. So, I took out my money and I walked right up to the Avon and checked in there. No water view, just a window onto Elizabeth Street."

"Did you enjoy it?"

Another sigh. "Honestly, it wasn't as much fun as I expected. Truth is, one night was enough. I missed the House. I've made friends here. Miss Lindsay is a good sort, and for the most part, the food is tasty. So, I came back. Why waste my money?"

"Thanks for telling us, Mrs. Brodie. I'm sorry it didn't quite work out."

"Oh, I learned a lesson, and that's always worth it, isn't it? Now, if we can put these men behind bars, I will be even happier."

"Good. I think we can switch on the siren. I'll do the same with the beacon, shall I?"

And that's how we arrived at the police headquarters.

CHAPTER THIRTY-EIGHT

THE ROOM USED for the identification parade was on the second floor of headquarters. It obviously doubled as an office, and several desks, held down by officious typewriters, had been pushed to the side. A long grey canvas hung on a wall, and white boards with large red numbers written on them were pinned on a rail near the ceiling. About ten feet or so in front and facing the canvas was a row of chairs.

Jack led Mrs. Brodie to the middle chair.

"I'm going to sit on this side of you, and Miss Frayne will be on the other. Shortly, we are going to bring in five men for you to take a look at. They will each stand below one of those numbers. The sergeant will call out each number in order, and the man beneath that number will step out. I ask you not to speak to the men or make any acknowledgement except to me when I will ask you to speak quietly if you recognize any one of them."

"Will they see me?"

"They will not. The light will be in their eyes, and we will be in the dark. All right so far?"

She nodded her head emphatically.

"In the interest of fair play, the men will all be dressed in a similar way. That is, each will be in a black jacket and dark trousers. The two men you have said were on Edward Street at the time of the robbery will be dressed likewise."

"Who are the others?"

"They are from various walks of life. They have volunteered to help with the parade." Jack gave her a smile. "Ready?"

Mrs. Brodie gave a little wriggle. She was indeed having a good time.

"Ready as I'll ever be."

Jack called over to the constable who was stationed at the door.

"Tell Sergeant Graves to bring in the men."

The constable stepped out to follow instructions, and right away a uniformed officer came in. He took up a position on the other side of the doorway, then turned and addressed those who were behind him, as yet invisible.

"Take up your positions. No talking. No gestures of any kind. When your number is called, you will walk out to that number, turn so you're facing the lights, and look straight ahead. You will remain in that position until instructed to step back, then you will stand beneath your number until dismissed."

He had the title of *sergeant* for good reason. He gave orders like an army drill sergeant.

He flipped a switch next to him, and the lights illuminating our portion of the room were immediately turned off. Simultaneously, the wall was illuminated with a dazzling light. We could have been about to watch a play. With those lights on, none of the men would be able to see us. I was a little relieved. I didn't particularly want to meet the angry eyes of Zav Genik, whom I had so recently whopped in the stomach.

"Number one," Jack called to the sergeant, who signalled to the constable. A man came out and began to walk slowly to the far side. I recognized him immediately as Genik's constant companion, Marko Ryga. He reached his number and turned to face us, blinking in the glare. Everything about him said *fear*.

"Take your time, Mrs. Brodie," said Jack quietly. "Do you recognize him?"

"Oh yes," she whispered. "He was with the other fellow. Saw them both two days ago in the yard. And before that on Edward Street. The other one's the trouble, though. I know it." She hesitated and continued to stare at Marko. "Funny, I feel as if I've seen him somewhere else as well."

"Where might that be?"

"Don't know. But it will come to me. Maybe he's just got the look of the Old Country. Black Irish."

"I believe he's Ukrainian. Shall we go on?"

She nodded, and Jack called out to the sergeant at the door. "Number two, please."

Next was a big, rangy fellow who strode out confidently. I recognized him at once. It was the constable from the hospital. Mrs. Brodie had no reaction. He took up his position, automatically taking on the stance of a constable on duty, legs apart, hands behind his back. The black jacket was too tight across his chest. Somewhat of a giveaway. I heard Jack sigh in exasperation.

"Next, please."

The third man resembled Marko Ryga. Intentionally, I'm sure. He was the same height, slim and dark-haired, clean-shaven. About the same age. The difference, obvious to me and not possible to disguise, was the lack of fear. He had his head lowered, but that made him seem shy rather than afraid. He took up his position.

"Don't know him," whispered Mrs. Brodie.

"Number four," called Jack.

The next man was tall, rangy, and had a droopy, reddish moustache. It was Zav Genik. Mrs. Brodie give a little gasp, then whispered to Jack.

"That's him. That's the one I saw. He's the one was at the House two days ago. And he was on Edward Street."

"You're positive?" Jack asked — unnecessarily, I thought. Mrs. Brodie could hardly have been more certain.

"Absolutely. I'd know him anywhere. He's an ugly piece of work."

She was right about that.

"There's one more, Mrs. Brodie."

"I don't need to see any more. It's him, I tell you."

"We have to bring on one more man, Mrs. Brodie. It's procedure."

"Very well."

Genik was in position, staring straight ahead. Rather to my surprise, he didn't look like the angry bully I'd encountered yesterday. He looked haggard and more defeated than anything else.

Jack signalled the sergeant. "Next, please."

The last man came out. He was sandy-haired, tall, but a heavier build than Zav Genik. Better nourished, by the look of him. Although he made an attempt not to be too obvious, there was no doubt in my mind he was one of the constables at the station.

Mrs. Brodie shifted in her seat. "Never seen him before."

Jack leaned into her. "Take another good look at all of them. Do you recognize here one or both men that you saw on the morning of March first on Edward Street near the corner of Elizabeth Street?"

Mrs. Brodie nodded vigorously. "I've just said that. It's number one and number four. No doubt whatsoever. They weren't wearing those clothes, but it's them all right."

"And you're not mixing them up with the two men who came to the casual yard two days ago, when you were with Miss Frayne?"

"Mixing them up? Not at all. I pointed out to her thems were the two men I'd seen, didn't I, miss?"

"You did indeed. And I can testify that the men we've seen today were those same ones."

"Good," said Jack. He called to the sergeant again. "Parade is dismissed. Have the two men in question remain in the holding room. Others can get back to work."

The sergeant repeated the direction, and the men began to file out. I heard Mrs. Brodie give a little giggle.

"I bet that number two is a copper, isn't he?"

Jack laughed. "Let's just say he was helping us out."

"And number five? Him too?"

"Another assistant."

"What about number three?"

"He's our janitor."

Mrs. Brodie pursed her lips. "Better watch out. He looked shifty to me."

"I'll take that under advisement."

"What now? Are you going to arrest those two?"

"We're going to hold them until tomorrow. In the meantime, we'll do a search of their residence. Hopefully, that will be conclusive." He turned toward Mrs. Brodie. "You have been marvellous. I'm going to have our matron get you a cup of tea, and then one of the constables will drive you home."

"Not you?"

"I've got to get going right away on the search, otherwise I would."

"You will make sure to come and tell me what happens, won't you?"

"I will. You are indispensable to our case."

I could see she liked that. Genuine appreciation goes a long way.

CHAPTER THIRTY-NINE

THE MATRON HAD taken Mrs. Brodie for her cup of tea. In spite of the grim circumstances, I thought she was having the time of her life. Lots to talk about when she got back to the House. She reminded me of my Gran. Same sort of spunk and resilience.

Jack turned to me. "I'm still having trouble writing. Would you be able to act as my recorder again, Charlotte? We can go directly to the address I was given and conduct a search. According to the information on the welfare card, they live at 37 Edward Street. It's a small salvage depot run by veterans. They have a room at the rear."

"Is Genik a veteran?"

"That's correct. The porter said he's one of a group of 'returned soldiers,' as they refer to themselves. 'Whiners,' he called them, but that might not be fair. Many of them haven't been given a decent pension by the government. They feel they made lots of sacrifices for this country and all the thanks they've got is poverty, unemployment, and indifference."

I didn't need to ask him what he thought. His sympathies were obvious. Jack Murdoch, my man Hilliard, Wilf Morrow, Calvin Greene — there was an endless list of men who could bear witness physically and/or emotionally to the toll the war had taken.

"Do you think there's going to be another war, Jack?"

He grimaced. "It's sure starting to look that way. This time, we mustn't stick our collective heads in the sand. We've got to be prepared."

He wasn't saying anything I hadn't already heard, but it was still a depressing thought.

"Let's get the car. But this time, if you don't mind, I won't switch on the siren."

We shared a smile at the delight our Mrs. Brodie had experienced as we'd raced along College Street, siren screaming.

JACK HAD ASSIGNED two constables to conduct the search, and they were waiting for us outside the house. Actually, it wasn't a house as such. It was a one-storey building with an adjacent yard piled with junk that, as far as I could tell, consisted mainly of rusted-out stoves, one or two crippled couches, and a few flattened motor cars. A painted sign over the door announced this was RELIABLE VETERANS SALVAGE.

Jack pulled the car up to the curb.

"According to the information I managed to extract from them this morning, they have a room at the rear."

If the state of the building was any indication, I wasn't surprised the two men had been given welfare chits to get meals at the House of Industry.

"They also function as night watchmen and general labour in the yard if needed," added Jack.

"I can't imagine this place gets much business. It looks like it's been salvaged from salvage. How much more use could you wring out of that couch, for instance?"

"There's always firewood, I suppose."

"It's sad to see what was once a pretty brocade come to this. Who knows, perhaps a young courting couple exchanged their first kiss on that sofa. Maybe a nice old auntie read a story to her little niece and nephew while they snuggled up in warmth and safety."

"What? What are you talking about?"

"Sorry, Jack. Places like this depress me. I'm just trying to paint a happier picture."

He burst out laughing. "Please refrain. I've got enough dealing with Detective McCready without you waxing poetic on me."

Good thing I hadn't shared my observations on the March wind that was pressing on us with great determination.

Jack called over to the two police constables. "Follow me. Let's see if there's anybody here."

There was no light showing in the front window, which didn't mean there wasn't somebody inside. The grime on the glass precluded any light being revealed.

There was no bell to be seen, so Jack thumped on the door. No answer.

He knocked again, but again there was no response.

"Let's check the rear."

The constables and I were about to follow him when the front door opened.

The reason for the delay was obvious. The man who answered was in an invalid chair. He greeted us in a cheery way.

"Good morning. What can I do for you?"

He glanced over Jack's shoulder and saw the two constables.

"Uh-oh. What is it today? I've paid my rent, and my licence is up to date. I swear I've got rid of the rodents. Has somebody complained again?"

"Good morning. I'm Detective Jack Murdoch. I'm here on a police matter. Are you the owner of this establishment?"

The man laughed. No mirth, believe me.

"Let's say my name's on the deed, but the true owner is the Bank of Commerce."

"I know what you mean, sir." Jack was being very polite. "May I have your full name?"

"Vasylyk. Dmitri Vasylyk."

"I understand this is the address of Viktor Genik and Marko Ryga."

"That's right. They've got a room in the rear. Why're you asking about them?"

Jack took the warrant paper from his pocket.

"At the moment, they are both being held on suspicion of breaking and entering. I have a warrant to search the premises."

Vasylyk took the warrant and studied it closely before handing it back.

"According to what I see there, you only have the right to search their room. Nothing else."

"That's correct. Would it be a problem if we extended that search to the entire building?"

Again, the man did his laugh that was not a laugh.

"You wouldn't find anything, believe me. I am in the front room. There's a privy that doesn't work properly next to that, and a cupboard that pretends to be a kitchen. The rest of the space is a warehouse where I store any goods that I have a remote chance of reselling. I know it doesn't look like much from the outside, but you'd be surprised what people throw out, even these days. Some of it's good stuff. All legit, I assure you."

He related all of this in a false, cheery tone that could not disguise the bitterness he was living with.

"How long have Mr. Genik and Mr. Ryga occupied the rear room?"

"Less than two weeks. They blew in from Manitoba with no money and no prospects. Turns out Genik and me were both serving men in the war, so I thought the least I could do was help out a comrade. They can stay in the room for free and in return do odd jobs as needed. They also keep an eye out at night."

He made a motion with his arms as if to lift himself out of the chair. He was probably in mid-life, but pain had etched deep lines on his face so that he looked much older. His legs were strapped down.

"I'm not too mobile, as you see, courtesy of a Kraut shell in the spine. There have been more times than one when I heard somebody scavenging in the yard, but I couldn't get out quick enough to catch them."

Again, Jack nodded sympathetically. "Do you know if the two men were on the premises last Monday morning, March first?"

"No idea. I often have to take some sleeping draught or other if I'm going to function." He tapped the chair harder, as if it was the cause of his troubles. "Many times I don't see daylight until ten o'clock or even later. So, they might have been in or they might not. Why are you asking?"

"That is the day of the alleged robbery."

"I can't say one way or another, to be truthful, but to date, I haven't seen them going out at that hour. I give them free lodgings, but I can't do board. I pay them when I can, but they mostly rely on customer tips. If it's been a real slow day, they head over to the poorhouse for some grub. But that's in the afternoon."

He looked up at us and did his peculiar lifting motion again. "I tell you, Detective, they're good fellows. Zav served his country with honour. He even got a medal. What are they supposed to have taken?"

"I'm afraid I can't reveal that information, Mr. Vasylyk. But I'd like to take a look at the room. Is there a key?"

"Ha. No key. No need. What would you be locking in or out?"

"All right then. How do we get in?"

"The back door is blocked off. You'll have to come through the front."

Jack gestured to the two constables. "Wait here, chaps."

Vasylyk waved his hand. For the first time, I saw the mutilation: on his right hand, all that was left was his thumb.

"It's a tight fit with my chair and all. You go and have a look-see. I'll wait in the hall. Like I said, you don't need a key."

Jack nodded at me. "Are you up for this, Charlotte?"

"You bet."

I just hoped we weren't going to enter the same kind of desolate hovel we'd encountered before.

The warehouse, which is what it was, was stacked with shelves floor to ceiling on both sides. A narrow passage led to the rear. As far as I could tell, the shelves were loaded with a bewildering variety of objects: kettles, tureens, fans, even framed pictures. I suppose if you were setting up your own home and were looking for a bargain, you might come here. I assumed Mr. Vasylyk could locate items for you. *How about an oven? Just needs a little spit and polish. You need a kitchen table? Here you go. Short of a leg, but that is easily fixed. Lean it against the wall. What's that you say? Some bedsheets? Got some good ones here. No need to worry about where they came from. They've all been fumigated.*

I must have been dawdling, because Jack turned around.

"Charlotte? Are you with me?"

"Coming."

He'd halted in front of a closed door on his right.

Vasylyk had been wheeling himself behind us.

"That's it," he called.

Jack turned the handle, and we went inside.

I have to say that what greeted us was completely unexpected.

Given our recent experiences with the boys' lair and the junk-filled warehouse, I'd expected to see the same. But this room was the exact opposite. It was neat as a pin — or a barracks, which is where I guessed Genik had learned to be so tidy. Small as it was, the space was used economically. A two-tier bunk bed took up most of the opposite wall. Brown covers, tightly tucked, reinforced the feeling of army accommodations. In one corner was a table, two shabby armchairs beside it. An empty fireplace and a washstand were in the other corner. A coat stand was currently unused. That was it. At first glance, there didn't seem to be anywhere one could hide even a pencil.

Jack frowned. "Okay. I doubt we're going to get much here, but let's have a quick look."

He walked over to the bunks. "When I was in the army, we had special footlockers for the few personal items we were allowed. And believe me, they were few. The footlockers were inspected regularly. Woe betide you if they were messy." He crouched down. "We stowed them under here, for the most part. Ah." He reached under the bunk and dragged out a small case. "If Genik had anything to hide, I'd say he'd put it in here."

The case was battered, reinforced with metal edges. It even had a couple of travel stickers on the side. One, I could see, proclaimed the owner had been in Valenciennes. On a fresher-looking label was printed the name *Viktor Genik*. There was a front lock and two rusty metal clasps.

Jack tugged at the lid, but it didn't yield.

Vasylyk had got himself to the door and was watching us. I wouldn't say he was exactly hostile — his situation was too precarious to antagonize a police officer he didn't know — but he was not going to co-operate if he didn't have to.

"I don't suppose you have a key to this, do you, sir?" Jack asked.

"No. Like I said, I let the workers stay here for free, but just because they aren't paying tenants doesn't mean they don't have the right to privacy."

"In other words, no. You don't have a key."

"Correct."

"Well, I need to open it. Miss Frayne, will you kindly make a record of what I am doing and exactly what we find? Mr. Vasylyk, I will show you a copy of the printed report, and if it comes to any court action, you can affirm all was as declared."

Jack was losing his polite shield.

He took a penknife from his pocket and opened out a thin blade. I had removed my notebook and pencil from my purse, and I noted down what he was holding. My shorthand was a little fuzzy but still available to me.

Jack snapped the clasps on the case, pried open the lid easily, and lifted it.

He removed something that was wrapped in a thick, white-striped shawl. He opened it up, and there was Dr. Brandwein's silver menorah, gleaming and dignified.

That was it. There was nothing else in the case except a rolled pair of socks and a small black book. Jack held it up.

"A prayer book courtesy of the army chaplain." He grimaced. "All departing soldiers of the British Expeditionary Force were given one of these. I've still got mine."

Jack rocked back on his heels and addressed Vasylyk.

"The shawl and the menorah have been declared to be stolen. I will be confiscating them as evidence."

He rewrapped the menorah and replaced it in the suitcase.

Vasylyk remained in the doorway. "Can I expect to see the lads anytime soon? I need their help, like I said."

"I don't think you can count on it. You should think about hiring somebody else."

"Won't be hard. There's lots of veterans around who want honest work." Vasylyk did his lift with his arms. "I'll get back to the front, then. I assume you and the constables won't be lingering. I don't want to scare away any potential customers."

"We'll be leaving in a few minutes."

"Good."

Vasylyk reversed the chair and rolled himself away down the passageway.

Jack nodded at me. "I'd say this was pretty conclusive, wouldn't you?"

"Very much so. The Davies boys are exonerated."

Jack sighed. "For this, perhaps, but why did they have Dr. Brandwein's silver matchbox in their possession?"

"Leroy swore he found it in the laneway."

Jack snapped the suitcase shut. "We'll bring this with us. I'm going back to the station. Maybe Mr. Genik will be more forthcoming. Anything else we should look at, Charlotte?"

"What about the washstand?"

Like the rest of the room, it had a purely functional appearance. On it was a plain white water jug and bowl. The latter sported a significant chip on the brim. Beside them were a bar of yellow soap in a dish, a tin of tooth powder, and a pot containing two razors, a scraggly shaving brush, and a toothbrush.

"Nothing that you mightn't expect." He indicated the single toothbrush in the pot. "Do the two of them share this, do you think? Do they fight over whose turn it is to use it?" He pulled open the single drawer and crouched down to take a look. He whistled between his teeth. "What's this then?"

He held out a small velvet-covered jewellery box, and he grinned at me. "Do you think it contains an exquisite engagement ring? One that Genik was going to offer to his one true love if only he could convince her that he could once again be gainfully employed, no longer dependent on charity?"

He was speaking ironically, of course. A former soldier, now a policeman, completely conflicted about the state of his comrades who had fought to make the world a better place and who were now, all too often, making it worse. He handed me the little box.

"I'll let you do the honours. You open it, Charlotte."

I did so. There was no engagement ring inside that spoke of a broken heart, but there was something that almost took my breath away. There, nestled in a bed of white silk, was a single gold cufflink. It was twin to the one I had seen in Mr. Toban's pawnshop. The same initials were engraved on it: H.M.

I was not prone to swearing, but in this instance, I couldn't help it.

"How the bloody hell did this get here?"

CHAPTER FORTY

MR. VASYLYK WASN'T too happy that we were removing items from the room and demanded to examine the warrant again. Jack obliged him, and he had no recourse but to let us leave with the suitcase. He also denied any knowledge of the contents. I asked him if he'd seen the little jewellery box before, and he said he hadn't. He asked again if we thought his helpers would return anytime soon, but Jack couldn't answer. We both knew it was unlikely. However, he agreed to let Vasylyk know what the outcome was after further interrogation.

We were in the car on our way to the police station. Jack had been rather quiet, and I myself wasn't exactly chatty. The appearance of that little cufflink had been utterly unexpected. I was keen to get an explanation.

"Are you still up for taking notes?" Jack asked.

"I wouldn't miss it."

We headed for the station, and, once parked, Jack hurried us into his office. He asked for Genik and his companion to be brought to the interview room, which was on the same floor as where we'd done the lineup.

"I don't know about you, Charlotte, but I'm in dire need of a cup of coffee and a smoke."

"Coffee, yes. Smoke, no thanks."

The station had a room in the basement where the officers could take a break. A help-yourself coffee urn and a hot water urn for tea were on a table. There wasn't much else, and I gathered the officers brought their own sandwiches and cookies. No coddling for these stalwarts. From the quality of the air in the room, I assumed that they preferred to spend money on cigarettes and tobacco.

"Do the two of them require the presence of a solicitor?" I asked.

"Not this round. If they offer a confession, then we'll bring in the resident paralegal. That's next stage."

"What about the boys and their sentence? Can we get that changed right away?"

"I'll present a petition to Judge Carter as soon as he gets back from banging his balls around a golf course."

I raised my eyebrows at the expression but made no comment. My friend was definitely rattled and exasperated.

We finished the coffee — no sandwiches — and went up to the interview room. I had my notebook at the ready. Rather like a shield, I suppose. I didn't know how Genik was going to react.

A constable let us into the room, where both men were already seated at either end of a small table. My immediate impression was similar to the one I'd had earlier during the lineup. Genik's head was bowed, and he seemed like a defeated man. The younger one's head was also lowered.

"Afternoon, fellows," said Jack.

We sat down across from them, me slightly behind Jack. The constable stationed himself by the door. He was the same officer who'd been in the lineup.

Genik noticed me, and I was rather gratified to see the look of shock on his face.

"You know who I am," said Jack, "but allow me to introduce Miss Frayne. She will be acting as our official record keeper. She will be taking notes on our meeting for future police reference."

"I didn't know you were with the cops," Genik said to me. "You get around, don't you?"

"I try to," I answered, cheery as all get-out.

The younger one didn't speak, but he too looked surprised and nervous.

"All right then," said Jack. "Let's get down to it."

He put the suitcase, a.k.a. footlocker, on the table and removed the shawl with the menorah still wrapped inside.

"We found these items in this suitcase in your room at the salvage yard. They were reported stolen last week from the residence of Dr. Morris Brandwein, who resides on Edward Street. I have to ask you if, in fact, you stole these same items?"

Genik raised his head and stared for several minutes at the ceiling. I wasn't sure if he was going to say anything at all, but finally he did. He looked at Jack.

"I have told you we did not rob Dr. Brandwein. We are not thieves."

"How did these items come to be in your possession, if that is the case?"

Genik sighed and spoke in the tone of somebody addressing a rather slow pupil.

"Because, Detective, Dr. Brandwein gave them to us."

CHAPTER FORTY-ONE

THE CONSTABLE WAS too disciplined and too much in awe of his superior officer to make his reaction obvious, so he quickly turned his spontaneous guffaw into a cough. Jack flashed him a warning glance.

"Please explain yourself, Mr. Genik."

"Sometime last month, the gentleman in question came to the scrapyard. It's really a second-hand goods place, and Vasylyk buys and sells all sort of goods — mostly household, no jewellery or clothes. So a gent introducing himself as Dr. Brandwein comes in — don't ask me what day it was, I don't remember. One day melts into another, as far as I'm concerned." He paused. "I don't suppose I could have a smoke, could I?"

Without answering, Jack slid his cigarette case across the table, and Genik took one hungrily. In turn, he offered one to Ryga, who also helped himself, but less frantically. He hadn't said a word so far.

Jack gave Genik the time to light up and take a deep drag. He retrieved the case.

"Please continue. You were saying that Dr. Brandwein came to the salvage depot. What did he want? Was he buying or selling?"

"Selling. He said he was planning to move in the near future and wanted to divest himself of unnecessary possessions.

He wanted somebody to visit his house and do an appraisal. Vasylyk couldn't go himself on account of him having no legs, so he said Marko and I would come and do it. He thought as how we'd been at the depot long enough to get a sense of what sells and what doesn't and therefore what price we might offer."

Genik was punctuating all of this speech with deep draws on the cigarette. The room was rapidly filling with tobacco smoke. I wasn't sure how long I was going to last. Jack must have sensed that, and he gave the duty constable a signal to open the window. Whew.

"Go on."

"So, Marko and me got up bright and early as requested and went to see the doctor. He let us in but apologized as he had overslept and wasn't ready for us. He wasn't even dressed, for Lord's sake. Waste of bloody time, it was. Oh, he apologized and all that, but it was a waste. We said we'd come back next day if he liked. 'Not yet,' says he. 'I don't think it's safe for any of us Jews to go to Germany. I'll let you know if that changes.' I didn't have a clue what he was yammering about, but I gathered he was intending to leave the country. Anyways, we were about to leave when he said he wanted to give us something to recompense us for taking our valuable time or some such malarkey." Genik shrugged. "I wasn't going to fight him on that, was I? So then doesn't he pick up one of those Jewish candelabras that was on a shelf in the kitchen, grab some kind of shawl, wrap it up, and hand it to us. 'Here,' says he. 'Take this. Of course, you can sell it or pawn it if you want — it's your gift — but I hope you won't. I'd like you to keep the menorah safe on your shelf. The shawl is a prayer shawl, but it will keep you warm when you need it.'"

At this point, the younger man sat up straight. "I didn't like it. He seemed so nervous. I mean, we're Catholic, both Zav and me. What would we do with some Jewish stuff? Was he trying to convert us or what? I've heard of Jews trying to do that."

I had to stop writing for a minute. I had never heard of that, just the other way around. Some zealous Christians intent on converting Jews. They got them into a group called "Jews for Jesus." Had Dr. Brandwein converted to Christianity? Was that why he was giving away his Jewish artifacts?

"In spite of your misgivings, you accepted the gift?" asked Jack.

"Course we did. Good silver, it was. And a nice wool shawl. We wasn't going to turn that down."

"Go on. Dr. Brandwein says he wants you to have this gift, you accept, and then what?"

"No 'then what.' We left and went back to the depot. Ask the man himself, if you don't believe me."

"We can't. He has suffered a severe stroke and at the moment cannot communicate at all. There is some doubt as to whether or not he will even live."

Genik was good at showing no immediate reaction.

"Sorry to hear that. He was fine and healthy when we left."

"According to the information we have been given, he would have had the stroke that morning. Did he surprise you in the act of breaking and entering? Is that what brought on the stroke?"

This time, Genik did react. He glared at Jack. "What I've told you is the truth."

"What time were you there at the house?"

"I dunno. Early. Just getting light. He said he wanted us to come early, so early we came."

"And when you left, you swear to me that Dr. Brandwein was fine?"

"Absolutely."

"And there was nobody else in the house?"

"Can't say, can I? We met him in the kitchen. Might have been somebody upstairs with him. Come to think of it, maybe there was. A bit of crumpet, perhaps? Maybe that's why he was so keen to get rid of us. Mind you, he didn't strike me as that sort of person. Bit long in the tooth to be throwing his leg over, but you never know, do you?"

He managed to send this in my direction. I kept my eyes on the notebook. If he was telling the truth, it was by no means impossible. Working for Mr. Gilmore had taught me that. The human desire, especially the male desire, knew no age limits. Was it relevant?

Jack went on. "When our detective arrived at the house, he said the back door was open, and it looked as if the lock had been forced. How do you explain that, Mr. Genik?"

"I don't. We went to the front door and rang the bell. The doctor came down and opened said door. He told us to come around to the back, which we did. He was there on the doorstep."

"Had the lock been forced?"

"How would I know? He let us in and let us out."

Abruptly, Jack turned his attention to the young man, Marko Ryga.

"Do you corroborate what your friend is saying, or do you have a different story?"

Ryga shook his head. "It happened exactly as Zav has said. We didn't rob anybody."

"When did you report to Mr. Vasylyk that Dr. Brandwein cancelled the assessment? Did you tell your boss that he gave you a rather special gift?"

"When we got back to the depot, Vasylyk was not yet up.

He has to take opiates for his pain, and he sleeps a lot. So, in answer to your question, we did not tell him until later in the day. We were busy by then — nice drop-off from an estate sale on Orde Street — so he didn't get too bothered about the cancellation. And I forgot completely to mention the gifts. It didn't seem important."

My task was to be inconspicuous and take notes in my rusty shorthand, but I could no longer be silent. I suppose it was seeing similarities between Mrs. Brodie and my dear departed Gran that did it.

"Excuse me, Detective, I'd like to ask the gentleman a question if you don't mind."

Jack looked a little startled, but bless him, he nodded at once.

"Please do, Miss Frayne."

"Mr. Genik. You say you are totally innocent of any kind of burglary at Dr. Brandwein's house, but you were seen by somebody. A Mrs. Brodie, who was delivering some of her work to a client on Edward Street. You have been most anxious to contact her since that time — to the extent, I must add, of making threats to myself just last night. Why do you want to speak to her?"

Genik waved his cigarette in the air to accentuate his point.

"She looked scared when she saw us leaving Brandwein's house. I could tell she thought we were up to no good. I wanted to reassure her, is all. Explain what we were doing. I saw the two of you together at the window of the casuals' yard. I thought she was pointing us out." He actually smiled, and, to my surprise, it was a rather nice smile. "I'm not a fool, Miss Frayne. I put two and two together. I guessed she was telling everybody we was thieves. Am I right?"

"It's true. She does think that."

"See? And I apologize for frightening you. I didn't mean to. My face looks that way. Nothing I can do about it. A gift from the Front." Again, his face twitched. "I must say, you can take care of yourself. My stomach is still sore."

I honestly didn't know what to say, and I turned back to Jack.

"Thank you, Detective. I don't have any more questions at the moment." In reality, this wasn't quite true. My brain was flooded with questions, but they didn't directly relate to the present matter. What was his wartime experience? How did he get to know Marko? He was old enough to have started a family. Had he?

"Thank you, Miss Frayne." Jack reached down into the evidence box.

He took out the little jewellery box and snapped it open. "How do you explain this? We found it in the washstand drawer of your room. A cufflink such as this one has been reported stolen." He held it out so they could see what it was. Marko immediately reached out for it, but Jack snatched it away.

"Not so fast. I'm waiting for your explanation."

"That's mine," spluttered the young man.

"Is it? How did you come by it?"

"My mother gave it to me. It belonged to her father."

"Really? It's initialed, I see. What were your grandfather's initials?"

"R.O., most likely."

"That's not what's here. Where did he get it?"

"I haven't a clue. He wasn't the most talkative of men. All he ever said was it was a special gift and it had belonged to a special man."

"Is your grandfather still alive?"

"No. He died two years ago. He was seventy-four." Marko looked wistful. "I wish he'd said more about his life. He was from the Old Country originally, but he never opened up. When he passed away, my mother inherited it. She gave it to me when I was on the Trek. She made me swear to keep it safe. She said if I ever lost it, a curse would come down upon me and the entire family. So, I take it everywhere."

"A single cufflink isn't that useful, I would say."

"There is only one. I don't know what happened to the other one."

As far as I knew, the twin was currently sitting in a pawn-broker's shop on McCaul Street.

Genik spoke up, angry. "Ever since I've known Marko, he's had that cufflink. And that's going on four years now. Who says it's stolen?"

"Never mind that, for now." Jack closed the jewellery box and put it to one side on the table, then he turned back to address Genik. "There is also a silver matchbox that belonged to Dr. Brandwein and has been reported as missing from the doctor's house. Do you know anything about that?"

"No! I tell you, we are not thieves. It's the government who are the thieves here. Took away the best years of our lives and promised us a better world to pay for the sacrifice we made. But it hasn't happened, has it? They're the thieves. We're the ones who've been robbed."

And suddenly he was gasping for breath and struggling to get air into his lungs.

Marko caught his arm.

"There, there, Zav. It's all right. Just take a deep breath. That's it. Good. Now another. We'll be all right."

It only took a few minutes for Genik's anxiety to subside. His shoulders slumped.

"Sorry about that. It happens to me sometimes if I get too worked up."

Marko looked at us indignantly. "He was a war hero, he was. Got two medals. Not just one. Two. One at Ypres. One at Vaillencourt. And look how the country's treated him. Shameful it is."

"Well, are you going to charge us or not?" Genik's voice was raspy but steady, the storm gone as quickly as it had arrived.

Jack drummed his fingers on the table. "Let's say I'm going to release you for now. You mustn't leave the city without notifying your local police. We will continue the investigation until we are satisfied."

"Does that mean we can take our things?"

"It does. But as I said, you mustn't leave without letting us know."

"Wouldn't dream of it. Besides, where would we go? We've got some steady work now." Genik touched his forefinger to his forehead. "Thanks. And let's hope Dr. Brandwein makes a proper recovery. He seemed like a decent bloke. He'll tell you what I said was true."

Jack beckoned to the constable to escort the two men back to the front desk and check them out. As they were going, Genik smiled the stiff, crooked smile at me.

Frankly, I still couldn't determine if he was indeed an accomplished liar or a damaged man who was telling the truth.

CHAPTER FORTY-TWO

WHEN THEY HAD left, Jack turned to me.

"What do you think, Charlotte?"

"It's hard to know. It sounds utterly improbable. A Jewish man handing over a menorah and prayer shawl to two strange men who are essentially homeless. He could have presumably given them money if he thought they were in need. Why an important artifact like a menorah and a tallit? On the other hand, Genik is darn convincing. Ryga was too."

"I agree on both counts."

"Jack, I'm wondering if anybody did, in fact, break in? What was it McCready said? *The door was open, and the lock looked as if it had been forced.* In what way did it look forced? And where, if anywhere, do the Davies boys enter the picture?"

"It's not out of the question that they came later, found Dr. Brandwein already unconscious, and seized the chance to steal something: the silver matchbox."

"Logically, that is possible, but why would they even be at that house? At least Genik supplied us with a reason."

"They are newspaper boys, Charlotte. Perhaps they were delivering a paper."

"Why didn't they say that to McCready?"

"I don't know."

"Why did Dr. Brandwein cancel the assessment? And is that relevant?"

"Again, I have to say, I don't know."

"Was he alone? Or he was indeed having a little dalliance, and if so, is that at all relevant?"

"Charlotte, for the third time, I have to say, *I don't know.*"

"Okay. Let's suppose for a moment the two boys arrived at the house right after Genik and Ryga left. They went to the back door even though, if they were delivering a newspaper, they would have simply left it on the front doorstep. Then they entered through the back door, with no other intention but to steal. Why walk all the way to the front of the house where the den is located? Surely there must have been other objects close at hand to be easily picked up. And even in the den, there must have been some valuable items. You yourself possess a handsome silver cigarette case. I would imagine Dr. Brandwein, a committed smoker with his own special room to inhale, would have had all the accoutrements, fancy cigarette case being one of them. Is the housekeeper certain nothing else was missing? According to the report, she doesn't sound too sure of anything."

"The times don't fit either. Just say Genik and Ryga are as innocent as lambs. They leave with their gifts, then the two boys arrive right afterward. If, in fact, they *were* there. Leroy is denying it. But just say he's lying. For reasons as yet unknown, they arrive at the house. Do they encounter the doctor? Is he already on the floor unconscious?"

"Mr. Glozier is sure he saw the Davies boys about eight o'clock leaving the front yard. Or rather running from the yard. Dr. Brandwein was found unconscious at just after eight-thirty, but he could have had a collapse earlier. Was that why they were running?"

"One good thing is that we can at the least confirm Genik's version of events," said Jack. "Theft or gift? Dr. Brandwein will tell us himself."

We were interrupted by the flashing light on the intercom. Jack picked up the telephone.

"Yes? ... Oh, right. Put him on."

Jack put his hand over the mouthpiece of the receiver and said to me, "I called the hospital earlier, and it's the doctor replying." Then into the phone, "Yes, Doctor. Detective Murdoch here. Thank you for calling back." A pause as the doctor spoke. Jack's expression changed, and I knew he was not hearing good news.

"Right. Thank you, Doctor. Yes, I'm sorry too. Very sorry."

He hung up the telephone.

"Don't tell me ...?"

"I'm afraid Dr. Brandwein won't be confirming anything. He passed away without regaining consciousness."

CHAPTER FORTY-THREE

JACK IMMEDIATELY FLIPPED a switch to connect with the main switchboard.

"Forbes, who's on duty desk? ... Tell him to hold those two men. I'll be right there. Don't let them go.... What? They've already gone?" He slammed the phone back. "They've been released."

"What are you going to do, Jack?"

"Not much I can do at the moment. Without Dr. Brandwein's corroboration, we've only got their word for the gift-giving." He drummed his fingers on the desk. "On the other hand, I couldn't legally hold them any longer. Not without more evidence."

"What about Mrs. Brodie's identification?"

"That's no longer in doubt. They have admitted they were on the street, and Genik says he saw her too. But were they guilty thieves running from the scene of the crime? Or were they just, as they said, in a hurry to get back to their digs and stow their gifts?"

"And the Davies brothers? How do they fit in? They do have at least one article that belonged to Dr. Brandwein."

Jack shook his head like a dog shaking off water. "I sure would like to find that Leroy."

"And I'd like to have another chat with Rosa. She directed us last time; maybe she has other ideas as to where Leroy might go to ground. I'll see if I can get Cal to come with me. He might be able to find out things I can't."

"Good idea. And I'm going to get McCready to come to Dr. Brandwein's house and revisit the scene of the crime. It might look different to my dull eyes. I'll also bring in the young lad, Howard Zweit, who found Brandwein. He might have more to say if he's not talking to an officer who is captivated by the drama of the scene."

I could see McCready was one officer who would not be recommended for further promotion by Jack Murdoch.

"Charlotte, what do you want to do about the cufflink that Marko Ryga says is a family heirloom? He's taken it with him, I'm sure."

"That's next on my list. I'm going to pay Mrs. Calder another visit. I feel as if I've stuck my fingers into a spider's web. All the strands are sticky and interconnected. At some point, the spider will fall out."

"It's a tangled web, all right."

Groan.

CHAPTER FORTY-FOUR

THE SECOND SITTING was almost done when I arrived at the café, and it was jammed as usual. It looked as if they had squeezed in a few more places at the long table. There was definitely a sense of sated hunger. People were chatting to one another in a friendly-looking way.

I went in by the side door. Gramps was at the kitchen table, peeling potatoes. He didn't hear me come in, and I went over to him and shouted in his ear.

"Hey! You're supposed to be resting!"

He hardly paused. "Hey yourself. I'm not deaf. And I am resting. This is a very relaxing job."

Cal was disposing of some dinnerware at the sink, and he looked over his shoulder. "He's on work-to-rule orders. He isn't allowed to hurry or get tense. If there is the slightest sign of either, he'll be sent back to barracks."

Gramps dropped one of the naked potatoes into the bucket Cal had provided for him. "I have to relay a message to you from Hilliard. He had to deal with some pressing business, and he will see you later today."

"What pressing business?"

"He didn't say."

"The children?"

"Maybe."

Another shorn potato fell into the bucket.

"Speaking of pressing business, how did it go today?" Gramps added.

"Dr. Brandwein has died."

Cal heard me, and he turned around in shock. "Sorry to hear that."

"We still don't know where the Davies boys fit into the picture. I was wondering if you could come back with me to the UNIA Hall, Cal. It is really important that we locate Leroy. Unless we clear this up, the doctor's death can make things worse for them."

"I was going to tell you, I did drop into the Methodist church, but they didn't have any information. The minister is very much aware of who comes to the church, and he didn't know the boys. So, no go there."

"Okay. Thanks for doing that anyway."

Cal started to remove his apron. "Give me ten minutes and we can leave. Mr. Frayne, I'm leaving you in charge. When Pearl finishes with the cash, tell her everything is prepped for dinner. She doesn't have to do a thing. Wilf is out all afternoon, so he won't be here to interfere, and if Hilliard gets back before I do, just say I've taken off with Charlotte." He winked at Gramps. "Make sure he knows what that means and doesn't get the wrong idea."

Gramps made a face. "A little competition never hurt the wooing. Increases the appetite."

"What! Cut it out, you two. I'm beginning to feel like a morsel or something."

They both laughed. Men!

Cal was as good as his word and was ready to go in five minutes. We went out via the side door, but this time I was ready. I made sure there was nobody heading toward us on the sidewalk. The lone man who was walking in our direction was actually reading a book as he walked. Good story, I presumed. It was us who had to avoid a collision. Out of the way, all you bookworms.

We hurried on. I filled him on encountering Rosa and how she had directed me to the hovel where we'd found the boys had holed up.

"We can go back there and check, but I doubt he'd return to the same place. He's on the run."

"I agree. Let's see what Charley has to say first." He glanced over at me. "Sorry I ran out on you last time. There was somebody I needed to talk to."

"Violet?"

"Er ... yes, as a matter of fact."

"I had the feeling you both sort of fancied each other. Was I wrong?"

He stuttered again. "No. I suppose not."

"Why don't you ask her out? I'll bet she'd be only too happy."

He didn't answer for a moment, and I wondered if he'd even heard me. I was about to repeat what I'd said when he spoke, so quietly I almost didn't hear him.

"Where would it go, Charlotte? What future could we possibly have?"

"I don't know what you mean. You have a good, steady job. I'll bet the fellows would take you on as a partner if you wanted. It wouldn't be lucrative for you — they don't make a big profit, as you know — but they're well respected and popular. That counts for something, don't you think?"

He had an expression on his face I couldn't quite read.

"It's got nothing to do with my wage-earning capabilities."

254 • MAUREEN JENNINGS

"What then?"

"Let's just say I'm not good marriage material. Women get to see that pretty quickly."

I didn't have a clue what he was referring to, but it was clear any further pushing on my part would be intrusive. I let it go, and we continued on without speaking.

CHARLEY DYER WAS in his office and welcomed us warmly.

"No sign of the lad?" he asked me.

"Not yet, unfortunately."

"How's his brother?"

"Still not good. But given his state, the police might be willing to suspend sentence against Leroy on compassionate grounds."

This was not likely, but I thought I knew Jack Murdoch well enough by now to know he would do everything in his power to make it so.

"Is Rosa here?" I asked. "She seems to be a friend of the boys'. We thought if we talked to her again, something new might emerge."

Dyer shook his head. "Haven't seen her. Not since you were here last. Matter of fact, several of the young folk haven't turned up since you were here. I guess you might call them officialdom shy."

"Good grief. I hope that's not a permanent thing."

"Probably not. We'll have to see. I've always maintained a place where they don't have to worry. Where they can be themselves, if you know what I mean."

I did and I didn't. This was new territory to me.

To my relief, Cal stepped up to the plate.

"Charley, did you notice either of the lads with a particular friend? Somebody who might know where he'd hide out? It's really important."

Dyer lifted his chin and contemplated the ceiling. Then he returned to earth and beamed at Cal.

"You know what? It just came to me. A few months back, there was a fellow who was coming quite regularly. He liked to sit in on the discussion groups mostly. Leroy seemed to take to him and vice versa. He looked like he was teaching the young fellow something or other. They'd sit for hours on end, heads together, Leroy writing down notes in a notebook the man gave him. Mind you, I'm not what you'd call a political man. Can't be in this job. But I was getting a bit worried at one point because I did know this man was a follower of that anarchist philosophy."

"He was an anarchist?" I said. "What was his name?" Dyer didn't answer. I could see he was ambivalent about whether or not to let me into the inner workings of his club.

Cal tried another approach to the question. "Does this fellow still come here?"

"Haven't seen him for weeks. I mean, this centre is open to anybody. It's mostly funded by the city. That said, as you can see, a lot of Black folks come here regularly. It's a real meeting place for them. People who aren't Black aren't always comfortable with that, and they don't stick around."

"Charley, this could be important," Cal said. "Do you remember the man's name?"

"Hmm. Richard something … Fox? No, that's not right."

He stopped. I helped him out.

"Wolfe? Was it Richard *Wolfe*?"

CHAPTER FORTY-FIVE

OF COURSE IT was, and it made complete sense that Wolfe had indeed helped the boys escape from the jail. Richard Wolfe, the anarchist who was in the cells at the same time as Leroy and Jerome and who rooted for them as they made their escape. If he'd had this prior close relationship with Leroy, I was positive he would know where we could find him.

Dyer had no address for Wolfe, but he suggested we check with the Young Communist League headquarters on College Street.

"He's likely on their membership roll."

It wasn't too far away, and Cal and I headed there immediately.

Dyer seemed to have warmed up to me; I wasn't sure why, but he shook hands heartily.

"Come back and visit. We could set up a talk for you. I'm sure the kids would be interested in hearing about your line of work."

I didn't know about that. Lost jewellery? Lost lovers? Lost hopes? However, I told him I would be in touch.

ON THE WAY there, I explained to Cal how I had come to be acquainted with Rick Wolfe. He laughed.

"You're a little tiger, aren't you? Let's hope he doesn't sue you."

"Not with this aiding and abetting suspicion hanging over his head, he won't. Never mind that he's with a dicey group and I'm an upholder of the law."

"Funny thing is, Charlotte, I've always been attracted to the anarchist philosophy. Quite idealistic and Christian, when you get down to it. Equality for all."

"Maybe. Too bad they don't always practise what they preach."

He shrugged. "Who does?"

THE YOUNG COMMUNIST League was located in an unpretentious building squeezed between a florist shop and a Romanian grill, currently closed. The florist shop was named Evergreen. We didn't wait to ascertain if they were a thriving concern but went straight into the foyer of the building, which had the rather grand name of Balmoral Chambers.

According to the notice board in the foyer, Balmoral Chambers housed an eclectic mix of tenants, each with an intellectual bent. On the first floor was the Jordan Chess and Bridge Club. The adjoining space was taken by the Lord Reading Club, and next to that Mr. Oscar Clarke offered vocal lessons. The Young Communist League occupied two rooms on the third floor. Cal and I climbed the stairs — no elevator here. Everything seemed clean and well cared for, but it was quiet. Nobody practising their scales with Mr. Clarke; nobody running off to deliver the latest issue of *The Young Worker*, which, according to the sign on the door, was published here.

We paused at the landing to catch our breath.

"Shall we?" I said to Cal.

Without discussing it, we fell into a reversal of roles. It was my turn to take the initiative.

I rapped hard on the door. It had a bevelled glass panel, and there was no light coming through. No sound either.

I knocked again, and this time I tried the door handle. The door opened at once without protest. I went into the room, Cal close behind me.

The space was long and narrow, lined on three sides by bookshelves. There was a table in the centre and several chairs. Handy for earnest meetings. A desk with a typewriter sat by the far window. No people. No diligent secretary typing away. No dedicated communist, young or old. I glimpsed large framed photographs on the wall. One of them for sure was the dignified and hirsute Karl Marx.

"Hello? Anybody home?"

There was no answer.

"What do you think, Cal?"

"Let's try that one."

He indicated another door just to the right of us. There was a large sign at eye level that said, PRIVATE.

"Let me," said Cal, and he stepped forward, rapped hard, and called out loudly. "Hello! We're looking for Richard Wolfe. Rick? Calvin Greene here."

This was not the time to question him about his acquaintance with the man we were looking for, but I was jolted. He certainly hadn't admitted to it earlier.

"Rick?"

The door was opened almost at once, and on the threshold was my former adversary, Richard Wolfe himself. He stepped out and closed the door behind him.

He peered at us through his thin glasses. "Yes?" He saw Cal, and he actually smiled. "Calvin. What are you doing here? Don't tell me you've seen the light."

Cal grinned back. "You'll be the first to know if that

happens, Rick. I'm here with my friend Miss Frayne. I believe you've already met."

Wolfe scowled at me and lifted his little finger. "We have indeed. And I'm still considering a lawsuit."

"We've come to talk to young Leroy Davies. Is he here?" continued Cal.

"What makes you think I would know?"

"We went to UNIA Hall, and Charley Dyer said you and the lad were good pals."

"So what? I've got lots of pals, and I don't know where they all are every minute of the day."

It was an impasse, and we were all awkwardly clustered around the door at this point.

Cal addressed Wolfe. "Listen, Rick. Can we sit down and talk about this? I can vouch for Charlotte's honesty and good intentions."

Another scowl. "Good intentions are usually as effective as goose farts."

I hadn't heard that expression before, but I got the point. I thought Shakespeare would have appreciated it.

I shifted ever so slightly to be closer to the door and raised my voice. "I am in touch with the Davies case, and the situation has changed. Some new information has come forth."

"Such as?"

I don't know how things would have resolved, but at that moment, the door opened. Leroy poked his head out.

"What information?"

Wolfe tried to push him back. "I told you to stay quiet."

Leroy didn't succumb. He was looking at me desperately.

"What's changed?" he asked again.

"Jerome's condition is listed as stable. It's not that. It's something else." I indicated the table. "Can we sit down?"

Wolfe addressed Leroy. "All right, comrade? Do you want to hear what she has to say?"

"Yes, please."

Wolfe didn't look too happy about the boy's response. I think he preferred intractable opposition. He knew how to deal with that.

"Okay then. We've got thirty-five minutes until the secretary returns."

We trooped over to the table, Wolfe taking the chair at the head. Leroy sat at his left, and Cal and I took the chairs across from him. All we needed was a gavel and perhaps a couple of wigs.

Leroy's gaze was fixed on me.

"I'm so sorry about what happened at the hospital, Leroy. I didn't know there was a constable on duty."

He gave a small shrug. "I saw what you did. Thanks."

Wolfe leaned his arms on the table. "I should establish for the record, Miss Frayne, that I am now acting as counsel for Leroy and Jerome Davies. It is utterly shameful that they were not allowed representation previously."

"I agree with you, Mr. Wolfe. That is why it is so important that Leroy agrees to return to custody. The case has taken on a different twist."

"Which is?"

"Two men have been questioned concerning the break-in of Dr. Brandwein's house. They claim that two of the articles that were alleged to be stolen were in fact given to them as gifts by Dr. Brandwein."

Wolfe leaned back in his chair. "Pull the other leg, why don't you? Don't tell me the doctor has gone along with that."

"Unfortunately, Dr. Brandwein can't corroborate anything. He died this morning."

That knocked the wind out of his sails. Temporarily.

"At least you've got two other culprits in the picture. And you said you have recovered two of the articles allegedly stolen. What were the other things?"

"One other. A silver matchbox. It was found in Leroy's rucksack."

Leroy burst out. "I told you, we picked it up in the laneway. We didn't pinch it."

Wolfe reached over and put his hand on Leroy's arm. It was a kind gesture, and I liked him better for it.

Leroy stared at me. "Is it true what you said, that Dr. Brandwein has kicked the bucket?"

"Yes, it is true."

"How? What happened to him?"

"He had a stroke. He was found unconscious in his house. He was taken to hospital, but he didn't recover."

"When was that? I mean, what time of day was he found?"

There was a note of urgency in Leroy's voice, and I saw Wolfe picked up on that too. Once again, he touched the boy's arm. This time more as warning than comfort.

"According to the police report, Dr. Brandwein was discovered by one of his pupils, who came to the house shortly after eight-thirty. The police officer was of the opinion that the doctor disturbed the intruders in the act and the shock is what brought on the stroke. We don't know if that is true. The two men who have admitted to being there say he was fine when they left."

I could see Leroy was working out something in his mind, but I had no idea what it was.

"What time was it when the two guys came by the doctor's house?"

"They say it was just before eight o'clock."

"And he was alive when they left?"

"So they say."

"But they could be lying?"

"Yes."

Wolfe asserted himself. "Look, miss. Leroy here is mightily upset about his only brother. He has agreed he will go back to the coppers if he can see his brother first. You said previously you would guarantee that, but it didn't seem like you could."

"I'm sorry. I didn't know there would be a constable at the hospital."

"She helped me," said Leroy. He actually grinned. "Good trick, miss."

Wolfe made a little *harrumph* sound. "Be that as it may, as I am now Leroy's counsel, I want to make sure that doesn't happen again. How can we make sure it would be safe for him?"

"Is there a telephone here? I can ring the detective in charge and see what he advises."

"Is that Murdoch?"

"Yes."

"All right. He's one of the few cops I trust. But make it clear, Leroy will only come in if he's allowed to see his brother."

"Okay."

I knew Jack Murdoch was thoroughly honourable, but he was also restricted by laws. I dearly hoped I wasn't making another empty promise.

"In fact, it's better if I talk to him myself," said Wolfe. "You make the connection, and I'll do the talking."

"All right."

"Telephone's over here."

Wolfe directed me to the desk. There was a small timer beside the telephone and a tin labelled "English breakfast tea."

MARCH ROARS • 263

"I'll have to charge you ten cents a minute," said Wolfe, and he wound up the timer at the ready. He must have caught my expression because he shrugged. "Not up to me. The League keeps track of every penny. Telephone lines are expensive."

He dragged over another chair and pulled it close to me. I was glad to be put through to Jack Murdoch quite quickly.

"Hello, Charlotte. What's happening?

"Jack, I am in contact with Leroy Davies."

Jack whistled through his teeth. "Where is he? Can you tell me?"

"Not at the moment. Richard Wolfe is now his counsel."

"*The* Richard Wolfe?"

"One and the same. He's sitting right beside me, as a matter of fact, and he would like to speak to you himself. Is that all right?"

"Put him on."

I handed the phone to Wolfe and moved out of the way.

His voice became loud and hearty.

"Jack. Rick here. Yes, as Miss Frayne said I am now the counsel for the Davies brothers. They clearly need to have proper representation in court if these charges are to go through ... Yes, I know they shouldn't have run off the way they did ... He's sorry. He has agreed to turn himself in ... Yes, I'm glad too. However, there is one condition. He will have the opportunity to see his brother first."

There was a rather long pause, and I wondered what Jack was saying. Both Cal and Leroy were watching us.

"All right. Yes, I will be the guarantor. No running off this time. Okay. We'll come to College Street ... Yes, I agree to those terms ... Yes, she's right here." He held out the receiver to me. "He wants to talk to you." He got up quickly and went to the table. "Come on, Leroy, we're going to the hospital."

I took the phone. "Yes, Jack."

"Charlotte, I'm going out on a limb bargaining like this. Legally, the boy's a fugitive. What's your sense? Will he try for another runner?"

"I don't think so."

"All right. I'm sending a police car to pick you up. I'd feel better if you went with them. Are you okay with that?"

"Yes, I am. Absolutely."

"Good. I'll allow them an hour at the hospital, then they will come here. I'm going over to the Brandwein house right now to have another look for myself. I'll meet you back at the station."

"Excellent."

"Oh, by the way, are you at the Young Communist League centre?"

"Yes."

"Thought so."

We hung up.

"We'd better hurry," said Wolfe. "I said we'd meet them on the street. He's sending a police car. I don't want them to know we're in here."

We hustled out, and as we went past the portrait of Tim Buck, I swear he winked.

As we were leaving, the secretary arrived. It was young Rosa, the brilliant musician who obviously had to make a living somehow. She looked startled to see me, but there was no time to have a chat. I assumed she had helped arrange the present refuge. Wolfe hustled Leroy out of the door, but he managed to give Rosa a sweet smile and a hurried, "It'll be all right."

CHAPTER FORTY-SIX

CAL SAID HE had to get back to the café. I knew he could have more time if he wanted, but I guessed he had no desire to get into a police car.

He reached out to Leroy and ruffled the boy's hair.

"You'll be all right, little brother. I promise."

With a salute to me, Cal strode off. Leroy watched him for a moment. They were indeed brothers.

The police car came into sight almost immediately and pulled up to the curb for us to get in.

A uniformed officer was driving. Nobody I'd met before, and he was rigorously proper. I took the passenger seat, and Wolfe and Leroy climbed in the back. The officer introduced himself as Constable Bosen.

"I will drop you off in front of the hospital. I will return in one hour to pick you up. I will be waiting in the same place. From there, I will take you to police headquarters to meet with Detective Murdoch."

He didn't say, *Is that clear?* But he might as well have. He had his instructions.

Leroy didn't respond, but I could tell he wasn't too happy with the brief amount of time he was being allotted. Wolfe nodded his acknowledgement. We drove off along what was now a busy College Street. There was no siren wailing, no light flashing. Nobody noticed this extremely fraught trip.

JACK HAD OBVIOUSLY telephoned ahead to prepare the hospital, and Dr. Sterling himself was waiting in the foyer. I made the introductions.

"The young man is still under sedation, so he may be a little unresponsive, but we have seen some progress today. He has more sensation in his legs." He was addressing me the entire time. "He has a speech impediment, I notice. A cleft palate." I nodded. "Should have had that taken care of at birth. Might be too late to do much now, but when he's recovered sufficiently from the concussion, we can see what we can do."

Leroy stiffened, but Wolfe was keeping a tight grip on his arm, and he didn't say anything.

"We can only have two people at a time in the room. Too much equipment. Who's it to be?"

This time, Leroy spoke up. "Her and me."

I wasn't sure what this meant exactly, but I agreed. Dr. Sterling led the way through the now docile swing door.

"I'll be right here if you need me," said Wolfe.

The hospital room was the same as when I'd seen it last. Jerome was the same inert figure hooked up to an oxygen-dispensing machine and a heart monitor. Leroy had entered the room ahead of me, but he stopped so suddenly in his tracks we almost collided.

"Is he alive?"

Dr. Sterling was right behind us, and he came forward and walked over to the bed, bent over briefly, then, for the first time, smiled at Leroy.

"He's sleeping, or rather he's in a half sleep. Speak to him clearly and loudly and he will be able to hear you."

Leroy didn't move. "What shall I say?"

"Anything. Say who you are first." He beckoned. "Come closer. No need to be nervous. Miss Frayne, why don't you take that chair over there. I'll get out of the way. Come, Leroy. You can hold his hand if you want to."

Rather slowly, Leroy approached the bedside.

"That's right," said the doctor encouragingly. He leaned over the injured boy and spoke in his ear. "Jerome, it's Dr. Sterling here. You've got a visitor. Your brother has come to see you."

Jerome had seemed to be so deeply asleep nothing would have wakened him, but even from where I was now seated, I could see his eyelids begin to flutter. The doctor stepped back and indicated to Leroy that he should come closer.

Leroy moved over quickly, enfolding his brother's limp hand in both of his.

"Jay, it's Lee here. How're you doing? What a silly sod you are. How could you crack your noggin like that? What am I going to do with you?" He perched on the edge of the bed so his face was close to Jerome's. "I suppose you expect I'll look after you now for the rest of your life. Well, forget that. We're brothers, remember. I'm the oldest. You're the one supposed to look after me in my old age. So, liven up, you silly darkie. Time to rise and shine."

His words gushed out of him until there were no more.

After a few minutes, Jerome managed to come to the surface sufficiently to say something that only Leroy could understand. It was an effort, and he fell back into sleep right after. Dr. Sterling patted Leroy on the shoulder.

"Keep talking to him. We think people can still hear even if they don't respond. I'll be back shortly."

Leroy sat beside his brother, not letting go of his hand, continuing to talk, making promises, scolding him lovingly, reminding him of the adventures they'd had together. More were to come. I made myself as invisible as I could. At first, it seemed as if Leroy would go on forever, but even he finally ran out of steam. We sat in silence, and he held on to his brother's hand.

Finally, Dr. Sterling reappeared, examined the boy in the bed, checked the vitals machines, and then smiled at both of us.

"This has been good for him, but he also needs his rest." He patted Leroy's shoulder. "Try not to fret too much. He's got a good strong constitution, and I'm sure he'll pull through." He addressed me again. "I'll give you a few more minutes, then you had better join that other chap in the foyer. I promised the detective I'd have you out of here within the hour."

He left.

Leroy looked over at me. The anguish in his eyes ripped at my heart.

"He's all I've got, miss. I don't know what I'll do if he goes. It's like he's being swept out to sea and there's nothing I can do about it."

I offered him what meagre comfort I could. "The ones we love are those we come back for."

CHAPTER FORTY-SEVEN

NOBODY SPOKE DURING the drive back to the police station. When we arrived, there was another constable waiting, and he directed us to Jack's office immediately.

Jack was back to wearing his sling, and I thought he looked a little haggard. He stood up at once.

"Please sit down, everybody."

We did, even Rick Wolfe. He had his hand on Leroy's arm the entire time. The boy had withdrawn into some interior space since seeing his brother, and when he sat down, he stared at the floor.

Jack bent toward him. "Leroy. I first want to say how sorry I am about what happened to your brother."

No response, then Wolfe spoke for him.

"We have seen Jerome, and as agreed, Leroy has returned to custody. However, as his counsel, I request an immediate release to my recognizance."

"I have already arranged that," answered Jack. "You will need to go the duty desk, and the constable will take down the particulars."

"Will I have to go back to the cells?" asked Leroy, his voice low.

"You will not. As of today, Mr. Wolfe will be responsible for your complying with the court conditions until such time as they change."

"When will we get a hearing?" asked Rick.

"Hopefully as soon as two days hence. In the meantime, I assume you have somewhere Leroy can stay."

"I've got a spare room in my flat. He can stay with me."

"Good. I should say, I have also brought in the Children's Aid Society. If necessary, they will do an assessment of your living arrangements."

"Ha. Won't be necessary. I know them. They know me."

Jack addressed the boy. "Leroy, do you agree with this arrangement?"

Leroy looked up at him and, for a moment, there was a flash of the spunk I'd seen before.

"Is it a choice between staying with Mr. Wolfe or going into the cells again?"

Jack answered him patiently. "No. You can go to the Children's Aid shelter until the case is settled, if you prefer."

"No thanks. We was there before. Worse than prison, if you ask me."

"All right then, Mr. Wolfe it is."

Wolfe tapped Leroy on the head. "Smart decision, lad. We'll get along just fine. I've got lots of books you haven't even read yet."

Rather to my surprise, Leroy looked happy to hear that. I presumed Mr. Lenin awaited.

"Rick, I will keep you apprised of any new developments," said Jack. "Expect a court date within the next two days."

The constable came to the door to escort the two of them to the duty desk. Just as they were going out, Leroy turned to Jack.

"Am I still going to get the strap? And will they strap Jerome when he gets better?"

I could see Jack clench his teeth. "Let's say I will make sure you are not punished for something you didn't do."

It wasn't an unequivocal answer, and the boy knew it. I understood the position Jack was in, but my own anger flared up again. Sometimes, the law is truly an ass.

Jack closed the door behind them and returned to his desk.

"I've got some quite good news. Or, I should say, better news."

"That would be welcome."

"I went to the Brandwein house and did a careful walk-around. The back door lock was indeed not operating, but it looked as if it was stuck rather than in any way forced as my good fellow McCready reported. The doorjamb itself was quite unmarked."

"Why did the Zweit boy and the officer both think there was a break-in?"

"I have pressed McCready to be as specific as he is capable of being. He said that the boy declared the door was ajar when he went into the kitchen. They all seem to have jumped to the conclusion that there had been a burglary. Master Zweit said the menorah and the tallit were both missing from the shelf, and this confirmed it in McCready's mind. He was only too willing to go with a more dramatic story than the one that is more likely. Given that the lock is faulty, it makes sense that the doctor didn't close the door properly after Genik and Ryga left. He collapsed in the hallway. We don't know what time, but it seemed as if he was heading away from the kitchen."

"He might have been going to the telephone."

"True."

"Have we determined whether not there was anybody else in the house?"

"I was able to question the housekeeper, Mrs. Ricci. She was shocked to the core at the very idea that her employer might be having any kind of dalliance. Dr. Brandwein was a most respectable man. A widower. Kind and generous to a fault."

"Did you broach the idea that he had given his menorah and tallit as gifts to two down-and-out men?"

"I did. All she could say was that he had seemed to be in a strange state of mind recently. He was most upset about the news coming in from Europe and commented to her on more than one occasion that it was dangerous to be a Jew these days. She herself is a Methodist, and she indicated that she would approve of Dr. Brandwein changing his faith. This had not been broached between them, however. This does add a touch of plausibility to Genik's story of being given the articles as gifts."

"So now the only concrete piece of evidence linking the boys to the house is the matchbox?"

"Correct."

"Not deserving of ten strokes of the strap, surely?"

"I agree. As I said, I have put in a requisition to Judge Carter to suspend the sentence until such time as we have completed the investigation."

"Do you think he will agree?"

"I'm not sure. He has a reputation for being very set in his ways. Once his mind is made up, he's not easily swayed."

The intercom buzzed and interrupted us. Jack answered. "Yes. Good. Bring him down, please." He hung up and smiled at me. "The young lad who found Dr. Brandwein is here. I thought we'd go over his statement again. See if there is anything new we can determine. I'm not too hopeful, but you never know. Will you be my recorder again, Charlotte?"

"Wouldn't miss it."

There was a discreet tap on the door, and the constable ushered in Master Howard Zweit. The young lad was extremely nervous and actually stumbled over his own feet as he entered. He was wearing a cloth cap, which he pulled off immediately, releasing his thick, dark hair into a shock of curls.

"You asked to see me, sir?"

"Have a seat. This is Miss Frayne, who will be taking notes while we talk. You'll be able to see them afterward and see if they are correct."

"Yes, sir. Thank you, sir."

Jack took McCready's report from the folder, placed it on his desk, and skimmed through it. He was not being intimidating in any way, but Master Zweit was almost disintegrating before my eyes. He was desperately twisting his cap.

Jack addressed him. "When the police officer questioned you, you said you had come to see Dr. Brandwein for a tutoring session."

"Yes, sir. That is correct, sir."

"Isn't that rather early in the morning for tutoring?"

"We meet at that time so I get to school for my first class."

"Were you late for your tutoring session?"

"I beg your pardon, sir?"

"I was asking if you were late. You say you found Dr. Brandwein unconscious on the floor, and you immediately went to the telephone and rang for an ambulance. Our station did not report receiving a call until eight-forty. Given a reasonable delay in ascertaining the nature of the situation, I would say you arrived at the house past eight. Hence my question."

Howard twisted his cap even harder, and his face had turned red. "I might have been a little late, sir. I didn't actually check the time. When I saw what state the doctor was in, I ran to the telephone, but it took me a few minutes to find the right telephone number."

Jack leaned toward the boy. "It's not a crime to be late for a tutoring session, Howard. I was always late for school when I was your age. My father despaired of me."

I caught the look of relief that flitted across the lad's face. This was safe territory. The cap-twisting slowed down.

"There is something I am more concerned about," continued Jack. "Dr. Brandwein had a silver matchbox in his den. It appears to have been stolen. Would you know anything about that?"

Howard gulped. "Why do you say it was stolen, sir?"

"Because it was found in the possession of a newsboy. Mrs. Ricci says the last time she saw it was in the den, on the table."

"Has the newsboy confessed?"

"He says he and his brother found it several days ago in the laneway nearby. Can you say anything about that?"

For a moment, Howard stared down at the floor. He muttered something that I couldn't hear.

"Sorry, would you mind repeating that?"

I don't know if he was startled by the question or if I'd suddenly stepped into his mother's shoes. Regardless, he straightened up. A man of honour ready to receive his punishment.

"What I said, miss, was that I was the one who took the matchbox."

"You're saying you stole it?" Jack asked.

"No, sir. I borrowed it. I like to smoke, you see. But my mama doesn't approve, so I only have a cigarette when I'm far from the house. Last week, it was Dr. Brandwein who was a little late. I was waiting in his den. I really craved a ciggie, so I thought I could have a puff before he came down. I had a cigarette, all right, but I realized I had no matches. I picked up the matchbox, but before I could strike a match, I heard him coming downstairs. I put the box in my pocket, intending to light up later. Dr. Brandwein never used it. He had one of those fancy new lighters." Howard was starting to weep. I felt sorry for the lad. As the situation had developed, his little act of borrowing was serious, but it was nowhere near as catastrophic as he was currently experiencing it.

Jack gave him some time to collect himself, and finally Howard continued.

"After my lesson, I headed back to school. I was hurrying, but when I stopped so I could have my fag, I discovered I had dropped the matchbox somewhere along the way. Probably in the laneway. It was too late to go back and look for it that day, so I went on to school. After school, I came back and searched for it, but I couldn't find it."

"Did you tell Dr. Brandwein what you had done?"

"No, sir. When I came for my next lesson was when I found him on the floor."

"At any time, have you encountered two young negro boys delivering newspapers?"

"No, sir. Never, sir. There is never anybody about when I come."

Again, Jack leaned forward, and his expression was stern.

"I want you to have a look at the matchbox we have in our possession, and you see if it is the same one that belonged to your tutor. If you are sure it is, then you must say so. If you are not sure, then you must declare as much. All right?"

"Yes, sir."

"How many matches were in the box?"

"Five, sir."

"Are you positive?"

"Yes, sir."

"Very well, Howard. You have done well to own up to this." Jack paused, and his expression was stern. "But what you call borrowing, I call stealing."

"Yes, sir. But I was going to return it, I swear. I didn't even realize I'd put it in my pocket until after."

Frankly, I thought it more likely that Master Zweit had been counting on Dr. Brandwein not noticing the box was missing. But I still felt sorry for him.

"Will you tell my parents, sir?"

"I don't know. We'll have to see what happens next. For now, we'll leave it. Your statement will be typed up by Miss Frayne. I will ask you to look it over and sign the bottom to say these are your own words and what is recorded is true. Do you understand?"

"Yes, sir. Perfectly. Thank you, sir."

"Good. Now I will send for my constable, and he will take you to another room. We will come and get you."

"Yes, sir."

Jack called for the constable, and Howard was led away. When the door closed behind him, Jack grinned at me.

"I remember my first cigarette. I was thirteen, and I *borrowed* it from my father, not realizing how obvious I was being. He caught me in the act. Naturally, he didn't want me to start smoking that soon. His answer was to make me smoke an entire package of cigarettes one after the other. I got violently sick. He thought that would cure me. It did for a while, but when I signed up for the army, smoking was so much a way of life it would have been impossible to resist."

He took his cigarette case out of his pocket and tapped on it. "So, here we are. Fiona doesn't like it, the children beg me to stop, but I can't seem to give it up." He shook out a cigarette then looked over at me. "You don't smoke, do you, Charlotte?"

"I tried when I was young, and it seemed so grown-up and glamorous, but I didn't like it. The smoke burned my throat."

"Does it?" exclaimed Jack. "I suppose you're right. You just get used to it." He lit his cigarette. "Anyway, back to business. What young Howard has said totally corroborates Leroy's statement about finding the matchbox in the laneway." He blew a smoke circle in the air and put his finger through it for emphasis. "I'll go and inform Wolfe. Let's hope Judge Carter will see the escape and assault of a police officer as an understandable attempt to avoid unfair punishment."

"Jack, it seems pretty clear that the boys aren't guilty of theft or breaking and entering, but I'm concerned about one other thing."

"Glozier's statement that he saw them leaving the house?"

"That's it. He was adamant. Not just close to the house, actually coming out of the front yard."

"I don't know what to make of it. Leroy seemed to get pretty intense when we were trying to ascertain the time sequence of Dr. Brandwein's collapse. Did you notice?"

"I did. I'm afraid he's hiding something. It doesn't seem to be theft, so I don't know what it is. Perhaps it's minor."

"Okay. One step at a time. Let's get the poor scamp out of this place."

He left me to type up my notes. The police typewriter had been made available for me, and it was smooth and fast. Better than the dinosaur I had to use back at the office. I thought I'd put in a request for an update. Which reminded me: I hadn't yet heard from Mr. Gilmore. I wondered how he was doing with his mysterious mission.

I sat down at the desk, fed in the paper, and stopped. For fun, I typed the heading: A GRAVE INJUSTICE AVERTED. Detective McCready, move over.

CHAPTER FORTY-EIGHT

ALL THIS TOOK up a couple of hours. Jack filled out the requisition for payment for my services, which was appreciated, and I left. He offered to get me a ride, but I declined. I needed fresh air and a brisk walk.

There was also one more knot in the thread I needed to sort out.

I headed for Gerrard Street. A chat with Maria Johnson, Mrs. Calder's housekeeper, was in order.

The night was dark, although the wind had not yet given up. I had to hold on to my beret. The trees in the park were tossing and swaying like live creatures.

I didn't know what I would encounter at the Calder residence. The front room lights were on, the curtains drawn, and I was only too happy when Maria answered the door in prompt fashion.

"Mrs. Calder isn't at home." Her tone had reverted to unfriendly.

"It's you I wanted to speak to, Maria."

She frowned. "What about?"

"I'd rather not talk to you while I'm on the doorstep."

"I'm busy. I'm preparing for tomorrow's dinner. What is it?"

"It's about Mr. Toban. Or more specifically, your visit to Mr. Toban yesterday. The pawnbroker."

That got through, and she stepped back quickly.

"Come in. The mistress is at her club, and she won't be back for another half an hour."

I followed her into the hall. My comment had thrown her into great agitation.

"I'm in the kitchen; follow me," she said, and she led the way, almost running down the hall.

Once there, she closed the door. She actually picked up a rolling pin that was on the counter, and I had a fleeting fantasy that she could easily clobber me on the head. However, I could see she had been in the middle of rolling out some pastry, and she wasn't hostile so much as upset.

"I'm making some veal pies for dinner," she explained. "The mistress likes them, and they'll keep for a few days."

I wondered if she had submitted the recipe to the cookbook.

She started to wipe her hands on her apron. "What did you want to talk to me about, miss?"

I saw no reason to beat around the bush.

"I happened to be in Mr. Toban's shop on another case, and I saw that he had a cufflink that exactly fit the description that Mrs. Calder had given me. She'd said it was stolen from her jewellery box. There was also a charm bracelet. It had to be the one Mrs. Calder had described to me. She claims it too was stolen. Then I see you going into the shop some time later. What else could I think, Maria, except that you were, in fact, the thief and that you had taken the items to be pawned. Is that the case?"

Maria didn't look at me but concentrated on smoothing out the pastry.

"No, that it is not the case."

"What is, then? Mr. Toban said that he received the items from a woman who was dressed in widow's weeds. Well-to-do, by his account. By chance, I saw you entering the same shop. That is true, is it not?"

"Yes, that was me, but it's not what you think."

"All right. Enlighten me."

"I was just there to retrieve the things. I'm not the one who brings them in to pawn."

"Who is, then?"

"The mistress. Mrs. Calder."

"What? You're saying Mrs. Calder pawns her own things? Why?"

Maria wiped her face with her apron. She left a smudge of flour on her cheek.

"I've been with Mrs. Calder for almost twenty years now, and she's been very good to me. However, not long after her husband died, she started to act quite strangely. Finally, me and some of the ladies from the Pioneer Club persuaded her to go to a nerve doctor. He said she was suffering from something that happened long ago. He had a word for it. *Torma*, or some such."

"Trauma?"

"Yes, that sounds like the word he used. He explained it as some kind of hurt to the brain."

"Do you know what he was referring to?"

"No, she didn't either. He said she had buried the memory somewhere in the bottom of her mind, but it was coming to the surface and causing her to do strange things. Don't ask me what he meant by that because I don't know. She's always going on about her dear father who was so good to her. She's been well-off all her life. No children to worry about. A lovely home. I don't know what could have bothered her like that."

Maria rolled out another piece of pastry with great thumping and vigour. However, she seemed eager to unburden herself.

"The nerve doctor gave her some medicine, but it doesn't seem to have made much difference. What she has got to doing, you see, is taking things to the pawnshop. The odd thing is, it's always the same two things. Sometimes it's the charm bracelet and sometimes it's the cufflink that belonged to her father. Sometimes it's both."

"Nothing else? No other jewellery?"

"No. Nothing. Just them. When she first said the bracelet was missing, I turned the house upside down. Couldn't find it. Then, mysteriously, it turned up. I just thought she'd misplaced it and was embarrassed to admit it. Nothing more was said. Then, about three weeks or so later, wouldn't you know, the darned thing vanished again. This time, she said the cufflink had gone too. More searching. Nothing. Then, miraculously, both things showed up. Nothing said. Lo and behold, didn't they vanish again a fortnight later. That's when the mistress started to say as how somebody must have stolen them. She went to the trouble of hiring a private detective like you. An older woman, it was. As soon as she started to make inquiries, didn't the bracelet and the cufflink reappear. But not long after, I was brushing off the mistress's coat and didn't I find a ticket in her the pocket. A pawnbroker's note. As you can imagine, miss, I didn't know what to make of it. She doesn't need money, I know that for certain. So I decided to visit the shop myself and see what was what. Sure enough, there was the bracelet and the cufflink. I didn't ask questions at that point, I just paid the pledge and got them back. I returned them to the jewellery box. The mistress didn't even seem to notice. Two weeks later, same story. That's when she hired you."

"How many times has this happened?"

"At least five. So, you see, nothing's stolen. If you'll just give me your bill, Miss Frayne, I'll do the same with you."

"Have you tried to confront her?"

"I've been afraid to. She can get so highly strung. She'll collapse for a week sometimes, usually because she thinks somebody in her club has been rude to her. It's never true. I thought it better not to say anything. She forgets, you see."

She lifted the pastry and placed it on top of the pie dish and began to flute it.

"What do I owe you, miss?"

"I don't think my job is over yet, Maria."

I wasn't totally sure what I meant by that, but to my mind, this story wasn't finished. Although Maria was scornful of the nerve doctor, as she called him, I thought there might be truth to what he'd said. I knew similar things happened to returned soldiers. If so, what was the long-ago shell shock that was infecting Mrs. Calder's mind? Besides, I couldn't get the strange coincidence of Marko possessing the other cufflink out of my mind.

Maria was busy with the pastry shell.

"Does the name Marko Ryga mean anything to you, Maria?"

She hardly paused. "No. Should it?"

"Not necessarily. Another question, if you don't mind. In what year was Mrs. Calder born?"

This put a temporary halt to the energetic pie-making.

"What? Why do you want to know?"

"I'm just trying to work out some things for my own sake."

"She was born in 1865. March 15. I know that exactly because her birthday is coming up soon, and she likes it when I make her a special cake. She invites her Pioneer Club. Every year."

That would make Emmeline seventy-two years old this year. She'd said she was nine when her father died suddenly.

Did this have anything to do with what the doctor called an early trauma? Had to be. I didn't yet see how that explained her strange behaviour, but I knew I was on to something. Of course, that did *not* explain how the young Marko Ryga, recently arrived from Manitoba, had supposedly come into possession of a family heirloom that was identical to the one belonging to Mrs. Calder. I believed him when he said he'd inherited the cufflink in his possession from his grandfather. He'd mentioned that his grandfather had died two years earlier at the age of seventy-four.

That would make the grandfather and Mrs. Calder roughly the same age. This could mean nothing or everything, I'd yet to find out. Perhaps my two cases were linked after all.

CHAPTER FORTY-NINE

I DIDN'T STAY any longer at the Calder residence. Maria repeated that Mrs. Calder was due home at any time, and I had no desire to encounter her. I promised to come back the next day to settle my account, and I left.

It had been a full day, and I was only too happy to slip through the side door of the Paradise and walk into the warm, bright kitchen. Clean-up had pretty much finished by now, and I was greeted by a chorus of shouts and various exclamations from the men who were seated at the table.

Where've you been? was the dominant theme.

"Earning a living, unlike you lie-abeds."

Hilliard had been putting away clean dishes in the cupboard, but he came over at once and gave me a gratifying hug and a kiss.

"You're late, and you look tired. Come and sit down."

Cal too had stood up, and he went immediately to the stove.

"She needs some hot soup. I'll heat it up."

"As long as it's nothing fishy, Cal. I've been dealing with something fishy all day." That brought a burst of laughter from all of them. My Gramps hadn't stood up, but he waved at me to join him. Unfortunately, laughing at my feeble joke had brought on his cough. Hill pulled me in close, not dropping his arm from my shoulders, and we went over to the table.

"I'd better get you home, Gramps."

"Don't fuss. I'm fine. I want to hear what you've been up to. I'm sure we all do."

Cal brought over a bowl of soup.

"Pea soup. Recipe courtesy of Mrs. Henderson, one of your Pioneer ladies."

"How did the stewed eels turn out?"

That gave Gramps his opening. "They slithered down real good."

Cal gave him a playful swat on the back of his head. "They did not slither."

"True," Hilliard joined in. "In fact, they were rather chewy and not slithery at all."

Cal gazed at him in dismay. "Chewy? Nobody said they were chewy."

Dissection of the meals was an ongoing sport here.

Gramps jumped in to calm the waters. "I, for one, was skeptical, but I liked them a lot. Very subtle fishy taste, but it was more like eating ..." He tailed off, at a loss for words, but I was glad to have missed this particular dining experience. The pea soup, on the other hand, was delicious.

"Wilf had second helpings," said Cal.

"Oh, he'll eat anything," added Hill, rather tactlessly.

This was all very jolly, but I knew how seriously Cal took his job. If the customers weren't almost licking their plates, he worried. I did a little redirect.

"Where *is* Wilf, by the way?"

"He went upstairs," answered Hill. "He said he needed to do more work on his script."

"So, you're going with the play? The one about the strike?"

"We haven't decided. He says now he wants to do something about the demand for justice that resulted in the trek to

Ottawa. As we know, that was a disaster. I still think we need to present something more uplifting."

"I could recite my new limericks," said Gramps. "They're uplifting."

I paused my spoon ostentatiously in mid-air. "Oh no. I thought we'd cured you of writing limericks, Gramps."

"Not at all. I was just resting. Now I'm back to full strength. All creative people need to take a little break between inspirations."

We all groaned at him.

"Go on, then," said Hill. "Give it to us."

"All right." He struck a pose. "Mary had a little lamb, she named it Adolf Hitler. But everywhere that Mary went, that lamb, he always bit her."

We laughed. "I'd say that's awfully prescient of you, Gramps," said Hilliard.

"If I knew what the word meant, I'd say thanks," answered Gramps. "Do you want another?"

"Okay. If you must."

"The last line needs some tinkering, but anyway, here it is: Mary had a little lamb, who learned to be a miner. His job finished, sad to say, when he went on strike for proper pay."

"Oh Lord, Arnie. I thought these were supposed to be uplifting."

Gramps shrugged. "It's what's happening, though, isn't it?"

"Can't you at least make it *glad* to say instead of *sad* to say? Who the hell'd want a miner's job?"

It was my turn to stand up. I carried my bowl to the sink and rinsed it out, dodging Cal on the way, who wanted to do it for me.

"Let's get going, Gramps."

"I thought you were going to tell us what happened today."

"Professional confidentiality forbids it."

"Ha. You mean you want to get home to bed."

"True. Maybe tomorrow morning I'll break the rules and let you in on it. All I am allowed to say now is that our prime minister says Canada will stand with England if there's a war."

"Did he consult with you?"

"Something like that."

"Oh, boy. I'd better go and get my trench tool," said Hilliard.

"Trenches! Don't bother," spluttered Gramps. "There won't be another war. The workers will go on strike and refuse to fight."

"Hey, Mr. Frayne. I suggest you make up another limerick about that. Then we can say *glad* indeed."

"Here's one more." We all sighed in unison, but I suddenly realized that my Gramps's expression had changed. He looked very sad. Hilliard hadn't noticed.

"Go on, Arnie. I'll brace myself."

This time, Gramps didn't strike a pose. "I made up this one a while ago, but it's depressingly relevant again." He bent his head. "Mary had a little boy, who signed up to be a soldier. A letter came one mournful day; her son wouldn't ever be a minute older."

I put my arms around him and pressed my cheek against his.

He was talking about my father.

HILLIARD DROVE US home, and we both fussed over Gramps like two concerned parents. I rather liked the experience, other than being worried about my grandfather. Hill made the night-cap while I put up the goose grease poultice and the oregano steam. Arnie being Arnie, he complained about the unneces-sary fuss, but it was a token protest. His cough was a little better, but in spite of the teasing and the jokes, I knew he was upset by the war talk. Even touching briefly on the loss of his only son always brought back the pain. I had never met the young man who'd fathered me, so it didn't exactly upset me in the same way. I just felt the usual twinge. What would it have been like if Philip Frayne had returned from the war?

I finally tucked Gramps into his bed.

"I don't suppose you're going to tell me a bedtime story as well."

"Finish your drink first ... I'll take the glass. Close your eyes."

He settled himself further down in the bed. I dropped a kiss on his head and switched off the light.

"Once upon a time there was a grumpy old man named Arnie. He had one special and delightful granddaughter who was often forced to take charge of this stubborn old man. In spite of this serious failing, Arnie was so kind and generous, not to mention funny, that all around him loved him dearly ..."

The smile faded from his lips, and he was asleep.

HILLIARD AND I braved the discomfort of my single bed, and as we were finally both drifting off to sleep, he murmured in my ear.

"I enjoyed playing Mom and Dad tonight. We'd make good parents, don't you think?"

He fell asleep before I could answer, which was a good thing because the question had struck a bolt of fear in my heart. I'd avoided marriage and parenthood so far in my life. I couldn't imagine a more daunting job.

CHAPTER FIFTY

Friday, March 12, 1937

THE NEXT MORNING, Hilliard was up and away early. He had to get back to the café. I didn't wait much longer, but as soon as I knew Gramps was mobile and breakfasted, I too left. Maria Johnson had said the usual breakfast hour was eight-thirty. I'd agreed I'd give Mrs. Calder time to enjoy her pancakes and syrup before I returned. I didn't want to wait any longer. There were some matters to be settled, and the sooner the better.

On the way there, I had to make a stop at the House of Industry. I needed to talk with Mrs. Olivia Brodie.

I hoped I was making the right decision. I was going on an intuition that she would want to know what I had to tell her.

I'd jotted down the questions. Not that I would forget, but writing them in my notebook gave them a sort of professional, businesslike air.

Question One. What was your maiden name?

Question Two. Where did you live as a child?

Question Three. (The big one.) What was the grave injustice perpetrated on your family?

BREAKFAST AT THE House was finished by the time I got there, and Miss Lindsay, gracious as ever, told me Mrs. Brodie was once again in the sunroom.

"I'm happy to say she's in much better spirits today. She has opened up to the other residents, and they have all been

enjoying the story of her adventures with the police officers."
Miss Lindsay chuckled. "She hasn't told us where she was
when she left the House. She's being most mysterious about
it so far. Her right, of course, and I'm sure she'll tell us when
she's good and ready. It's been quite the topic of conversation
here." She glanced over at me. "Any ideas?"

I dodged the question. "As you say, she'll reveal it when
she wants to."

Once again, Miss Lindsay surprised me. "Is it in connection
with her disappearance that you want to talk to her?"

"No, not at all. It's something quite different. There is a
confidential matter I would like to discuss with her. It may be
that I will ask her to accompany me on an important visit."

"Can you elucidate? I must keep the welfare of our residents
uppermost. It's not just their physical welfare — some of them
are quite fragile, mentally. Mrs. Brodie appears to be of a
sturdy cast of mind, but I wouldn't want her to be unnecessarily
upset."

I admit I was a bit pulled up short by this, but I kept seeing the delight on Olivia's face as we screamed along College
Street. I hoped I was right in assuming that what I had to say
would ultimately benefit her.

"I promise I will take good care of her."

"Very well. I must trust you. As you requested, I have
reserved the private visitor room. I will fetch her."

My talk with Olivia took about an hour, and, to my great
relief, after a short period of shock while she absorbed what I'd
told her, she agreed to come with me. There was not the same
excitement as she'd shown when we'd set out with Jack Murdoch to the police station, but she was adamant she wanted to
deal with things.

It seemed an imposition for Olivia to have to walk to

Gerrard Street, so I had the receptionist at the House ring for a taxicab. When she heard that, Olivia's sombre mood lifted a little.

"I've never ridden in a taxicab before," she whispered to me.

The driver raised his eyebrows when I gave him the address where we were going, but he knew better than to pry. He probably thought we were doing business with the mistress of the house — which, in a manner of speaking, was true.

I'd had no opportunity to speak further with Maria Johnson, and I was crossing my fingers that she wouldn't refuse us admittance. A protector indeed.

We alighted from the taxi, and Olivia stood on the sidewalk, contemplating the house.

"So, this is where she lives. Not as grand, is it?"

Maria answered the doorbell right away. Olivia was dressed in her Sunday best: tweed coat, hat this time a discreet navy. But there was no way to hide her social status, and Maria pegged her immediately.

"Madam is waiting for you, Miss Frayne. She is in the drawing room. Would ... er, would this lady like to wait in the kitchen?"

I moved a little closer to Olivia. "She'll come with me, thank you, Maria."

"How shall I announce her, madam?"

"Her name is Mrs. Olivia Brodie. You can say she is my companion."

"Very well."

Maria was emanating old-fashioned snobbery, but my status, however transitory, trumped hers as housekeeper. Barely.

"Please come this way."

I was glad to see that Olivia wasn't intimidated. She'd no doubt gone into grand houses like this before, but probably not through the front door. However, as we followed Maria down the hall, she shrank a little closer to me. It wasn't the rich furnishings or the flocked wall covering — a holdover from a previous era. Not the thick, lush carpet, nor the cut glass chandelier that tinkled with the door opening. All were necessary trappings of wealth and position.

I knew she was nervous about what she was about to encounter.

Maria gave one rap on the door of the drawing room, waited to be admitted, then, with an efficient thrust, opened the door and ushered us in. At the same time, she said in a voice worthy of a butler, "Miss Frayne to see you, madam. And Mrs. Brodie."

Mrs. Calder was seated by the fire, which was lit. It wasn't cold out, but there was a feeling of chill in the air. She had returned to her at-home colours, and she shimmered as she stood and turned to greet me, speaking immediately.

"Miss Frayne. Do come in. I will settle your account right away. I must apologize for that appalling scene the other day. Those ladies mean well, but they do seem to pry into my affairs in the most dreadful way. I have learned to tell them nothing."

Olivia had been almost obscured behind me, but she now stepped forward.

"Hello, Miss Emmeline. Do you remember me?"

Mrs. Calder's hand flew to her throat, and she stared at her. "Surely it can't be."

"It is. I'm Livvy. Olivia O'Rourke, as once was."

To my dismay, Mrs. Calder promptly fainted. Or at least she pretended to.

The next several minutes were, to say the least, chaotic. Maria, who seemed to have mastered the art of closed-door listening, came rushing in, and we both helped Mrs. Calder into the chair. Olivia herself made no attempt to interfere, but she waited quietly until Emmeline made her recovery.

Finally, when order was restored, Olivia said, "My apologies. I didn't intend to shock you in that way."

At which Mrs. Calder burst into tears. This time, I thought they were genuine.

"I thought you were dead. I thought all of you were dead."

"As good as, thanks to you," answered a grim-faced Olivia.

MUCH LATER, WE finally left to return Olivia to the House, leaving Emmeline to lie down with a strong sedative and Maria's ministrations. Olivia didn't talk much on the way back, and I was having many, many qualms about what I had initiated.

After a while, Olivia said, "I suppose I can't blame her entirely. We were children, after all. The problem was the grown-ups weren't willing to believe such a well-brought-up child with so many privileges could create such trouble. When it comes to a choice of dismissing your servants or calling your only child a wicked liar ... well, there is no choice really, is there?"

I reached over and squeezed her hand. "I'm sorry, Olivia. Perhaps we should have let sleeping dogs lie."

"Absolutely not. I don't believe in that. Wrong is wrong. Injustice is injustice." It was her turn to comfort me. "Don't fret. I've got a lot to think about, but I'll be all right."

I made sure she was safely delivered to Miss Lindsay, said I'd return tomorrow, then I made my way to the Paradise.

I HAD TO wait until the second sitting of lunch was finished before I could debrief, but everybody was all ears as I related my tale.

294 of MAUREEN JENNINGS

"I suppose you could call it a deadly mix of tragedy, neglect, and jealousy. Mrs. Moorhead, Emmeline Calder's mother, died when she was a child, leaving her to the devoted but erratic care of her father. As a government minister, he was called upon to travel a lot, work long hours, and so on. The servants were in charge of the little girl. Her physical needs were taken care of, but not her emotional ones."

"You can't expect paid servants to do that," burst out Wilf. "Why should they?"

"Can you give Charlotte a chance to tell us what happened?" said Hilliard, his voice sharp.

Wilf shrugged, undeterred.

"Then, not too long after Mr. Moorhead became a widower, the cool but caring housekeeper also passed on. Moorhead hired a young Irish woman to take her place."

I paused. I had everybody's attention.

"This young woman was herself not long widowed. She had two young children: a boy, Sean — pet name Rory — and a girl, Olivia. Usually called Livvy. Mrs. O'Rourke was the new housekeeper's name, and she was a recent immigrant from Ireland. Right off the boat. Mr. Moorhead took quite a fancy to her. Made pets of her two children. He paid special attention to the boy, who was on the cusp of manhood."

I saw Gramps raise his eyebrows.

"That was the expression used," I answered.

"Good, I like *cusp of* ..."

"The two children were roughly the same age as Emmeline."

I paused to sip my tea, which was getting tepid. Wilf seized the moment.

"I can guess where this is heading. It's the age-old story. Exploitation of the workers by those who hold the power. Did he seduce the comely young woman?"

I put down my cup, not missing the expression on Gramps's face. My own mother had been a comely young Irish immigrant. In her case, the seducer, if he could be called that, was the man who sired me, Philip Frayne.

"No, he did not. One dark day, Mr. Moorhead went into his study and discovered that all of the money he kept in a special box for the household expenses had gone. There was at least twenty dollars."

"Wouldn't go far these days," chimed in Cal.

I was getting fed up with all the interruptions. "Do you mind if I tell this my way without the commentary?"

"Sorry. Go on."

"Mr. Moorhead gathered everybody together. Valet, cook, housekeeper, the children. The whole lot. Could anybody shed light on this? Nobody could. Then young Emmeline spoke up. She had seen Rory O'Rourke coming out of her father's study that very evening. Perhaps they should take a look in his room. He shared the attic room with his sister. Mr. Moorhead and his valet both went to the room and, lo and behold, there they found the wallet with the money still in it underneath the boy's pillow."

I paused again. "Everybody with me so far?"

"Let me guess," Cal said. "The lad claimed he was innocent, but they wouldn't believe him."

"Exactly. The evidence seemed incontrovertible. Emmeline stood by her accusation, Rory stood by his denial. His mother, Brigid, defended him. Little Livvy could only watch in horror. Given all the turmoil, Mr. Moorhead had no choice but to send Brigid packing. She was to leave the very next day. With her children, naturally. However, that same night, the boy, Sean, ran away. When Mr. Moorhead awoke, he discovered the boy of whom he was so fond had taken one of his monogrammed cufflinks with him."

It was Hilliard's turn to question. "Did they call in the police?"

"They did not. Mr. Moorhead declared he was so devastated and betrayed by a boy he had favoured that he just wanted to bury the incident. Brigid left the house as ordered. She had virtually no resources, and she soon fell upon hard times. There were no such things as pensions back then, don't forget."

I surveyed the sombre faces of my audience.

"Sorry, folks, there's more. Three days after the incident, Mr. Moorhead had a fatal heart attack. Mrs. O'Rourke died from consumption two years after the expulsion. Livvy was left an orphan. She was ten years old."

Gramps held up his hand. "Stop, Lottie. This is too sad. Are you saying that all this dreadful tale came out when these two women met?"

"I'm putting it together for you, but yes, this is the story that emerged both when I talked to Olivia earlier and when we met with Mrs. Calder."

"What happened to the boy?" asked Cal. "Were they reunited?"

"Alas, no. Nobody in his family heard from him from that day on. I should say, by the way, that when I was first examining Mrs. Calder's jewellery case, I came across an old postcard that was from Rory. He'd intended to send for his mother and sister. Olivia was in no position to trace his whereabouts."

"You say the mother died. What happened to Olivia?"

"She was taken into service and moved with that family to Sudbury." I couldn't resist a little jab at Wilf. "Contrary to what you insist on believing about employer-servant relationships, Wilf, she was very well treated, and she was happy there. Eventually, she met a good man — he worked in the mines. They married. No children. She remained in Sudbury until last year."

Wilf interjected. "Okay with the sagas. What's the true story of the thefts? Or do you want us to guess? A dollar for the correct answer?"

"Before I get into that, I need another cup of tea."

"And a fresh cookie, by the look of you," said Cal. "I'll get it."

That gave me sufficient time to gird my loins. The scene that had happened in the decorous drawing room between the two women had been harrowing. I could have done with the services of Dr. Freud himself.

CHAPTER FIFTY-ONE

OLIVIA STOOD UP and moved a few feet in front of Emmeline. She wasn't loud, but her voice was strong and steady.

"You lied, didn't you? You lied when you said you saw Rory coming out of the study. You took that money and planted it in his room. Why? You had everything; we had nothing."

Surprisingly, Emmeline offered no resistance. In fact, I thought she was relieved to finally admit what had happened. She was crying, but quietly, unchecked tears rolling down her cheeks.

"I'm sorry. I'm so very sorry. After dear Mama went to heaven, Papa was always so busy. I hardly saw him from one month to the next. Then you arrived, and he seemed to pay you both so much attention. Especially your brother." She rubbed at her chest as if the pain of that memory still burned her. "How many times did he say, 'Dear Emmie, if only you'd been born a boy. We could have had such good times together'? So, there he was, the boy he'd always wanted. I couldn't bear it. I thought I would just make some trouble. I didn't expect what would happen. Then Papa died so soon afterward. His doctor said he had a weak heart, but I knew better. I knew that the shock had killed him."

She was so pale at this point I was afraid she might pass out. She continued speaking more and more frantically.

"Rory wrote, but I burned the letters. There were five in that year. Then no more."

"Did you also plant the cufflink?" Olivia asked.

"I did not. He stole it. It was Papa's prize possession. I think that hurt him even more than the theft of the money."

"The supposed theft."

With a taste for the dramatic that seemed built in, Emmeline slid off the chair and, kneeling, clasped her hands together, prayer fashion.

"Yes, indeed. The supposed theft. Can you ever forgive me, dear Livvy?"

Olivia was still steady, but she stepped back.

"I don't know."

Emmeline was even more frantic. "I will make it up to you, I swear. I will pay any amount you think is right for recompense."

"Money won't change the past. I don't want your money. My life has been as good as it could be given the circumstances. It is you I pity."

EPILOGUE

IF YOU HAD asked me how I spent my time for the next week, I would have said something along the lines of "picking up stitches," a metaphor I got from Olivia, who never seemed to stop her knitting projects. She claimed to be slowed down by arthritis, but she still managed to finish the back and front of a sweater she was knitting for me. It was a colourful Fair Isle pattern. I visited her every day to help with the other non-woollen stitches.

There was one meeting that was crucial.

I brought Marko Ryga over to the House. I didn't tell him why until we were in the visiting room where an equally mystified Olivia was waiting for me. She was curious as to the presence of this young man she'd last seen in the police lineup. I proceeded cautiously.

"Mrs. Brodie. You've already seen this young man. His name is Marko Ryga."

"Yes, I remember. He and his partner have been released, as I understand it."

"That is true."

"But thank the Lord the two boys are not under suspicion anymore."

"Also true."

She looked at me. "I'm sorry, Charlotte, but I don't know why you have asked me to meet him. You have been rather mysterious."

"I don't know either, Miss Frayne," said Marko. "I thought everything was cleared up."

"There are a couple of loose ends, but they are important ones."

There was no way around it. I plunged in.

"You see, Marko and Olivia, I believe you are related to each other."

Almost simultaneously, they both exclaimed.

"What! I don't have a family," said Mrs. Brodie.

"Me, neither," said Marko. "Zav Genik is the only person I'd call family."

"Well, I have what I sincerely hope will be good news to both of you. Olivia, meet your great-nephew. His grandfather was your brother, Rory."

She actually turned pale. "Rory? I thought I had lost him long ago."

"He remained in Winnipeg. His daughter, Bridie, who would have been your niece, married Filip Ryga, and they had this fine young man, Marko."

Olivia still didn't move, and Marko also seemed transfixed.

"Is your grandfather alive?"

"I'm afraid not. He died a while ago."

She turned to me. "How can I know this is true?"

"Marko's mother gave him an heirloom that had belonged to her father. Will you show the cufflink to Mrs. Brodie, please, Marko?"

I'd asked him ahead of time to bring the jewellery box, and he took it from his pocket and handed it to Olivia.

She snapped it open and stared at the cufflink for a few moments.

"So, Rory did steal it?"

Marko shook his head. "He always said it was a gift from somebody he referred to as a 'special man.'"

Olivia closed the box with a snap. "Let's say the case is closed, shall we?"

Then she held out her arms.

"Dear boy. Come and give your auntie a hug."

Marko was only too happy to oblige.

"I knew you looked familiar," said Olivia. "Now I can see why. You are the spitting image of your grandfather as I knew him." She hugged him closer, her face beaming. "Oh, I have so wanted to have my own kin near me."

I left them to it. Olivia already wanted to introduce him to the other residents. As she'd said, she now had kin of her own.

MRS. EMMELINE CALDER was put under a doctor's care and was, so far, showing no further inclination to go back and forth to the pawnbroker. The nerve specialist, Dr. Jones, described her behaviour as *ritualistic obsessive-compulsive*. He said it had probably been precipitated by the death of her husband, but the real trauma was the death of her beloved father — something for which she felt responsible. The doctor emphasized she was not really in a rational frame of mind when she trotted off to the pawnbroker with fantastic stories. He said, "Any obsessive ritual has this element. Especially if they are secretive. Some people can't leave the house without turning around three times and crossing their fingers. Omit the ritual and they get anxious."

Emmeline had set out to get rid of Brigid O'Rourke and her children, and she had succeeded at a terrible cost. As Olivia had put it to me, "a grave injustice" had been committed.

To ease the pain of that childhood loss, Emmeline secretly disposed of her precious articles then restored them. Over and over. Gone and restored. Gone and then restored. She had felt robbed of her father's love, and now she was compelled to accuse others of robbery. In the end, the objects returned. Nothing was lost.

The reunion with Olivia and the relief of confession appeared to have ended the compulsion, but it remained to be seen if that would stick. Dr. Jones said he was going to write a paper about it for *The Lancet*. One of these days, I intended to look it up.

Mrs. Calder was insisting on giving money to the maligned family. She swore she would ensure Rory's grandson was looked after as long as he needed. He was happy with that and even pushed her to include Zav Genik in any legal settlement. An injustice put to rights, as best as it is ever possible.

Did Dr. Brandwein willingly hand over his menorah and tallit? We'd probably never know. Zav said he intended to keep them as mementos.

SECOND STITCH. LEROY came to live at the Paradise under Cal's mentorship. He was thrilled with the idea of being an apprentice to a chef. "Lots of future possibilities," was his comment. Jerome was moved to a special wing for rehabilitation. We didn't know how much mobility he would finally recover, but for now the brothers were together and safe. After much pressure from Jack Murdoch, Judge Carter had agreed to stay all charges. Leroy was put on probation for six months, but at least there was to be no strapping.

After a little — I hope, gentle — prodding, Leroy finally admitted he'd told a small fib, as he put it. He and his brother had indeed gone to Dr. Brandwein's house that Monday morning.

"Okay, I'll bite. Why were you there?"

"I was delivering a copy of *The Young Worker*. The doctor was a member of the Communist Party, but he didn't want anybody to know. It's not something a man like him can always own up to. When he didn't answer the door, I thought he might have changed his mind, so we left. I didn't know he'd had a stroke. I just thought he wasn't up yet."

"So, Mr. Glozier did see you?"

"He did, but he jumped to the conclusion that we had been doing something bad. Which we hadn't. We were hurrying because we were late picking up our papers."

"Why didn't you tell Detective Murdoch the truth?"

"I didn't want to get the doctor into trouble." Leroy looked upset at this point. "He was a good man. We had some good talks."

And a young boy in serious trouble was willing to pay the price of loyalty.

THIRD STITCH. MR. Gilmore returned, harried and troubled. He said the situation for the Jews in Europe was getting worse every day. He had connected with an organization that was helping children get out of Germany while they still could. They were in desperate need of money.

I thought it was a project that was right up the alley of the Ladies' Pioneer Club.

FOURTH AND FINAL. The road to St. Patrick's night at the Paradise was a rocky one. There were many squabbles between Hilliard and Wilf about what shape the entertainment should take. Finally, they compromised. Wilf wrote a powerful drama based on the On-to-Ottawa Trek a couple of years before. He agreed to have the men sing a few lively Irish songs when they were riding in the boxcars. He grumbled that most of

them were Ukrainian, not Irish, but he found a songbook with
workers' songs and was happy.

The night of St. Patrick's, the café basement was jam-
packed. The audience seemed to love everything: the vivid
drama of brutality and promises broken; vigorous songs; and,
perhaps especially, homemade beer and free biscuits that Cal
had coloured green.

As we were about to start, the door opened, and in came
Jack Murdoch.

He had his wife, Fiona, and his two children with him. And
an older man I didn't recognize.

I was at my station, collecting tickets, and Jack brought
him over. Like Jack, he was tall and slim, with wavy grey hair,
nice brown eyes, and a pleasant smile.

"Charlotte, I'd like you to meet my father, former detective
William Murdoch. He's here for a visit."

ACKNOWLEDGEMENTS

There are always so many people to thank for support, encouragement and information along the way, it would take half a book to write down all of their names. Hopefully they know who they are. Many thanks are due to Carl Dyer for sharing his experience of Marcus Garvey and for his enthusiasm for this topic and my work in general. Especial thanks are due to Keara Langford, my brilliant research assistant; to my wonderful publisher Marc Côté and to the incredible Sarah Cooper who offers sage advice and good cheer no matter what I'm moaning about. To Barry Jowett for editing this book and for being both meticulous and tactful — no mean feat. And to Andrea Waters for tidying up the manuscript in such a careful and thorough way.

And by no means least, thanks to Nick Craine for creating fabulous cover art for the series.

We acknowledge the sacred land on which Cormorant Books operates. It has been a site of human activity for 15,000 years. This land is the territory of the Huron-Wendat and Petun First Nations, the Seneca, and most recently, the Mississaugas of the Credit River. The territory was the subject of the Dish With One Spoon Wampum Belt Covenant, an agreement between the Iroquois Confederacy and Confederacy of the Ojibway and allied nations to peaceably share and steward the resources around the Great Lakes. Today, the meeting place of Toronto is still home to many Indigenous people from across Turtle Island. We are grateful to have the opportunity to work in the community, on this territory.

We are also mindful of broken covenants and the need to strive to make right with all our relations.